STUMBLING IN
THE SHORE SERIES
BOOK 3

STUMBLING IN

THE SHORE SERIES
BOOK 3

M.R. JOSEPH

Stumbling In

Edited by Kathy Krick

Elaine York- Allusion Graphics

LLC/Publishing & Book Formatting

http://www.allusiongraphics.com

Jennifer Kearney Photography 2015

http://www.jenniferkearneyphotography.com

Formatted by:

Indie Pixel Studio

http://www.indiepixelstudio.com

ISBN: 1514364069
ISBN-13: 978-1514364062

DEDICATION

To my mom
For teaching me right from wrong and from wrong to
right
For letting me be who I am and not judging
For always encouraging me to strive for greatness
even in moments of weakness
Thank you for being the strong woman you are and
for setting the example of what a strong woman
should be.
I love you, mommy

ACKNOWLEDGEMENTS

Thank you to my biggest pimp out there. My loving, adoring husband/book cover designer. Thank you for all that you do for me. Nothing I do would be possible without your love, patience, and support. My love for you and your talents is immeasurable. I love you with all that I am. Forever.

To my kiddos for always telling me how proud you are of me. But it's really you who I am so very proud of. Mommy loves you with all her heart.

Thank you to my family and friends for being there for me and understanding and supporting this dream of mine. Love you all.

Thank you to my betas for giving me such encouragement and fun suggestions with Max and Willow's story. Especially Marla Knob, Wendy Shatwell, Julie MacIntyre, and Kristine Barakat, and of course my Smut City crew for 'stumbling' along the way with me on this journey as always.

Thank you to my author family for just being you. I love being a part of a family who cheers on each others successes and who are there when the bumps in the road get in the way. I feel blessed to be a part of such a crazy, fantastic world.

To the bloggers who are the butter on my bread, the cream in my coffee, and the noodles in my soup. Without you there wouldn't be the stories I write. My appreciation for all that you do goes beyond words.

Thank you to my editor, Kathy Krick for all of

your hard work and for being such a sweetheart. I appreciate everything!

Thank you to Elaine York at Allusion Graphics for putting the cherry on top of the Sundae. Thank you for all your hard work.

Thanks to my dear formatter, JB McGee at Indie Pixel Studio for doing another great job with this book. You're awesome!

To my fan-freaking-tastic photographer, Jennifer Kearney for your eye. You know how to create some magic. I'm very grateful for your talents, expertise, and friendship. I can't wait till we're back at the beach for another masterpiece.

Thank you to my cover models, Carmen Carangi and Chantal Brown for your beautiful faces. Thank you for gracing the cover of this book. You both are amazing and gorgeous! Thank you for your time and for making our photo shoot so much fun!

Lastly, to the readers. I can't write this without thinking of all of you. Thank you for taking a chance on me by reading my words and believing in me and in my stories. Thank you for taking the time to write reviews as well. I do this because of you.

PROLOGUE

May 2014
Max & Willow~

"Oh, my God, my head. What the hell? Max get the fuck off of me."

"Huh, what? What the... Willow, why the hell are you in my bed and why am I looking at your naked boobs?"

"What the hell is going on? Where are my clothes? Where the fuck is your clothes? Pull that sheet up on yourself. You think I want your Mr. Winky looking at me? Do it!"

"Stop yelling and let me try to get my head around this. My head hurts so badly. I still may be drunk."

"You smell like it."

"God, could you be an even bigger bitch? You think you smell like roses? You should see your face. It looks like it's been through a car wash."

"Shut up, you little shit. You are like a gnat that's constantly flying around me and no matter how many times I swat at you, you never go away."

"Oh, no."

"Ugh, what?"

"Condom wrappers."

"Where?"

"There. All over the floor."

"There's so many of them. I think I'm going to puke."

"Don't do it here. In my room. And how did you wind up here anyway?"

"I don't know, asshole. I drank a lot. Apparently, so did you."

"Oh, my God. My head. I need water and something greasy to eat."

"What was the last thing you remember?"

"Being at Jax. Singing with the band. Watching Harlow walk in. Watching her and Cruz getting back together and making out on the dance floor. You?"

"Shots. Lots of shots."

"Yeah. They feel much better going down rather than up."

"Ugh. Stop talking so loud!"

"I'm not. It hurts to talk."

"Shut up, Max."

"You shut up, Willow."

"Ahh... shit. Why'd you push me off the bed? God, Willow."

"Because."

"Because why?"

"Because you are a royal pain in my ass, that's why."

"Oh, and you're a picnic in the park."

"I thought I told you not to yell."

"I'm not yelling. BUT I WILL IF YOU CAN'T HEAR MEEEEE!"

"Oh, my God! Are you nuts screaming in my ear like that? I should punch you in the dick for that."

"Now why would you want to go and do something like that? I'm sure my dick and I treated you nicely last night. I haven't heard any complaints thus far."

"Ugh. Gross. I can't even wrap my head around this, and your dick is the last thing I want to think about."

"Well, thinking about what's under the sheet you're holding is not making me want to write a sonnet, ya know."

"I hate you, Max. I can't even be in the same room as you without wanting to slit my wrists."

"Feeling is mutual, ice queen. Hand me my underwear, please."

"Oh, now we are resorting to name calling. You are no challenge for me, little man."

"Little man? I see no little man here."

"Oh, please. Don't adjust your boner in front of me either. I doubt there's anything there anyway."

"Ha. Funny one. Why don't you get out of that bed and try to walk and we'll see how my 'nothing' makes you limp like you've been riding bareback on a horse for a week."

"Don't flatter yourself. I'm sure my vagina said 'Oh, no here comes a baby thumb. Ovaries, take cover.'"

"You know what you are?"

"What? Enlighten me."

"A spoiled, rich, whiny, and impudent child."

"Oh, really! Well, you are a talentless, scrawny, leprechaun-sized sea urchin."

"Nice, Wills. Really? You think of that right off the top of your head? May I commend you on your exemplary comeback skills. Truly amazing."

"Go fuck yourself, Max."

"Oh, Willow, I'm sure you took good care of that for me last night."

"I'm going to throw up."

"So glad my lovemaking skills make you nauseous."

"You make me nauseous."

"That's a first."

"I highly doubt that."

"Listen, let's just cut the crap. It happened, Willow. We can go around and around with the insults, but it's not getting us anywhere. There's nothing we can do about it."

"If only I had a time machine."

"Tell me about it. I'd go back two years ago and tell Porter never mind, I'm not staying next door to a crazy person all summer."

"Don't talk about Harlow that way. She didn't do anything to you."

"Oh, is that a small smile I see? That, I must admit, was funny, Wills."

"It wasn't a smile. I have gas."

"I never met a girl with so much class. You are just a breath of fresh air, aren't you?"

"Stop talking and let me think."

"About what?"

"About what we are going to tell people."

"We tell nothing. As far as you and I are concerned, it never happened. If someone asks, I slept in here and you slept in your car. It's early enough that you can sneak down to your car then walk back up."

"Why the hell should I pretend I'm some homeless thug sleeping in the back seat of a car? You do it."

"No, you do it, Willow."

"No, Max. You."

"You."

"You."

"Okay, stop. We don't have to fight about this. Just go back to your house and tell Harlow and Thea you got locked out and that I was still up last night when it happened so I told you to sleep on the sofa."

"Now you're talking. Nice going, brainiac."

"It'll work. They won't suspect a thing."

"We can never speak of this, Max. Never. No one can ever know."

"Agreed. Should we... um... shake on it or something?"

"I think we did enough touching last night, don't you think? A verbal agreement will suffice."

"Understood. We'll forget this ever happened and go on with our lives — keep on hating each other. Right?"

"Um, yeah, exactly. Max?"

"Yeah, Wills?"

"You're standing on my panties."

"Oh, jeez. Sorry. Here."

"Can you turn around?"

"Sorry, sure."

"Okay, you can turn around. I found my clothes."

"This never happened, Max. Remember."

"I won't forget. And it will never happen again."

"Never."

"Never ever."

"Exactly. Never ever again."

CHAPTER 1

I Do Not Sound Like A Fucking Cat
Willow~

Sneaking out of my aunt's house and out of Max's bed (insert gag here), was easier than I anticipated. Our plan was foolproof. All the scenes were strategically in place. The actors took the stage and with a little tiptoeing around it was successful. For some reason my house is unlocked when I push the sliding door open and I creep inside. I go right to the fridge hoping I left some kind of beverage that contained electrolytes and caffeine. No such luck. Just fucking water. Fuckity, fuck, fuck, fuck.

I tip my head back and drain the bottle, praying that this headache goes away as soon as I am rehydrated.

I slept with Max.

I had sex with Max.

I fucked Max.

Max fucked me.

Am I happy about it? Would I be if I

remembered that it happened?

Am I in love with Max?

What is love anyway, really? I don't know what being in love with someone is supposed to feel like. I know my parents are in love. I've watched them and know what it at least looks like. But Max hates me and I hate him too. He does annoy the living shit out of me, but I am strangely attracted to him. When he sings on stage with his band, my panties feel like they will spontaneously combust. Just by looking at the way his lips are so close to the microphone stirs something in me. Sometimes he sticks his tongue out and licks his lips when he takes a break to play his guitar during the instrumental. Then, when he's about to start singing again and he throws his guitar over his shoulder — still strapped to his body — he runs his hand over his small, close-cut mohawk. Beads of sweat branch out onto his forehead from the heat of the stage lights. That and the vivacious way he plays causes that stirring. Then he goes back to making love to that fucking microphone.

Damn microphone.

Okay — like I said, I'm strangely attracted to him. No judgement, bitches.

Yeah, yeah, yeah. I know, so un-Willow of me, right? Well, I'm human. I have feelings like everyone else. I bleed when I'm cut, and I put my $200 jeans on one leg at a time like everyone else. People think I'm incapable of showing true emotion — they think I'm just this hard ass with the witty comebacks — and I am, trust me. I'm fucking hysterical with the one-liners and total sass that would shame the rich and stun the poor.

And I'm scared.

What scares me? Feeling something for someone, especially for Max. There are a lot of reasons to dislike Max. I'll give the rundown.

He's shorter than me. He is what I call a brainiac because he thinks he knows everything. He chews with his mouth open. He loves Irish whiskey — which I despise. He's poor. He thinks he's funny when he's truly not, and his fashion sense is not something to be desired. He actually dresses hideously. And did I mention he's poor? I can't even imagine taking him to the country club my parents belong to. He'd probably wear those black, worn-out Vans he has and some stupid novelty t-shirt that says something dumb like 'Do you want two tickets to see the gun show?' There would be a picture of a guy flexing on it and Max would try to dress it up with some sort of suit jacket from some poor person's donation store.

He'd probably look cute, but like I said, he's a pain in my ass — the yeast infection that won't go away no matter how much cream you apply.

When I'm with him and we are hanging with the gang, most of the time I want to punch him, then he'll say something witty or adorable and all I want to do is kiss him. I'm messed up. I know I am. I'm contradicting myself. And this is why I can't let anyone know what happened. I treat him like dog poo on my Louboutins.

God, how I wish I could remember last night. All I see when I shut my eyes are all those damn condom wrappers on the floor. There had to be at least six or seven. So I'm guessing no whiskey dick for Max?

Alcohol. Damn alcohol.

I down my water, and on the last gulp I realize it does nothing to quench my thirst but I know I need to drink.

A hand touches my shoulder and I jump, spitting water out into the sink in front of me.

"Oh, my God! Thea, you scared the crap out me."

She covers her mouth, stifling a laugh.

"Sorry 'bout that. Why are you still in your clothes from last night? Your bed is still made."

I knew there would be a line of questioning. Usually it's Harlow, but I imagine she's still caught up in the sheets with her man candy. It's about time.

"I, um... got locked out and slept on the couch next door." Thea just shrugs and believes the lie. Thank God. I mean why would she suspect anything in the first place. It is Porter's place and he is my cousin.

I go to grab another bottle of water. I see that Harlow's door is still closed and I don't hear anything coming from there so I'm assuming there's no romp fest going on.

I motion to Harlow's bedroom door. "I'm guessing those two aren't up yet."

"Nope. It was a late night last night. Let's just let them sleep."

I think about it... for literally a split second.

"Nah."

I go to Har's door and turn and wink at Thea

and then proceed to bang on it like there's a fire and I need to get them out.

"Let's go, Dickcop. Put away your package and get your asses up, dressed, and out here. Pronto."

I hear something hit the door from the inside and a few groans and not ones of a sexual nature.

I hear the sweet sounds of Cruz telling me to fuck off. Ah, music to my ears.

"What did you say, Cruz? Can't quite make out what you're saying?" I yell at the door and giggle. The thing that makes me most happy is busting that man's balls. But I will give him credit for one thing — he didn't give up on Harlow. He fought for her and got her back. Was I ever a huge fan of Cruz's? No, but the softer side of me — that doesn't come out often — saw how much he loved her. I really don't know what love like that is like but from the looks of it, it's what Cruz and Harlow have.

Thank God my best friend is okay. Thank God she remembered how she felt about him and didn't wind up going to England with Daniel. I mean, Daniel was a good guy and when she didn't remember her and Cruz's relationship, I sort of egged her on about moving on. I'm protective that way. Harlow and what she has been through — yeah, I knew I needed to keep my opinions to a minimum. I knew she loved him once she began remembering their relationship; with some things I knew Harlow had to figure out on her own. I feel sort of bad for Daniel. Even though at the bar last night, Harlow told me how it all went down. He

11

knew deep down her heart belonged to someone else. It all happened so fast and she made a hasty decision but her head was still not on straight. I'm still not sure it still is. That's my worry. Not about how she feels about Cruz — I know she loves him and they are meant to be — but I still worry about her mentally and physically. I've known her for half my life. She's my best friend.

See what I mean?

Love. It's too confusing. It's messy. I'm not sure I could handle it in my life.

Thea and I go sit in the living room. Thea makes some coffee and the smell of it makes me nauseous. I'm still nauseous. I sit on the sofa and wrap myself up in a blanket and rest my head on the armrest. I close my eyes for a second but the room is still spinning. I hate hangovers and this one I feel like is the king of them.

A tap on the sliding door makes me open my eyes. Porter walks in looking like how I feel. His normally perfect hair is tousled and he has sheet creases embedded in his face.

When he walks in he just moans and plops down next to me and tries to steal my blanket. Not happening.

"No way, cousin. Get your own."

I pull it away from him as he continues to moan.

"Why are you so mean to me? I just want to cuddle."

I look at him like he's crazy. "Ew, Porter. I do not cuddle with my cousin. That's just wrong. Go cuddle with someone else." I look behind me at

Thea leaning on the counter looking at her reflection in a spoon. She's smoothing her hair and removing smudge marks from under her eyes. She puts down the spoon and takes a sip of her coffee.

"Thea, come over here and cuddle with Porter. He needs the comfort of a woman."

She starts to cough and choke on her sip of coffee and it flies out of her mouth. Porter jumps up and makes his way over to her, patting her on her back.

What is she doing?

"You okay?" Porter continues to pat her on the back. After a few moments, Thea regains her composure, clearing her throat.

"I'm... I'm fine. Just went down the wrong pipe, I guess." I'm still looking at her and Porter and even though she's okay now, Porter continues to rub small circles on her back. He looks over to me and snaps his hand away and runs his hand through his hair, making his way back to the sofa with his head hanging down.

Another tap on the door and Max enters. My eyes go to him as well as his going to mine, but I quickly look away and rest my head once again on the arm of the sofa. I feel heat rise up in my cheeks. Unfortunately, his scent invades my brain. He's showered and smelling... delish. His smell does not nauseate me, but when he opens his mouth it does. He motions to Porter and me.

"Jeez, you two. You both look like shit. I can smell you from here, Willow."

All I can do is extend my middle finger to

him. That's all I can muster right now.

He's lucky.

Max goes to Thea and asks for some coffee. Then both of them join us in the living room once they grab their mugs and sit on the smaller sofa opposite of the one Porter and I are on.

I try my best not to make direct eye contact with Max as we all rehash the events of the night before. It's difficult because I know what we did — well, at least I'm imagining what we did. It makes my palms sweat. I can't decipher whether it's the booze exiting my body or my nerves.

I close my eyes again when Max starts to speak.

"I know Daniel seemed like a good guy. I kind of feel bad for the dude. That must have hit him hard."

I groan. "He'll be okay. She's meant to be with the asshat in the other room."

"How do *you* know he'll be okay, Willow? You don't know what that must have been like for him. I mean, don't get me wrong, I love Harlow and glad she came to her senses, but still, that had to be a major kick to the balls."

I raise my head up with much effort and look over at Max.

"Because I know, you twit. Harlow said he had a feeling that she had her doubts. He made it easy for her. He went back to England anyway. She'll never have to see him again."

Max shakes his head at me and he eyes me like he has more to say.

Unfortunately.

"What, Max? What? You know something I don't."

"Easy for her? I can't imagine that being easy? And, yeah, I do know, sort of. Craw is still seeing Daniel's sister Ally. Did we forget that? Don't you think that's going to cause a bit of a problem? Especially this summer?"

I'm annoyed. Not only by his comments but because I feel like shit as well. I get up from the sofa to get more water. I almost fall from being dizzy and I have to remind myself to pace my drinking this summer. I can't have another night like last night or a morning like this. And I can't allow alcohol to make poor decisions for me like the choices I made with Max.

I wave my hand, shooing Max's comment off like a fly.

"She'll have to get over it. It is what it is. You win some, you lose some."

I hear him let out a huff.

"You have the heart of an icicle, Wills. You really do."

I slam the refrigerator door and stand there with my one hand resting on it.

"Keep your opinions about me to yourself, little man. No one asked for your two cents. And who says my heart is cold? I'm happy for Harlow and Dickcop. That's a lot for me to say. Plus, I could care less about Craw's woman. I hardly know her. She has a problem with Harlow? Like I said, she'll have to get over it. Harlow and Daniel are done. Acabado."

"Acabado?" Porter asks.

"Finished, Porter. I'm a Spanish teacher, remember?"

Max tries to dispute me.

"It is going to be *our* business this summer though. Craw's going to be here a lot and he's Harlow's brother. If you think that it's going to be easy and that girl is just going to be okay with Harlow dumping her brother at the airport then you are as crazy and delusional as I always thought you were anyway — maybe even a little more."

I grab the nearest thing off the counter, which just happens to be my empty water bottle from before, and chuck it at him from across the room. He ducks because he already knew I had the preconceived notion to throw something at his stupid head.

"You want to see crazy and delusional, go look in the mirror, dumbass." With that, I turn to go back to my room and run into a shirtless, tattooed cop's chest. Gross.

I swipe at my face and hear that butthole chuckle.

"Oh, come now, Willow. It's not that bad." Cruz winks at me and flexes.

I take it back. Harlow hasn't come to her senses.

"You wish." I mumble.

I see Harlow beaming as her arm is wrapped around Cruz's waist.

"Jeez, Wills. You don't look very good. Hung over?"

I nod to Harlow. "You could say that. It's

about time you two got up. Are we going to have to disinfect your room from all the bodily fluids that were exchanged last night?"

Cruz nudges me aside to grab mugs for him and Harlow and he starts to pour them both coffee.

He looks over his shoulder at me. "Nah, we're not done yet. We'll take care of it later, right, Turnip?" He winks at Harlow, who rolls her eyes at him as he hands her the coffee.

Harlow takes a seat on the sofa and Cruz sits next to her. That's where I was sitting! Damn him! There's only one seat left besides the floor and the empty seat is next to Max and I'm so not going there. I'll stand.

"What was all the yelling out here?" Harlow asks as she sips her coffee.

Porter motions both his thumbs towards Max and me. Harlow just nods without surprise on her face.

"I figured as much." She looks to me and shakes her head. "When are you two going to get along? For the sake of us. All of us. If not, it's going to be a long summer and it really hasn't even started yet."

I can feel Max's eyes on me from where I stand, beckoning me to answer. Why doesn't he do it? And, he does.

"We get along. This is just like foreplay, Har. No worries."

I feel the heat rise up in my cheeks and I swear I'm going to hurl. I'm waiting for my face to give away the secret of last night but they all just laugh.

Crisis averted.

Porter yawns and stretches his hands above his head. "Did you guys hear that cat outside all night howling? I mean it went on for hours and hours. I swear it was right outside the house."

Cruz nods his head in agreement. "I know. It sounded like it was coming through the walls. It wouldn't shut the hell up, and damn was it loud."

Max snickers and I hear him quietly say, "Oh, it was coming alright." Max's eyes peer up slightly towards me through his long lashes and he may have winked.

Now before when I said that I might hurl, I think I just did a little in my mouth because I know that stupid comment was meant for me. I will fucking crush him like an ant.

Harlow motions for me to come over and sit. "Come over here, Wills. It hurts my head to have to keep turning to look at you. Besides, we have to talk to you guys."

I walk over reluctantly and sit in front of the coffee table facing Har, Cruz, and Porter. I try my best not to get into Max's line of sight. I don't succeed. Immediately my stomach feels a little funny with worry because Harlow looks serious and I'm hoping she's okay.

I am on full alert and temporarily forget about how bad my head hurts as well as the soreness I feel from last night. Damn it to hell! If the sex was that good, why can't I remember it but can feel it!

"What's wrong?" I ask as I chew on the corner

of my lip anticipating the bad news.

Harlow smiles and looks at Cruz, who is still shirtless and smiling back at her. Does the man own clothing?

"Nothing's wrong. I just have a few things to say to you guys." She looks around and scrunches up her face. "Where's Craw?" Everyone looks around like that is going to diffuse any bombs. Any ones that are about to explode will do so whether anyone likes it or not.

Porter tells her, "I'm pretty sure he and Ally got a room downtown last night."

"Why?" Harlow asks with hurt in her voice.

Porter shakes his head. "Not sure. A lot of last night was a blur. A whiskey-infused blur. I remember seeing them by the front door of Jax talking and then I didn't see him for a while. When I was at the bar getting some shots, I saw him leaving and I asked where he was going. He said he and Ally were leaving and he didn't look happy. Craw said they were getting a room and he'd see us today."

Harlow looks really upset. She scratches at her little scar that's on her head and with a tight-lipped smile she turns her toward Cruz. He winks at her and rubs her back with his hand.

"Turnip, we knew this part wasn't going to be easy for Craw. He's dating Daniel's sister."

"I know it's going to be a challenge but I don't want to tell... oh, never mind. I can't do it without Craw here."

Everyone's eyes look inquisitive.

If she thinks she's not going to tell us because

Craw isn't here, she's...

My eyes go wide and when Harlow moves her hands from her lap to rest on her chin - that's when I see it and all I can do is stare.

A fucking ring.

I can't speak. I can only point. Words no longer exist because I know what that is. Some inaudible sounds squeak out and I watch as Harlow and Cruz — especially Cruz — enjoy the fact that I can't speak.

He sits there, smirking at me. He sits up and perches his elbows on his knees and leans inward.

"What's wrong, Wills? Speechless. That's one for the books. A silent Willow Taylor. Miracles do happen." He chuckles.

Harlow smacks his arm and suddenly everyone's eyes are fixated on Harlow and Cruz on the sofa.

"You hush." Harlow wraps her bare hand around Cruz's bicep and holds out her ring-clad finger, displaying a blue-colored ring.

"Guys, we got engaged last night." Cruz smiles and kisses her temple. Thea gasps and I hear a 'holy shit' come from Porter's mouth. I look around the room and Max says nothing. He actually has a blank look on his face.

Harlow looks a little upset — I'm imagining it's because we are all shocked.

"Wow, guys. Thanks so much for the congrats and all the excitement. Try to calm down a little."

Thea hops up and goes straight to Harlow on the couch to hug her. Harlow stands and so does Cruz.

"I'm so happy for you, Har. I'm just surprised is all. But you guys are meant to be and the ring is gorgeous." She goes from hugging Harlow to giving Cruz the same affection.

Porter gets up and follows suit, grabbing Harlow into his arms and giving Cruz a bro hug.

"I'm sorry. I feel the same way as Thea. That was just... fast. Was this planned?"

Cruz wraps an arm around Harlow's shoulders. "I bought it a while ago. I just kept it with me in case she came back, and she did. I never lost hope." Harlow tiptoes up and kisses his cheek.

I'm pretty sure it's not the alcohol that may make me vomit.

"When did this happen? We were all together last night. As far as I can remember," Porter asks.

"We took a walk down to the dock once we got back. I did it there. It was almost sunrise. Ring was in my pocket. It hasn't left my pocket since she almost left."

Yeah, here comes the vomit.

Now I think I have some words.

"I'm all for you two being together. I mean I pushed for it once you started to remember, Har. I hated the fact you were going to England, not that I didn't like Daniel, but I didn't want you to go. Now you guys are engaged? Fast isn't even a word." I stand up, not steadily, but I do it. I go over to Harlow and grab her hand, looking at the ring. Yeah, okay, it's gorgeous, but still. She's way too young. My nostrils are flaring, my eyes are burning, and I can feel the redness creeping up

21

my face.

"I mean have you guys figured out anything yet? Harlow, you have a job back home. Cruz, what the hell are you doing? Do you even have a job? Are you moving to Princeton? If not, are you just going to sponge off her until you find a job?" My voice is raised and I don't really realize it until Harlow yells above me and snaps my mouth shut.

"Willow! What the hell is wrong with you? That's our business. We haven't discussed anything yet, but we will."

In a sharp tone I snap back at her, "Oh, it's none of my business? So him dumping you and you crying on my shoulder for months over him was none of my business? And then when you almost died was none of my business? Then you losing your memory and not remembering you loved him was none of my business? And you remembering him finally was none of my business as well? Shall I go on?"

Cruz's voice roars — startling everyone in the room.

"That's enough, Willow. Shut your mouth and keep your fucking opinions to yourself."

That's all I need to make my exit. I wave my hand at them, aggravated. "Fine. I hope you're both happy. I'm going home. You two have fun figuring your lives out." I storm out of the living room towards my room.

I slam the door shut and the sound of it hurts my head because of my current hangover.

I grab my bag and start gathering my shit

together. I throw it all in not caring what condition it ends up. They don't want my opinion? Fine. They don't have to hear it and, yes, I know at one time I supported Harlow and Cruz's relationship. They are complete opposites but Harlow went through so much with Chad and I saw how much she loved Cruz so I just wanted her to be happy and she was. Then when her relationship with Daniel started…again, I just wanted her to be happy. All I've ever wanted was Harlow to be happy, but this — an engagement? It's way too much. Too much too soon.

I hear a knock at my door and I quickly do my best to pack the rest of my crap. I'm not quick enough because the door opens and Max walks in. As soon as I see him I roll my eyes.

I give him a warning. "You are the last person I want to see right now so do me a favor and get the fuck out."

He leans against the door, running his hand across the top of his short mohawk and I wait for my lecture.

But I don't get one.

"I agree with you."

I look up at him in shock.

"With me? You agree with me? Seriously?"

"Well, I don't agree with the childish, tantrum-type way you said it, but yeah, I agree. This is way too fast."

Max agreeing with me is the biggest surprise.

"Isn't that exactly what I need? You agreeing with me. No thanks, I don't need that from you."

I return to my task and I hear him breathe out

an aggravated sigh.

"Why do you have to always be such a royal bitch all the time? I'm fucking agreeing with you, Willow. And if you're lashing out at me because of last night..." I shush him.

"Be quiet. I don't want anyone to hear about the debacle that was last night."

"Fine. Whatever. But seriously, this is all way too fast. They just got back together. I don't get it, but I don't have to get it. Neither do you."

I turn to him sharply, trying my best to keep my voice down.

"But he's your best friend and Harlow is my best friend. Don't their lives mean anything to you? This could be a huge mistake. Besides them being so young, they have a lot to figure out."

Max walks over and sits on the edge of the bed, rubbing his temples.

"But Wills, that's for them to figure out. Why anyone would want to get married is beyond me. I mean, I know he loves her, but God, I just don't get it."

I sit on the other edge of the bed — not near him, of course — and nod my head agreeing with him.

"Yeah. Why? I don't get the love thing anyway. They have so much to figure out and what I think they don't realize is that love just isn't enough. Not to mention she's going to have to deal with Craw when he finds out."

Max looks over to me with a look of revelation. He pinches the bridge of his nose and shakes his head.

"I forgot about Craw. This is going to be messy."

"Sure is. That's why I won't do it. Ever."

He questions me. "What? Love?"

My hand flies around me. "Yes, the whole thing. A relationship, love, marriage, babies. Not for me. Way too much. I like the relationship I already have."

Max looks at me oddly. "What relationship are you in?"

"The one I have with myself. I like me and only me."

A huff sounding sarcastic comment comes out of his mouth.

"So typical you. You love you. Only you."

"That's so not true. I love my parents. I'm their only kid and there's a reason behind that."

Max lets out a small laugh. "Oh, I bet there's a reason for that. They could probably only handle one of you. That's why you're an only child."

With all my might I reach my arms out in front of me and shove him right off the bed. Max falls to the floor with a thump when he lands on his ass.

He stands up rubbing his backside.

"You bitch. Even if you wanted a relationship with anyone, who would want one with you? I suggest you get out in the living room and apologize to your best friend who's crying out there." I take my defensive stance and cross my arms over my chest.

Har's crying? Over what I said?

Max goes for the doorknob but waits and turns

back around to me.

"I'm keeping my feelings about Cruz and Harlow to myself. It's not worth it. Wait and see what Harlow looks like when you go out there, then you'll see it's not worth it. I'm sorry I even thought we could have a civilized conversation about this and I'm sorry about what went on last night. Big fucking mistake."

I throw a shoe at the door and I miss hitting him. That little guy is way too quick for me.

Dammit.

Screw him. I'm the one who made the mistake last night. I don't need him reminding me. But about Harlow and Dickcop? He's right. It isn't my business. If this is what they want, then so be it. I don't have to be happy about it but it's their life.

I make my way out to the living room — head up, but still feeling crappy I made her cry. When I reach the living room, I don't see Harlow. I don't see Max or Porter. I see Cruz talking with Thea and as soon as he sees me he stalks towards me.

Here we go.

"Listen you. You made her cry. You're her best friend and you made her feel like shit. It's our life, Willow. *Our* life, not yours. Mind your business or it's going to be a long summer. I'm not going anywhere." He points to the sliding door out towards the deck and keeps talking. "That girl out there is the love of my life. She's my *whole* life, so if I see her upset, I get upset and no one, not even her best friend, will make her feel like shit. You don't support our decision? Fine. But keep your comments to yourself." He excuses himself from speaking with Thea and walks out the door. I can see him go to Har and hug her and kiss the top of her head. I see him swipe at her tears and she smiles up at him, then he walks away. I turn to Thea.

"And I suppose you're happy about all of this?"

She nods. "Yes, Wills, I am. They love each other. Who cares how old they are and they're not getting married tomorrow. All of our parents were young when they got married. If they're happy, then so be it."

Porter walks in and shakes his head at me. He stands where we are and leans his hip on the counter, crossing his arms in front of him.

"What, Porter?"

"Nothing, Wills. I didn't mean to interrupt. Go ahead, Thea. Finish what you were saying."

She begins to stutter. "I was... um, I was just going to say that..."

Porter adjusts his body so he's looking right at her and no longer at me. She swallows hard and bites her lip.

"I was going to say... good for them. I only hope someday that someone falls in love with me like that. To feel what Cruz feels for her must be amazing. For someone to love someone that much... I... I'm going to take a shower."

Thea ducks out and goes down the hall to her bedroom and shuts the door.

I look at Porter like I just saw something out of the *Twilight Zone*.

He shrugs.

"Willow, go out there and talk to her. She loves you and no matter what, your opinion and your support matters to her. Remember how long it took her to find happiness? Well, she's found it and it's with that big tattooed muscle head. Just try to be happy for them. Think about it." He pushes off the counter and comes around to give me a kiss on the top of my head and ruffles my hair like we are kids. I shove his hand away and he laughs and walks out the door. I love my cousin and he may be right.

As I walk out onto the deck I see Harlow leaning against the railing, her back to me.

I hate admitting I'm wrong. I hate sucking it up but I have always been supportive of Harlow and I need to continue to do so.

I step beside her and mimic her stance.

She knows I'm beside her, but she doesn't turn to look at me. All I can see is her swiping tears from her face.

Shit.

"Nice ring. It matches your eyes."

I wait for her response but all I get is a sniff from her.

"I guess this means I have to plan a bachelorette party?"

She continues giving me the cold shoulder.

"You know this isn't easy for me, Har. I'm not good at apologies."

She turns to me finally with a mixture of tears and anger on her face and I know at this point I'm fully prepared to take my medicine.

She leans one hand on the railing and the other is placed on her hip.

"For years and years when anyone called you a bitch and asked me how I could be friends with someone like Willow Taylor, I always stuck up for you. I always said because she's my best friend and has always had my back. And you have, Willow. You were there for me so many times and I am so thankful for that and for the friend you have been to me, but sometimes you need to stop and think before you speak. So often you stick your foot in your mouth and don't realize the consequences of what you say."

I have no words. I want to defend myself and tell her she's wrong, but I can't. I just take it.

"You are smart and beautiful but sometimes you lack the sensitivity part. If you don't agree with me being engaged to Cruz, you know what, Willow? Tough shit. I love him. I'm so in love with him and I want to spend my life with him. I'm so glad that I remember how much I love him and I'm so grateful that he never gave up on me. And I don't care what anyone thinks about it. Except for you, Willow, and I have no idea why. You aren't giving me any reasons to care what you think."

What's happening to me? Why are my eyes leaking fluid? God, I'm crying. And why do I feel so icky?

Harlow looks at me with wide eyes.

"Are you… are you crying?" I turn away to collect myself.

"No. Don't be ridiculous. I'm hung over and

the sun is bright and it stings my eyes."

I stay silent as I think about what Harlow said.

"Willow, can I ask you a question?" I nod.

"Do you know what kind of person you are? Honestly?"

I shake my head back and forth.

Harlow wraps her arms around my shoulders and squeezes me. She rests her head on my back.

"There is no one in the world like you, Willow Taylor. You are a rich brat and you know you are, but you're more than that. You are a caring, loving, funny, and loyal person and I don't think I'd be alive today without you. But there's one thing I want you to try to do. I want you to take off the tough girl shield sometimes and try to let some kind of love in. You have no idea what it feels like. What being loved like this feels like."

I sigh. "I know what being loved is like, Har. My parents love me, my friends love me."

She laughs and I feel the vibrations on my back.

"Yes. You're right. All that is true, but I'm talking about being in love, Wills."

"Maybe I don't want to feel like that. I don't understand it. I don't know if it's necessary. I see how messy it made your life. I mean, yesterday you were going to England to live with another man and take care of his kid, now you're marrying Cruz. You understand how fucked up that sounds? I don't know if I want all that mess."

She turns me around to look at her and she's smiling now.

"It's not something I need, it's something I

want. I want Cruz. I want him because he wants me. He loves me and I love him and it's the greatest feeling in the world and I want that for you. Someday, Willow I want that for you. And you're right. I was about to make my life a total mess and someone else's life a mess by going with Daniel. I love the man Daniel is, but I was never in love with him. I could have ruined his life. I could have ruined Cruz's life. So, yes, love is messy, but it's so worth the mess once you realize how wonderful it is too."

I bite my lip and when I look at Harlow's face as she speaks Cruz's name, I begin to understand how she feels. Not that I feel that way, but I see the happiness he brings her just by talking about him.

Now here's the part when I need to suck it up.

"I know you love the big asshole, and I know how much he loves you. He never gave up on you and for that he's okay in my book. I guess I was just thrown off guard. It's your life, Har. If you're happy, I'm happy."

She throws her arms around me and she's so damn mushy sometimes. I roll my eyes and pat her back.

"Thank you, Wills. Thank you. I am happy. So, so happy."

She's cutting off my air supply she's hugging me so tightly.

"Okay, okay. Enough. I get it. You are in love and you're going to marry below you." I shake my head as she smacks my arm at my last statement.

"What I'd say? You grew up in a mansion. Now you're going to marry a cop who works part-time and makes minimal coin arresting people. Have fun with that." I wink at her so she knows I'm goofing with her. Even though I'm so totally not.

"Still love me, Har?" I playfully nudge her with my shoulder.

"Yeah. Pretty much. I can't get rid of you even if I tried. You're my family."

"Now I'll be stuck with Dickcop for the rest of my life, right?"

She wiggles her eyebrows at me. "Sure will. Get used to it." I get a wink and a smile and I give a smile in return.

Harlow turns to me before she walks back into the house.

"Willow, try to remember what I said about letting love in. I want you to do exactly that — try." I swat at the air at her, trying to dismiss what she says. I want to say yes just to appease her, but I don't.

"Oh, and Wills, be careful the next time you use your flat iron. You have a really bad burn or something on your neck. I don't remember seeing it yesterday when you grabbed me from the airport. Better put some kind of ointment on it."

My hands fly to my throat even though I can't see what she's talking about. Harlow walks into the house and I run inside behind her and straight to the bathroom. I slam the door and brace my hands on the sink before looking up at what I already know is on my neck. I didn't even use a straight iron on my hair yesterday. I knew it was going to be a frizzy mess with the salt air. My eyes travel up slowly to the mirror and I see it.

It's red and spotty and it's a hickey. From Max.

That little fucker marked me.

Wonder how much *Law and Order* or *Criminal Minds* I have to watch in order to plot Max's murder and get away with it.

CHAPTER 2

Willow Taylor Will Be The Death Of Me
Max~

Currently, the crazy broad who lives next to me is banging on my bedroom door. I'm going to be late for my set at Jax so I really have no time for her bullshit right now.

"Max, open the fucking door before someone comes in the house. I'm going to kill you and I have a very good reason to want to cut off your balls."

Oh, that's really going to make me want to open the door now. Knowing that death is upon me.

"Max, I swear, open the door now or seriously suffer the consequences."

I look around my bedroom and try to plan an escape route. I'm high up so jumping out the window isn't going to work. Hiding under the bed won't work either. She'll find me. I don't have many choices.

I open the door and I see her — face red with

anger — and I swear she has steam coming out of her ears.

"What?"

She stares for a split second — her eyes lingering on my shirtless chest — so I grab my t-shirt and pull it on over my head.

Willow pulls her long hair back and exposes her neck.

"This is what!"

She points out the quarter-sized red mark on her neck. Suppressing a smile, I press my lips tight as I look at my handiwork.

I look at it, then turn away and stick some goop in my hair to get it straight up the way I like it. I check the sides of my head in the mirror, eyeing the strands and smoothing the strays that I don't want sticking out.

Willow spins me around by my shoulder so I'm looking in her direction.

"So you have nothing to say about this? All you care about is your damn coiffure?"

I cock my head to the side and look at the mark, furrow my brows and shrug, which I know even before I do it will royally piss her off.

I go back to working on my hair and lather up on my man scent.

"It's just a hickey, Willow. I didn't give you some disease. Just put on some of the hundreds of dollars worth of makeup you own and cover it."

Through the mirror I can see her pace around my room like a maniac, clenching her fists as she looks like she's about to have a mental breakdown. I need to diffuse the situation quickly or she will drive me crazy and I'll be late for sound check.

I sit on the bed and put on my black chucks.

"Look, Wills, it's really not a big deal. If anyone sees it just mention you hooked up with someone else last night, you don't remember much, and you discovered it this morning. No one saw it, right?"

She stops pacing. "Harlow did but she thought I burnt myself with my flat iron."

I tie my shoes and shake my head because she's being dramatic as usual.

"So what's the problem then? Just use that excuse if you want."

She smacks the side of my head.

God, I hate her.

"What the hell did you do that for?" I smooth the hair she just tousled and now I'm not annoyed. I'm angry.

"I have to go home today and face my parents, shorty. If they see something like this on their angel… I… well, I can't let them see it on me. And I have to go to back to work for the last week of school and I work with a few thousand thirteen year olds who will clearly distinguish that this is a hickey and not a burn mark."

"Harlow thought it was a burn mark. Why wouldn't a bunch of teenagers think that?"

Willow flops on my bed in frustration. "Because, genius, they're exactly that. Teenagers. They'll know."

I get off my bed and turn and look at her laying on mine. Her long blonde hair is splayed across my pillow and her face is so flushed from anger and… she looks gorgeous. She is gorgeous. But this is Willow and I can't stand being in the same room as her, but I can't help it if I feel my dick twitch in my jeans at this particular second.

There's a beautiful girl lying on my bed who hates me and who I just happened to fuck last night. And the kicker? I don't remember it.

Was I good?

Did she like it?

Did I like it?

She had to have, right? I mean when I cleaned up around here after she left I found a lot of condom wrappers. Could it be that the brat who was born with a silver spoon in her mouth is a freak in bed? I'll never ask her nor would it ever happen again for me to find out.

Yeah, I wish I could remember more stuff about last night. I can sort of recall her tits bouncing up and down as she rode me like a cowgirl on a bull. I sort of remember the way her ass looked as I did her from behind. Tight and firm, I think.

Well, I guess I can remember what it felt like. But how we got to that point is blurry.

Why do I even care what Willow Taylor thought of me in bed?

I can't really think about this anymore. I have to get out of here. If we are late for one more gig, there goes my chances of playing at Jax all summer and I need the money so we can cut a demo.

Images of what she must look like naked on

my bed when I'm sober need to leave my brain immediately. I'll never go fishing in that pond again. Gin-soaked blood or not.

I check my watch. "Okay, now you gotta go. I need to get to Jax in, oh, about five minutes ago for a sound check."

She groans and sits up in my bed, swinging her legs over the side and pushes off. She flips her hair and I watch her go towards the mirror again and inspect the love bite that started this whole conversation.

"So you have nothing to say about this? I'm just supposed to go home and deal with it? It's huge. You couldn't have put it behind my ear or on the back of my neck. Typical of you to put it practically in the front of my throat for all the world to see. My neck is not a stage, idiot."

"Willow, really it's no big deal. A hickey isn't going to ruin your precious reputation." I grab my keys and my wallet-chain and hook it onto my belt loop.

She stands in front of me when I turn around, she's in her normal bitch stance. I try to dodge her from further interaction with me but she's way too fast and every move I make, she's right in front of me. Finally, after several attempts of trying to get my body around hers I stop 'cause now, at this point, I'm exhausted.

"Jesus, Willow. Listen, in a few days it will be gone and you will be picture perfect once again. And never will these lips be cast upon your skin. It will just be something that happened." In true Willow fashion she points at my chest and talks to me through gritted teeth.

"You got that right, little man. I will never drink whiskey again in your presence. I will never be in this room again, and I will never see what you try to pass off as a dick again."

I snicker.

"There's really nothing wrong with my dick, Willow. Seven condom wrappers proved that." I take my hand and gently tap her cheek.

Her hand comes up and smacks my hand away but she's as quick as a whip and before I can even stop her she takes a chunk of my heavily pomaded hair and pulls at it — hard.

"Ow! What the fucking hell, Willow!"

She has such a grip on my hair that I have to slightly bend over just to relieve some of the pain. She twists her hand and her body and I've never wanted to hit a girl before, but God help me, I want to now.

"You will never, ever remind me of last night. Your name and reference to your dick will never be spoken again in the same sentence."

"Okay," I growl out.

She bends down to my level, getting close to my ear. "What's that, Max? I can't hear you? Speak up, please?"

Now if I call her a crazy bitch she will surely pull harder and I will soon be bald. I take the easy way out. I just give in to avoid any more pain.

"I said okay, Willow. I will never talk about my dick again nor will I ever talk about you and my dick again."

That must have calmed her. She lets go of my

hair and smooths out her clothes as I check to see if there is any start of male-pattern baldness because of her hissy fit.

"Well, then, that's that. I will cover this up with my most expensive makeup and go on with my life." I push her aside so I can get out the door.

"Yep. Let's bury the body and go right back to where we were about five minutes ago which is hating each other."

Willow lets out a breath and instead of exiting my room, she tries to make some sort of small talk.

"I… um, sort of apologized to Harlow. I was just in shock about her and the big goofball."

Playing with the keys in my hand, I give her somewhat of a smile.

"Nice to hear. She loves you. I have no idea why, but she does." I place my hand on the doorknob to leave but something about the way she looks right now is sort of vulnerable. Like she wants to talk and something in me tells me I should ask what's up. Even though she just caused me extreme pain, I'm the one who is human in this room.

"Sorry about that last statement. You're a good friend to her, Wills." Her facial expression is blank until she raises her nose up in the air after my politeness. It's almost as though she thought about what I said and accepted and appreciated it, then realized that I was the one giving her the compliment and her demeanor has changed because of it.

"Um… so you got the job for the summer at

Jax?" She plays with a strand of her golden hair and bites the inside of her mouth.

I let out a slight chuckle. "Not if I don't get out of here right now." A ghost of a smile appears on her face.

"You going home today?" I turn and ask her.

"Yes. I have to finish grading finals. I didn't expect my best friend to call me from the airport yesterday to tell me she wasn't going to England to live and to come pick her up. I was in the middle of grading."

I nod in understanding.

"Last week of school then?"

"Yep. I guess I'll see you guys next weekend." Silence surrounds the room for a few moments.

I open the door and look at her over my shoulder.

"Be careful driving back to Princeton, Wills. And that really is a nasty hickey so you better put on some extra spackle."

I wink at her because I know she hates it, and she flips me the bird and gives me a tight-lipped smile, which is an endearing quality in her. She looks a mess but a gorgeous one. No use in denying it. Too bad she's the daughter of Satan.

I will never ever be able to win with Willow Taylor. No matter how nice or sarcastic I am. I'm just hoping that she takes mercy on my hair this summer. After all, it is my trademark.

CHAPTER 3

I'll Always Be Daddy's Little Girl
Willow~

I managed to get out of the house without any further crap from anyone about the way I reacted to Cruz and Harlow being engaged. Cruz was at his house and Harlow and Thea were getting ready for the beach. I really didn't want to leave but responsibility calls. I have finals to grade and I need to get ready for the last week of school. Harlow doesn't have to 'cause she's supposed to be in England. Now she has no job and no place to live since she sub-leased her apartment. Not that it matters right now because we'll be in Sandy Cove all summer. She could come and stay with me at my parents' when the fall semester starts. They have six bedrooms so there's plenty of room.

Yes. I still live with my parents. Why the hell not? I'm an only child and my parents' house is so goddamn big it's like having my own place anyway.

My parents — Bill and Tessa Taylor — live in a ten-thousand-square-foot, Tudor-style home in the swanky part of Princeton. I've lived in that home all my life. I have the whole east wing to myself so why move out? I have my own bedroom, bathroom, dressing room, and sitting room. We have a cook who prepares lunches and dinners for us Monday through Thursday because my parents run their own PR firm for a production studio in New York. They aren't home most nights during the week. Mom loves to cook so she does a lot of it on the weekends.

I'm the apple of their eye. Their princess. I'll admit that. I'm spoiled rotten. I'll admit that too. I've been given everything I've ever wanted from them. Clothes, a car, my education. Name it — they gave it to me. But don't get me wrong, it's not because they are trying to compensate for their absence — they just love me.

They never moved to NYC because they didn't want to uproot me. They wanted something more stable for their daughter. They saw how my relationship with Harlow developed into a sisterhood, and being an only child they didn't want to take that away from me.

When I walk into the house I see our maid, Lupe, in the large foyer of our home as she waters the many plants that surround it.

"Miss Willow. You are home. So good to see you." I drop my small Louis Vuitton overnight bag on the floor as Lupe comes in for a hug. I love Lupe and she's like a grandparent to me. I don't have a large family and she has been working for my family since I was a year-and-a-half-old.

"I'm home, Lupe. Not for long, but I'm here."

She smiles at me and takes my bag from the floor and I snatch it from her and roll my eyes.

"Lupe, I can get my bag. Besides, it's Saturday, why are you here? You don't work weekends?"

"Oh, Mr. Bill and Mrs. Tessa are having guests this evening and they wanted some extra help."

"Well, how about I help *you* out? What needs to be done and where are my parents anyway?"

We walk towards the back of the house where the kitchen is.

Lupe turns her head to me as she speaks, "Mr. Bill is on the phone in his office and Mrs. Tessa is in the kitchen."

When I enter the grand entrance to our kitchen, I see my mom's back is to me. Her hands chopping away at something and Al Green is on the grandiose sound system we have installed.

"Mother," I yell. She turns my way and sees me and smiles. She wipes her hands on a towel and comes right over to me and engulfs me in a hug.

"Hello, darling."

She releases me and looks at me, her forehead wrinkling up.

"How did it go with Harlow? Is she okay? I'm still so confused by the whole thing. I'm so surprised she walked away from that young man and his child. She must have been really confused to have done that. I talked to Annabelle this morning and she told me she would tell me everything tonight when they come over."

I sigh and go to the refrigerator and fetch an apple from inside. I plop down on one of the stools that surround the kitchen island. I inspect the apple and take a bite from it. Not really wanting to tell my mother anything, I just chew and roll my eyes.

"Willow? You're not going to tell me, are you?"

I finish chewing. "Nope. I'll let Annabelle tell you when she comes but it's a long story. Lupe told me you're having guests? Who is coming?"

"The Hannums, the Johnsons, and Aunt Addy and Uncle Paul."

Aunt Addy and Uncle Paul are Porter's parents and Addy is my mom's sister.

"Is it okay if I don't eat with you tonight? I have finals to grade and I'm leaving for Sandy Cove first thing Friday evening so I have to pack."

Mother strokes my cheek and smiles but shakes her head. "Oh, Willow. I'm so proud of you. You really have found your niche in teaching. But I will miss you this summer. Don't forget we have a family weekend planned in the Hamptons the weekend of the fourth. I really expect you to be there this year, sweetie. Last year you missed it and I would really like you to come."

I can't say no to her even though July fourth in Sandy Cove is so much fun. Maybe I can negotiate.

"Would it be okay if I just spent one night? We usually do a party on the fourth in Sandy Cove."

She looks disapproving which she doesn't very often. I bat my eyelashes at her.

"Please, Mother. Even if Porter comes with me for the night?"

Her lips twist and her face scrunches up a bit. Her hands go to her hips as she inspects my face.

"Well… I just don't know…"

I hear the front door open and my dad calls out.

"I see my little girl's car in the driveway. Is she home?"

I hop off the stool and run into the foyer to hug the ever-loving shit out of the only man in my life who matters. My father.

"Daddy." I leap to him and throw my arms around his neck and he wraps his hands around me, gently picking me up off the ground from his embrace. He sets me down as I let out a small laugh.

He holds out my arms and surveys me like Mother usually does. I smile boldly at him turning myself slightly back and forth.

"Oh, Willow. I know it's only been a few days since I've seen you but is it me or do you get more beautiful everyday? Maybe I'm just biased."

I shake my head. "No, Daddy. You're probably right." I'm not serious. I mean I love myself but I'm not that vain.

Well… maybe just a little.

We both laugh and he pulls me into the side of his body as we walk towards the kitchen where my mother is.

"So did everything get straightened out at the beach, sweetie?" I nod and tell him the long story even before he has the chance to ask me. He kisses my temple and goes right to Mother and kisses her cheek softly as she continues her chopping. He steals a chopped pepper right from underneath her eyes and pops it in his mouth. She smacks his hand.

"That's for my homemade salsa, Billy. Hands off."

My mother still calls her high school sweetheart of a husband Billy and it cracks me up.

Daddy shrugs and takes a seat next to me on one of the counter stools. He places his briefcase on the counter and pulls out a small box. A blue one. You know where from. He slides it over to me and winks. I look up at him with my jaw agape and then look to my mother as she gives me a look of encouragement to open the box.

I quickly go to work, undoing the bow and taking the top off the box. Inside lays a beautiful silver necklace with a round circle of diamonds and Roman letters. It's absolutely gorgeous. It's so shiny and beautiful and just so perfect but I'm sort of confused as to what it is exactly.

My eyes wander up between both my parents and they can tell I'm grateful but confused.

Daddy gets off his chair and takes the necklace from me and stands behind me. I move my hair to the side as he attempts to hook the necklace around my neck. I swing my hair to the side where that damn hickey is that Max gave me and do my best to conceal it with my hair along with the pound of concealer I put on before I left for home.

"It's a compass, my darling girl. It's to remind you that you'll always know what direction to go towards. We are so very proud of you for making it to the end of your first year of teaching, Willow. So very proud." He hooks the necklace and I hold it gently in my hands and run the pad of my thumb across the facets of diamonds.

"Mother, Daddy, you didn't have to do this. You always give me so much."

Daddy kisses the top of my head. "That's because it's well deserved and you are my one and only princess so I will give you what I want when I want. Anything for you, my sweet girl."

I kiss my dad's cheek and thank him and my mother.

Daddy grabs his briefcase and rubs his face.

"You look tired, Billy. You have a few hours till the guests come. Why don't you go lie down."

He nods, agreeing with her. "Yes, I am tired actually. I think I'll do exactly that. You joining us for dinner, princess?"

"I can't, Daddy. Sorry. I have finals to grade and I want to start packing for the summer." He looks a little sad. I want to spend time with him and Mother. I'd like to catch up with the Hannums and my aunt and uncle, but I have other priorities to attend to before I can actually not act like an adult for the next twelve weeks.

"Daddy, how about we do lunch this week before I go. Just us."

He nods happily and I see a gleam in his eye. "I like that idea. I'll see you later, my princess."

When my dad makes his way upstairs, I see a look in my mother's eyes that's not one of comfort. She studies him as he walks out of the room.

"You okay, Mother?"

She shakes out of her daydream.

"Oh, yes, darling. I'm fine." Her smile really doesn't reassure me, but I don't ask any questions. I excuse myself and go to my wing of the house to finish grading the finals. Grades are due on Wednesday so now I know it's going to be a long night. Harlow fucked my whole weekend up. These papers could have been done by now. I have to remind myself to smack her on the good side of her head.

With my music blaring and my bed covered in piles of exams, I'm making some progress with the grading. Every once in a while I hear my parents and their guests laugh loud enough to make me smile. I wonder if everyone in Sandy Cove is at Jax. I texted Harlow earlier but she hasn't answered me back. I feel nauseous just thinking about where I'm pretty sure she is. In the room next to mine at the beach house getting it on with the wannabe Vin Diesel.

Thea didn't answer me back yet either and the curiosity as to what everyone is up to is killing me. I call Porter.

He answers after a few rings.

"Hey, Wills. What's happening?"

"That's why I'm calling. I'm grading exams and going crazy thinking about what sort of fun everyone is having. Where are the girls? What are you guys doing?"

I hear a sigh come out of my cousin's mouth. "I'm at Jax working. Cruz and Harlow went to see Tony and Bella to tell them about the engagement. Thea is…" He cuts off and breathes out in frustration. "She's talking to some guy at a table on the other side of the room in some dark corner. She's laughing at him and he's touching her hand."

My ears perk up at that.

"Really now. Thea is flirting with a guy? She never does that. Good for her. Hope she gets some. Is he hot?"

Porter growls in the phone. "Willow, how the hell should I know if he is or not. She's laughing at something he's saying. That's all I know. Don't ask me about hot guys… and Thea."

So hearing the way my cousin says his last words makes me wonder why he sounds so frazzled. Is he jealous? Does he like Thea? Then I stop and think about how ludicrous that sounds. Porter looks at her like he looks at Harlow. Like his little sisters. We've been friends forever. He protects her — he protects all of us. His voice sounds like that because he's protective of her.

"Porter, she's fine. Let her have some fun. She never dates. Random tongue tangles and maybe a boobie touch but…"

"Enough, Willow. Not listening to any more. What do you want anyway? I heard my parents are there."

"Yep. I went down for a few minutes. The Johnsons and Hannums are here too."

"Yikes. How are the Hannums dealing with everything? They say anything about Craw?"

"They haven't spoken with him but they seem to be okay with everything. They think as long as Harlow's happy, that's all that matters. She's been through enough in her life and they love him…" I groan.

"Well, get used to him being in your life, Wills. He's not going anywhere and I'm glad."

I roll my eyes. "Yeah, yeah, yeah… so, um… where's Max?"

"Getting ready for his set. You guys didn't leave on the best of terms today, did you?"

"He's an asswipe, so basically… no, as usual. He annoys me."

"No shit." He laughs. "Listen, Wills. I have to go. See you Friday?"

"Yep. I'll see you Friday."

Porter hangs up and I stretch my arms over my head. I hear a knock at my door.

"Come in." It's Daddy with a bowl of something in his hand.

"Hi, princess, I wanted to bring you a treat since you're up here working so hard." He sits on the edge of my bed and hands me a bowl of my mother's famous and delicious creme brûlée. I crave it when I'm not home. When she and I are home on the weekend, she makes it for me. I adore it with fresh berries on top of it and that's exactly how she made it this time.

"Thanks, Daddy." He picks up one of the exams and looks at it and laughs pointing to an answer to a question about what something in Spanish means and the student wrote that it meant 'walking the dog in the meat factory.'

"Is this for real?" I laugh too.

"Daddy, they're in seventh grade. They try, but to answer your question, as far as I know, yes, this one is dead serious."

I dig further into the creme brûlée savoring each spoonful.

My dad gets up from my bed and walks towards the door.

"I'm going to miss you this summer, Willow, but it's the time of your life right now and I want you to have fun and be young."

My dad is a serious person but usually not with me, and I wonder why he sounds somber but at the same time telling me all of this.

I put down my bowl and criss-cross my legs and lean over.

"Daddy, I'll miss you, too, but you know I'll be back to visit. I'll see you for Mom's birthday and for the fourth." He doesn't seem at ease. I get up from my bed and walk over to him, wrapping my hands around his waist.

"Oh, Daddy. I didn't realize you were going to miss me that much. It's not so bad. I was away at school for longer periods of time." His cheek goes to my temple and he breathes out a sigh.

"I know, princess. I guess it's just that you're older and not a little girl anymore. It's quiet around here without you sometimes. I'm so used to you, Harlow, and Thea being here but now you're all working and adults and… well, it just reminds me I'm getting older."

I squeeze him a bit tighter.

"Daddy, you're not old. You're the most handsome and special man on the earth and I'll always be your princess. Don't ever worry about that."

He rocks me a little as we stand here. "What if someone else sweeps you off your feet and wants you to be their princess?" I nip that in the bud.

"Not going to happen. I'm not getting a boyfriend anytime soon. No marriage or babies either. Maybe never."

He pulls away from me and looks so serious. He holds me by my shoulders.

"Willow, please don't say that. I know you're young but never let the reality of love escape you. Think of the possibility. Marrying your mom was the best thing I've ever done. I fell in love with her from the moment I saw her. Seventeen years old and I knew she had to be mine. And she was and then so were you."

My dad makes me smile. Even if he worked sixty-plus hours a week while I was growing up, he used every second of his spare time for my mother and me. He's such a hard worker and wanted me not to grow up the spoiled rich brat everyone thinks I am. Spoiled… yeah, okay, but not to the point where I don't respect the hard work and the things he and my mother provide for me. So what if I have enough Tiffany jewelry to open my own online store and a kick-ass, suped-up Range Rover. So what if they took me to Europe for vacation every summer from the time I was six. Those factions were learning ones as well. I saw museums and experienced the different cultures. I learned so much on those trips. It wasn't just me laying on a beach in St. Tropez. They have the money to provide these things. People on the outside see all of it and automatically think 'rich brat.' You know what? Let them. I don't fucking care what other people think.

"Okay, Daddy, but like I said, not anytime soon." I don't mean a thing I say but I want to make him happy so I tell him I'll open my brain and maybe my heart to what he wishes for me. I'll never be anyone's center of attention like I am my father's and I'm not sure I ever want to be. I just want to always be daddy's little girl.

CHAPTER 4

Summa, Summa, Summatime
Max~

The beginning of summer is always the best. It's getting warmer by the day but the nights are hot, and by that I mean playing at Jax almost every night of the week. This place gets packed and the lights from the stage give me a burn unlike the sun. I live for this. I live for being on the stage and even though a piece of paper says I'm a mechanical engineer that's not who I am. I thought it was but my feelings change as soon as my fingers hit those guitar strings. I know I went to school so I could make something of myself but what pumps the blood within my veins is music. The degree is the basis of a future I thought I wanted. Music though is what has become my life. It's my existence. It owns my soul.

Settling in my summer routine is easy. Waking up late from being at Jax well past last call, beach time when I do wake up, then back to the bar.

Porter got Cruz a job at Jax as a bouncer since he lost his job as a cop. He also does some work at another bar for more money. He's also doing more online courses during the day. He takes a big risk bringing his damn laptop to the beach on the days we go, but I give him a lot of credit for being so focused. I admire him for that. He juggles work, school, and his lady.

Thea works for Harlow's dad during the week. She worked something out where she works a few hours longer Monday through Thursday. This allows her to have Fridays off in the summer so she's usually here by Thursday night. Harlow will be here all summer and seems to be doing well. Cruz takes her two mornings a week to a local facility for physical therapy for her legs. And Willow…

She's a bitch. We just don't get along. It's like Harlow and Cruz not liking each other when we all first started living down here a few years ago but times that by ten. She has zero patience for me. Every word that comes out of my mouth she hates. She comments about my hair, my stature, my clothes. I cook dinner for everyone the one night a week I don't work and she turns her nose up at everything I make. I'm a pretty damn good cook. Not all of us are lucky enough to have had a cook growing up and eat whatever we wanted at a moment's notice. I made Chicken Divan — my signature dish — last week and when I dished it out, she automatically took her plate and dumped it in the garbage and went back to her house. Which, of course, started a war between us. Why?

Because I fished it out of the trash can and then proceeded to dump it on her car from the deck above. Oh, she is feisty when she's pissed. Her face flushes this pink color and her huge green eyes fill with rage. Her knuckles go stark white from fisting her palms together. It's comical really. The difference is she can dish it out, throw it away, but when it's spilled back onto her, literally, she can't take it. One of us will kill each other by summer's end and it's only been two weeks.

Craw is coming today. He's been M.I.A. for a while. He has been here once. His girlfriend Ally isn't ready to be around Harlow and Cruz because of her brother Daniel so she has Craw on a very short leash. No, thank you. No girl is going to tell me when or where I can go and whom I can see. Especially if one of those people is your sister. No chick is worth that. When he did come over, most of the time it was he and Harlow discussing things. It all happened so abruptly and the engagement threw Craw for a loop. It's not that he doesn't like Cruz but the situation with Harlow and Ally is a tender one. I can understand why Ally doesn't want to be around Harlow. She broke her brother's heart, but Craw and Harlow are really close so she needs to understand that as well. It's not my business, but I miss hanging with Craw.

Today is beach day. It's gorgeous out and I have the night off. I'm going to soak it all in and enjoy the day.

I fall asleep on my towel for a few minutes and I'm woken up by a slight kick to my leg. I look up to my left and squint from the sun and see someone through the haze.

"Hey, man. Nap time's over." It's Craw. I hop up and give him a bro hug. Porter does the same and so do Thea and Willow. We all stand in a circle, happy to see our friend.

"Great to see you, dude. You just get here?"

He shrugs. "Nah, been here for a while. I was up at the house talking to my sister and Cruz."

I look at his face and I can tell it probably didn't go very well. They haven't been getting along from what I gather. I wish things were different. He's torn. I get it, to a certain extent. He has his girl and he wants to make her happy but her being around Harlow and Cruz is going to take some time, if it ever does.

"So, I'm guessing it didn't go very well."

Craw shakes his head and runs his hands over his short hair.

"I'm trying to make Harlow understand that Ally is really upset over the whole thing. Her brother has had his heart broken so much over the past few years and then she dumps him right there at the fucking airport. There's no goodbye to his son Henry, she just left. She didn't see what the repercussions would be."

I nod, agreeing with him.

"I'm sorry, but it's hard for me to be with Ally and see the sadness she has for her brother and I care about her a lot. Then I think about how irresponsible Har has been and it pisses me off."

Willow opens her big mouth and spits out her fury.

"You and your little play thing need to get over it, Craw. She's happy and your sister hasn't been happy in a very long time."

We all stare at her because her voice is so full of annoyance.

"What? What did I say that's so wrong? It's true. It's over and done. I'm not trying to be cold, Craw, but this is Harlow. Your best friend and sister. You can't allow some girl you just care a lot about ruin your relationship." She air quotes when she says 'girl you care a lot about.'

Craw's eyes go cold and hard — totally pissed at her words.

"Fuck you, Willow."

She throws down her sunglasses on her beach chair and her arms start to flail around her.

"Fuck me, Craw? Really? You're going to say that to me? Remember when she tried to kill herself over Chad? Remember staying with her day and night during that time? Remember when she was in a coma and the pain that caused you? How about when she forgot almost everything but her name? That's sadness and that's pain, Craw. So you want to say to me fuck you? Fine, but remember what *she* has gone through."

Their eyes square up and because she's so damn tall, they are eye to freaking eye.

"Don't you think I know what she's gone through, Willow. I was there. Every single fucked up part of the last few years of my sister's life. I watched her almost die, twice. I don't need your mouth. I don't need your opinions. I need you to mind your own business." Craw steps away from her and I don't think she's done with him.

Craw grabs a beer from our cooler and pops the cap off. He crashes his body down on the sand and drinks almost the entire bottle.

And just when I think that shuts her up — in true Willow fashion — her mouth still runs.

"She is my business, Craw. She'll always be my business. You should think about that instead of some stupid piece of ass that will most likely dump you before the summer is over."

Craw is like a puma, jumping up from his place in the sand right in front of her face.

"She's not a stupid piece of ass. I think I love the girl and I want it to work so I have to try to figure out how to fit these two people in my life. You wouldn't know anything about that 'cause all you do is love yourself. Brat."

I laugh and instantly get a death-stare look from her. Her head snaps so damn quick it's like she automatically knew I'd say something and she was fully prepared for it.

She points at me with hatred.

"You shut your mouth, Mini-Me."

My eyes go wide. I didn't say anything, I just laughed 'cause Craw called an almost twenty-four-year-old woman a brat and I kinda love it.

"I didn't say anything, but he's right, Willow. It's none of your business how Ally feels and you shouldn't say she needs to get over it. You have no idea what Ally needs to get over. Her brother is hurting and she cares enough about him to feel the way she's feeling. Craw is confused. He can't just get over it. It affects him all around. You want Harlow to get over the fact that she can't have kids?"

Slap.

Yeah, she slapped me. I don't see it coming but I do feel Porter hold me back and after I turn my head to look at her again I do see Thea gripping her arm.

"How dare you? How dare you say such a thing? How could you?" Her face is so serious and she looks hurt.

Maybe that was harsh, but I tell the truth. I don't say anything to her. My face is still stinging from her hand, which doesn't make me feel bad that my words actually hurt *her.*

I shrug Porter's hands off of me.

I hear his voice low from behind me. "Remember, Max, we don't hit girls."

Porter knows me and he knows that I would so knock her out if she wasn't a girl.

I stand right up to her, well, to her chin. I lick my lips as I look at her reddened face and eye her up. A cocky smirk on my face and I quietly speak as I calm myself down and remember she's a chick so I can't lay her out.

"Don't you ever touch me again. Don't talk to me for the rest of the summer. Pretend I don't exist."

Her expression is blank and all we do is stare at each other for a few moments. I back up after she has no comeback. I grab my towel and sunglasses and just tread up the beach to the boardwalk. I'll find a bar to hang out in or just go home and sleep the rest of the day away. Anything to get away from her.

"Don't worry, short stuff. That won't be a problem."

Bitch.

After the slap heard 'round the world, things are no better between Willow and myself.

Actually, they've gotten worse.

We play games with each other. I hide her keys or her makeup when she's not home. I sneak in the girl's house and I hide each piece of lipstick or mascara or all the rest of that shit around the house. Like an Easter egg hunt. It drives her crazy. She stole my favorite guitar picks and put them in a container of water then stuck it in the extra freezer in the garage. It took Cruz and me two hours and two hairdryers we borrowed from Thea and Harlow to thaw them out. Which made me late for my set at Jax one night. That's when I melted all her lipstick on the stove then poured the contents in her fancy expensive shoes. That night when she was coming up to Jax with the gang, she got a foot filled with melted and expensive lipstick.

That's when she put crazy glue in my hair wax. Porter had to cut my hand off my hair. Or the other way around. Either way, bye-bye mohawk.

She gives it to me — I give it right back but all the while keeping our pact not to talk to one another. I think the gang is getting used to it. They really have no choice.

I'll be on stage and see her at a table with the girls and she'll just hold up her middle finger and hold it there, and hold it there, and hold it there. Sometimes it's just erect and her eyes aren't even on me. She'll sense I'm looking, though. She'll just drink and laugh with her friends or flirt with guys but the middle finger will still be saluting.

This same night I see Willow talking it up with some guy who looks like he just stepped out of the pages of GQ for Spoiled Rich Brats - frat house edition. He's wearing a pink polo shirt. Pink. I mean, is she serious? Mr. Prep-school is making her laugh. What could he possibly be saying to make her laugh so hard? I can see her hand go to his forearm. When she takes a sip of her drink, she always darts out her tongue and circles it around the straw. She draws attention to her mouth with this move and it appears to work. I can see how she peers up at him with her big eyes and long lashes when she's sipping on her cocktail. And then her go-to move — the hair flipping to one side to show off her long, tanned neck. An invitation for this guy to lick it. I'm not stupid. I see her do this move all the damn time. It's like she practices in front of a mirror or something.

I see her push back her chair slightly and cross her one leg over the other. She faces pink shirt guy and runs her manicured nail around her knee cap. Okay, here we go again. Another move to now draw attention to her long, golden-colored legs. So smooth and soft. Yep. I remember what they felt like.

Well, kind of. And my pants begin to tighten in the crotch.

Dammit!

Dicks have minds of their own, I swear.

Pink shirt gets closer in her ear, the ear where the hair is swept away from. I see him look at her with wanton eyes. He licks his bottom lip and tries to go in for the kill. He places a small kiss on the exposed skin of her neck and he lingers there. A little too long. But that's all he does.

And she likes it. I can tell. I can also tell that this is not helping the current problem in my pants.

Why should I be sporting wood over some guy lusting over Willow? I'm certifiable.

Pink shirt places his hand on her hip and holds it there. They move in closer to each other. She whispers something in his ear and his eyes grow heavy with lust. Pink shirt says something else to her, then stands up and walks towards the bathroom. When he's out of sight, Willow goes in her purse, fetches her small compact mirror and checks her hair and face. Pink shirt guy high-fives a friend — I suspect — on the way to the bathroom so what do I do? I follow him.

I enter the bathroom and unzip my fly in front of one of the urinals. Pink shirt is in there talking it up with a guy in a more hideous purple-colored shirt. Don't these two have mirrors? And Willow says *I'm* a bad dresser.

I stand there and listen closely to their conversation.

Purple shirt asks pink shirt if he's going to tap that piece of ass in the bar with the legs and the hair. Pink shirt says yes, that he's going to give it to her so good, she'll still feel his dick in her for a week. Purple shirt asks pink shirt if he can have some of that when he's through with her tonight. Pink shirt tells him 'sure, why not?' He'll send him a text when he's done.

Now, normally I would just go about my pissing, but I'm not so comfy with the way these two douches are talking about her. I mean she's like jock itch to me but still. So I whip out my phone as I zip up my pants. Pink and purple are still talking and I pretend to answer my phone.

"Oh, hey, man. Sorry, phone was on vibrate. Yeah, she's here. Willow, yeah, yeah. I have no idea but the last time I went down on her it was like going down on a gorilla. Yeah, big 70s bush. I thought that went out of style years ago. I know, man. How am I supposed to get anything accomplished when her beaver is not lady-scaped. No, I doubt she did. She told me she doesn't believe in razors or showering everyday. Yeah, I know. You try to look past it, but it's impossible. Yeah, okay, man. See ya." I hang up with my pretend phone call and go to the sink to wash my hands. Pink and purple stand there with their jaws dropped, looking right at me through the mirror. Pink speaks up.

"Um, excuse me, man, but, um… I didn't mean to eavesdrop but were you just talking about that girl Willow who's sitting out there. The tall blonde with the legs?"

I nonchalantly lift my chin and nod to him. "Yeah. You know her?"

He laughs. "No, not yet but I was hoping to." An inquisitive look appears on his face. "Uh, but is it true?"

I dry my hands on my shirt. "Is what true?" *Douche.*

"About her, you know." He motions to his crotch with his hands. "And her hygiene."

My expression changes from being curious about his answer to one I can appear to vouch for fictionally.

"Oh, that. Hey, have you guys ever seen the movie *The Planet of the Apes?*"

They both nod yes.

I wave them in closer so no one else who may be in the bathroom would hear.

"Good. That's all you need to know." I shake my head and leave them looking nothing less than terrified.

I walk out pretty proud of myself and pass by Willow's table where she's sitting now with Thea. She eyes me quickly and gives me the one finger salute. I don't say a word. I just give her a wicked smile and walk away. I know this worked because a guy doesn't want to go down a girl's pants and find a rainforest between her legs. He wants smooth. He wants the pink. He wants a well-landscaped lady. Unless he has a fetish for old school porn, then we have a problem. But I think it will go in my favor.

Bye-bye, pink shirted-douche.

After our set I roll up to the bar for a drink. I'm hot and tired and tonight I don't plan on staying except for one drink. I feel a hand touch my sweaty shoulder as I lean on the bar and something sweet smelling breathing words in my ear.

"I really like the way you play. Are your hands good for anything else besides playing the guitar?" I bite the inside of my cheek and feel a twitch in my pants. I turn my neck while still leaning. A girl stands there and smiles at me. She's tanned with long straight brown hair. Her big eyes twinkle and her eyebrows raise at me suggestively.

Lazily, I answer, "My hands can certainly do other things. They sometimes seem to have a mind of their own." I wink at her and raise my glass of Jack and Coke to her.

"I like that. I'm Cassie."

I turn my body around and lean my back on the bar, my elbows resting on it behind me.

"Max."

"I know who you are. I'm here most nights you guys play."

"Oh, really. You like what we play?"

"I like what *you* play. I like to watch you play."

Her tongue darts out to lick her bottom lip. That's hot.

This could be interesting.

"Wanna grab a table and sit?" She nods.

We go to a table after I buy her a drink. We sit close. Real close. Cassie is from New York and here for the summer with her friends. She's a senior in college. Young and gorgeous. Killer smile, killer legs, and killer tits, from what I can see from the tight shirt she's sporting. Even though she was a little forward at first, she seems to actually be intelligent and sweet. When a girl approaches me like she did they're usually drunk and, well, so am I and I haven't gotten laid since… shit. Memorial Day weekend with… fucking Willow.

I'm going to change that. Tonight.

Cassie and I continue to talk as people start to exit way past last call. The gang is still here but they start to filter out. Cruz and Harlow leave first, telling me that Har is sleeping in his room tonight. That means I need ear plugs. Porter is still cleaning up the bar. Thea and "The Bitch" are still here but come to my table.

"Hey, Max. We're going back to the house. You going home with Porter or do you want to share a cab with us?" Thea asks and "The Bitch" stands there looking bored until she sees Cassie at my table.

"Let him find his own way home. I'm going to the bathroom before we go." A flip of the bird in my direction and she's gone. Thea rolls her eyes and mouths 'sorry' to me.

I'm used to it. I don't even think Cassie saw Willow's immature gesture at me. I wouldn't care if she did anyway. But I'd just have to explain our total and absolute distaste for one another.

"I'm going to go to the bar and wait for Willow. See you later." Thea walks away.

Cassie stands up and straightens her tight skirt. *Damn, she's hot.*

"Actually I need to go to the ladies room as well. Will you wait for me?"

I give her a wink and tell her, "Of course."

I wait longer than expected and I wonder why it always takes girls so long to pee. Guys are just quick. Whip it out, do what we need to do and out the door. Girls on the other hand…

I see Willow waltz out of the bathroom. A very satisfied, cocky grin on her face. She must have had to really pee. She breezes by my table and extends her favorite finger my way. She says something to Porter and his jaw hangs open, and then he shakes his head. She grabs Thea at the bar and they take off out the door. A moment later Cassie shows up. I stand up when I see her and I'm so ready to take her back to my house and do stuff to her with the hands she admires so much. I can show her things that would make her head spin.

"So do you want to go back to my place for another drink?"

She shyly tucks her hair behind her ear and doesn't look directly at me but speaks.

"Um… actually it's getting late and I have something to do early tomorrow. I'm sorry. I'll see you soon."

She leaves the bar with me having a semi-hard on and I'm pretty sure that was the weirdest thing I've ever experienced.

I'm stunned. I have no idea what the hell just happened. Maybe she got sick and she was too embarrassed to say anything.

Oh, well. Guess it's just me and a bottle of lotion again.

I pack up my guitar and head to the bar where Porter is stocking clean glasses behind it.

"P, can I grab a ride with you? My, um… plans for the night just changed."

He laughs. "I'll say." I look at him confused, crinkling my brows.

"Huh?"

"Guess Wills scared her off. Sorry, man."

I feel my blood pressure rise slightly as I come to realize "The Bitch" sabotaged any chance of me getting some ass tonight.

I look at him inquisitively.

"And what does that mean exactly? What did she say to her?"

He leans in to me, looking around so no one else can hear. "Now don't quote me on the whole conversation but she told me she was sending that girl home… alone. Oh, and said she told her your weenie was small and you had a case of herpes."

"FUUCCCKKK," I yell out. The remaining waitresses and bartenders turn and look at me.

"Relax, Max. This is just another one of her games. You two have been torturing each other for weeks now."

My fists are tight and I want to strangle her or hit something hard. Not her because boys don't hit girls. Porter gently reminds me of this again.

"She's gone too far this time, P. Paybacks are a bitch."

I don't even wait for a reply before I head out

the door and take off towards our house. I forgo my guitar and almost full sprint the twelve blocks there.

When I get there I stand in front of the house, bending over with my hands on my knees panting like a dog. I'm so out of breath but my hate fuel gives me all I need to confront Willow and her random acts of bitchiness.

The house is dark. I use the hidden spare key and let myself into the girl's house. It's quiet. I know Thea is sleeping and Harlow is at my house. When I reach Willow's door, I don't even bother to knock, I go right in. I try and still my anger towards her and my plan is to rip her out of her bed and give her a fight. I want to give her a battle. I want to give her fierce consequences, but I don't want Thea to wake up or the guys next door to hear me scream at her and be subjected to our WWE-type verbal match.

I walk to her bed and see her sleeping so quietly. Her blonde hair laying across the pillow, one of her long, lean legs wrapped around another pillow. She looks so peaceful.

Not for long.

Bitch.

I yank the pillow from under her head and it flops onto the mattress. She wakes up startled and hops out of bed and takes a karate-type stance.

"What the hell... what the... Max?" Realizing it's me she lets her hands down and backs up and switches on her bedside lamp.

Her hair is a tangled mess, her cheeks are flushed. Wearing a tight tank top and tiny boy shorts, she's a combo of flustered and… beauty.

She looks fucking beautiful.

"What are you doing in my room? Get the fuck out." Her voice is raised and I place my finger on her lips as I tell her to shush. She smacks my hand away from her face.

"You'll wake everyone up. I came here to settle this like adults, Willow. I know what you did with that girl in the bar. Very naughty of you."

I eye her up and down like some kind of meal and I have no idea why. Is it because I'm as horny as a toad or is it the color in her cheeks or her body, or the way she glares at me like she wants to rip my skin off and pounce on me like I'm prey and she's the Tigress. If that's a turn on, then I am one sick bastard. She realizes how I'm looking at her and the girl is half naked and has no shame. I'd fully expect her to grab a pillow to cover herself but not Willow Taylor. She's a 'fuck it' kind of girl.

"Hey, I did her a favor. She has no idea what kind of asshole she was going to go home with."

As she stands there looking so fucking sexy. As much as I try to control the rasping boner in my pants. I know my attempt is going to be unsuccessful.

"I could be fucking my brains out right now if it wasn't for your stupid, big mouth."

She lets out an exaggerated breath and laughs. She crosses her arms over her chest, accentuating her breasts in that tank top and sticks out one of her barely covered hips.

"Oh, please. One look at that minion-sized

dick of yours and she'd be running for the hills. I saved that poor girl from the disappointment of not having the multiple orgasms every woman deserves. With you, she didn't stand a chance."

"And I feel sorry for any guy who would even think about getting his dick anywhere near you — a spoiled, rich, socialite brat who makes Paris Hilton look like Mother Theresa."

The nostrils flare, the heat from the anger radiating off her body is felt even from where I stand. It surrounds the room. Thickly.

Willow Taylor is a hot piece of ass when she's all pissy.

Unfortunately.

My body is a ticking time bomb. My dick — ready to explode.

Why, why, why?

I step up to her. Our faces inches apart.

"Hey, assface, don't think I don't know about how you marauded that guy last week at Jax from coming home with me." I look quite confused.

"Hmm, Wills. Which one? There's been so many, I've lost count. Was it the scientist from M.I.T. or the rugby player from Scotland? Or was it pink shirt guy who was going to pass you along to his friend after he fucked you?"

So sue me for knowing about her hookups. I'm around all the time. How could I *not* know?

She looks shocked for a second but quickly recovers her expression.

"Nice hair, butthole." She pokes at my head. I try to dodge her but then her fingers go to what's left of my strands and she pulls.

Okay, that's it. She messed with my hair one too many times. This is war.

"You are the world's biggest bitch. You know that, right? Of course you do. What am I crazy to think you didn't realize what a stuck up, superficial, vain bitch you really are."

She bites her lip so hard I'm sure blood leaks inside her mouth.

"And I'm sure the world knows what a talentless, midget-like dipshit you are."

My breathing grows heavy. My chest heaves and my hand flexes. My fingers move of their own accord. In and out of a fist they form with nowhere else to go.

"I fucking hate you, Willow."

"You are the bane of my existence, Max."

"Go straight to hell, Willow."

"Go fuck yourself, Max."

Pink creeps up her cheeks and she snakes out her tongue that is the same color as her cheeks and licks her lips.

And then I lose all control of mind, body, and spirit. Pent up anger, sexual frustration, and hatred over take any road of common sense I should be going down.

"I'd rather fuck you."

Her eyes grow big and before her ugly mouth can protest my statement, I grab the back of her neck and crash my lips into hers. She doesn't pull away. She doesn't punch me like I would think she would. She actually grabs onto my ass and pulls me closer. Tongues crash, teeth clank, hands roam. My hands tangle in her bed head of hair. I nip at her lip and lick my way around inside her mouth. My mouth leaves hers and my tongue goes to her neck. I taste her skin, bite it gently, and tease her earlobe with my teeth. Her hands find my short hair and she digs her nails into my scalp. It hurts, but it hurts so good. Every time I lick her shoulder she moans. Every time my hands move to another spot she lets out a devilish sound of pleasure. My balls ache. I can't catch my breath, and all I can do is feel every inch of her exposed skin. It's so fucking soft and smells and tastes so good. Like candy. Sinful, bitchy candy.

I give her a chance to return any favors I have just given her.

Willow Taylor may be a bitch, but sexually, she's quite... giving.

She doesn't hesitate to work magic on the buckle of my shorts simultaneously tonguing my ear and licking my neck.

Fuck, it feels so good. She feels so good.

God, I hate her.

She pulls down my pants in one fast swoop and cups my aching balls. My head falls back and she continues to massage them. She claws at my chest with her free hand - feeling every inch of the bumps on my stomach from under my shirt and I think it's an invitation to rip it off.

We kiss again hard and violent. Hot and filled with lust. When she touches the length of my fully erect dick, she breaks the kiss and she looks up at me with wide, illuminated eyes.

"Holy shit. I lied to that poor girl. You're fucking huge." I laugh and tell her to lower her voice.

"Different now that we're sober, right?" She nods and a small smile appears on her face. I grip the edges of her tank top and raise it up slightly, looking to her for some sort of permission to continue. Like Willow always does, she takes matters into her own hands and grabs the shirt and pulls it over her own head.

Yeah, as I suspected… Willow's got a great rack.

Wish I could have remembered that from the last time.

I grab her and kiss her again after I take in the sight of her fantabulous tits. My arms snake up her back and I hold her and she repeats this motion with me. We bump and grind against one another. She rips her mouth from mine after our dry-humping is leading to zero.

"Are we really doing this?" I nod.

"Why?"

"'Cause we can." My lips reach hers again and all that's present are the sounds of our mouths fused together and the subtle moans and sexually gratifying groans we both display.

She pulls away.

"Fuck me, Max. Don't hold back. Just fucking fuck me."

I hope she knows what she's saying and by the way her lips latch onto mine, it tells me she knows.

Match, set, point Willow Taylor.

CHAPTER 5

Mergers and Other Kinds of Messed Up Shit

Willow~

This is happening. I mean this is really happening and I'm doing it completely sober. I'm letting Max invade my lady parts with his hands.

Oh God, he's making me feel so good.

I don't understand how someone I despise can make me feel like this. He kisses like an over-achiever. He uses his tongue like a weapon and his hands are pure immorality.

As we tumble onto the bed our bodies are nothing but sweat and muscle and lust-filled and I don't think I've ever felt this hungry before.

Or someone who is as hungry for me. It's a metaphor really.

The hate that builds and builds until one day it explodes and bam, here you are. In bed rolling around in the sheets with the person you loathe. The one person who's a nuisance to you in every way possible, and the one who you had drunk sex with… seven times.

And in about five seconds we can make that number eight.

I can't catch my breath. I can't see straight when I open my eyes. The wind tunnel going through my head is making all logical decisions I *could* make not even possible. But this is what I know:

Max Vincent can kiss.

Max Vincent has great hands.

Max Vincent has great fingers.

Max Vincent is hung like a fucking horse and I'm really pissed off at myself for being so drunk the last time we did this.

Max rolls on the condom that he fishes out of his wallet that has fallen on the floor. As he hangs over the side of the bed I have a few stolen moments to really think about what I'm doing. I contemplate the consequences if there are any. But he's super quick and my brain doesn't even have time to process what's about to go down.

He raises his head back up and I watch him methodically roll on the condom as he's perched on his knees and I see that humungous dangling participle that's between his legs. It's like a kick-stand on a bike.

Damn.

As I watch him, he watches me and I swear I'm about to spontaneously combust just from the sight of the whole thing. It's erotic. It's hot. It's downright making me crazy. His eyes turn suddenly and for a minute I think he may be changing his mind. I sit up on my elbows.

"Second thoughts?"

He shakes his head.

"Nope."

"Then why the look?"

He sighs but not in frustration. Maybe worry, maybe doubt.

"No look. I want this. I have no idea why, but I do."

He runs his hand over his newly cut hair, thanks to me, and I have the same feeling as well.

"Me neither." My eyes don't leave his when I say it and I want this so bad I can't keep my legs still. My knees hit one another and I try to keep them together and still. My boy short underwear is off and, for some reason, I don't feel like myself. I feel… vulnerable. It's not something I feel often. But in this situation I do.

As Max places his hands on my knobby knees, his grip is daring but gentle and he parts them, baring myself to him and I take a deep breath in and hold it as he gazes at the second best part of my anatomy. My hair, of course, being my first.

He settles there and holds his dick right at my entrance.

"Once this happens, there's no going back and it will be it. The last time."

I nod and oh God, I want him in me so bad and now I just want him to shut up and fuck me.

"Never again. So stop talking and do it already." That's all the invite he needs. In one hard as nails push, he's inside and I can't help but to cry out.

"Holy shit!" He covers my mouth after even I realize I'm way too loud and Thea is across the hall.

Each thrust sends shockwaves to all the right places and I dig my nails into his back and he likes it. I can tell by the way he says, 'Oh, yeah.' It's so drawn out even when he pounds away over and over again. I wrap my legs tightly around his waist and my hips meet each thrust. He rolls his hips and I snake my hands down to grip his tight, tiny ass. If I get a chance to get a good look at it, I'd bet it's smaller than mine.

Bastard.

He licks my neck and nibbles my ear while invading me and I'm trying to hold myself off from bliss.

He hits a really good spot and I feel it down to my toes, which, in fact, begin to curl on the sheets. My toes have never curled, and I've had enough sex in my life to know whether I've done it or not.

I yell out again and within a minute I hear a knock at my door.

Max and I stop. We remain still until I hear the knock again and then the doorknob jiggles but it never opens.

I whisper to him, "You locked it?" He nods with wide eyes. I can feel my heart coming out of my chest.

"Wills, you okay? Are you awake? Why's the door locked?"

I panic and mouth to Max, "What do I say?"

He shrugs and I punch him in the shoulder.

His mouth goes into an 'O' shape.

Quietly, he says, "Tell her you had a nightmare."

I roll my eyes. "What am I, five?"

"Just do it." He growls. So I do.

"I'm fine, Thea. I had a nightmare. Doorknob must be broke. Go back to sleep."

"But are you okay?" Her sweet, little voice comes through the door and I feel so bad 'cause she's concerned about me and I'm lying to her.

"Thea, I'm fine." Max rolls his hips again and sends me spiraling. I'm going to come if he doesn't stop. I keep mouthing for him to stop and he smiles and shakes his head no.

With every pump of himself rippling through me, my eyes roll back into my head and I know his plan is not to stop any time soon.

"Willow, do you want me to come sleep with you? You keep making these noises like you're in pain or something."

Oh, Thea. Pain is not what I'm in right now, that's for sure.

"Really, Thea. I'm fine. I'm going back to sleep. See you in the morning."

She says a small 'okay' to me through the door and I feel like a puddle of sweat.

Now the adrenaline of almost getting caught has revved up my sexual appetite and with all the strength I have in my body I hook my arms under Max and sweep his legs from underneath him and flip him over. I have zero idea how I do this but I'm on top this time and I quickly sink down onto him without him even putting up a fight. I'm used to being in control. I'm used to having my own way. I'm the bitch and I intend on riding this merry-go-round on *my* terms right now.

"Holy shit, Willow." Max's head flops down on the pillow as I ride myself on him towards release. My hands are on his pecs. I'm holding onto his skin so hard I may draw blood and by the look on Max's face I don't think he'd care too much. He grips my hips like they're pieces of rope that he has to hold onto before he falls off some wall or something like that.

He sucks in his lower lip and I see the whites of his eyes for a minute as he gasps with a few more 'Oh Gods.' Faster and faster I go, quickening my moves, riding his lap and I'm fueled by his words and his sounds.

"Jesus, Willow. You're fucking amazing."

I wink at him. "Well, thank you."

Keep it up, Max. Keep talking. It just makes it all the better.

He sits up on his elbows, temporarily releasing his hold on my hips. He grabs the back of my neck and pulls my mouth to his. It's unexpected and sexy as hell. The deeper the kiss goes, the closer I get.

I pull away from his lips as I fall off the edge. The edge of pleasure, the edge of bliss, the edge of confusion.

Max joins me two minutes later — trying to be as quiet as he can be — and because I'm still coming down off my high, all I can hear is the blood pumping in my ears so I can't tell if he's being loud or not. When I open my eyes he's staring at me and I suddenly feel very aware of everything. What we just did.

What did we just do?

I pop off of Max's lap and collapse next to him. We pant like dogs in heat and I pull my covers over my naked body. Max's hand is over his face and he starts to laugh.

Is he laughing at my body? Are my boobs too small so he's laughing? Do I have middle of the night breath? What the fuckity fuck is he laughing at?

"Shut the hell up, would ya? You want to wake Thea up again and maybe the guys next door."

He wipes the corners of his eyes and looks over at me — still laughing.

I smack his bare chest.

"Why are you laughing? What's so funny?"

"I just… I can't believe we just… I can't believe how… I can't speak."

I would have to agree. As much as I don't want to admit, it may have just been the single-most gratifying sexual experience I've ever had. And it was with Max.

Max.

Then I'm snapped back to reality. I just had amazing, mind-blowing, intensely orgasmic sex with the one person who's like a yeast infection — annoying and itchy.

I sit up abruptly and find my little robe on the chair next to my bed and put it on quickly. I turn around and look at Max lying in my bed. His one arm tucked under his head and the other resting quite comfortably next to him. A satisfied look gleaming in his eye.

I find his shorts and shirt on the floor and throw them at his head.

I point to the door. "Get out."

He takes the clothes off his face and grimaces. A little bit of a blank stare then an

'eureka' moment hits him.

He throws the blankets off and there's his huge peen staring me right in the face — again.

Max swings his legs over the bed and pulls his shorts on, then his shirt. He turns to me and I stand there with my head clutching my forehead. My mouth is dry and my knees still shaking a little. Maybe from nerves or from the overwhelming orgasm I just had.

"Okay, listen, like before, we keep this between us. I don't... I don't need anyone knowing... just shut your mouth about it and swear it's not happening again. A moment of weakness. That's all this was."

"On your part, sure. I'm not weak, Willow. I was just horny."

Yeah, I get it. Horniness overtakes common sense and that's exactly what this is. I gave him blue balls tonight by scaring off that little hussy at Jax and I just needed to get off. The end of the school year, Harlow getting engaged, Max and I tormenting each other — this was a tension tamer. A method of relaxation. Not to mention I haven't hooked up once since I've been here. Even though it's almost the end of June I still have high hopes that I would have gotten some by now.

I just sort of did, didn't I?

I wave my hands, annoyed at him but also the tone of my voice is somewhat agreeing with him.

"Okay, fine. Me too, but as much as I hate to admit it, it was also rather… enjoyable. And if you mutter one letter of that word to anyone I will remove your balls with a prison shank."

Coolly and calmly he goes to the mirror above the dresser and checks his hair. Still speaking to me as he does a once over, I stand there in my robe. Arms crossed, wanting him to leave and looking at the rumpled sheets on my bed in astonishment.

I need to wash these — asap!

Max turns towards me and for reasons only known to me, I can't look him directly in the eyes now. I mean, the man was just inside me and I can't even give him eye-to-eye contact.

"Wills, I got this. Let's not resort to violence towards my balls or any other part of my male anatomy. Whatever this was between us was just a matter of a ways and means. I was the way and you were the means."

Now all I want to do is kick him in that big dick of his.

I stroll over to him, calm and collected since it is after three a.m. and I can't scream at him so I put on my best debutante attitude and force a fake smile.

"Pardon me, but I am not a 'means' as you have just referred to me."

"Well then what would you call it?" I ponder it, placing my finger on my chin and looking to the ceiling.

"Let's just say we were in a sexual bind. I can admit I haven't hooked up since... well, you know..." Max lifts up the corner of his mouth.

"Yeah, I know what you're referring to and I have to say I've hit a dry spell. Actually, that could have been changed if it wasn't for you ruining my night with a torrid story about me having fictional herpes. Thanks again for that."

I curtsey 'cause I'm a smart ass.

"Well, it wasn't my best work, but it seemed to have worked in your favor." A smart-ass grin appears and I can't help but do the same just thinking about how I started the conversation with that girl in the bathroom. All I did was ask her if she knew him and she told me not really but she was just about to know him a lot better. Then I told her about the rumor I heard about his lack of penis and that everyone in Sandy Cove knew about it. Then with shocked eyes I knew I had her in my grip so I whispered that I heard he also had a scorching case of herpes and it couldn't be controlled with medication alone. She went green and tucked the cleavage she was coaxing out of her tiny shirt back in and that's when I made my exit.

"Well played, Willow. Well played." He suddenly looks out of sorts, a bit uncomfortable.

I twist my lips to the side and bite a part of the inside.

"So it's late and I better get going... far walk and all." I snort. Max gives me a courteous nod and walks towards the door. Quietly, he turns the handle and he's about to walk out the door with so many unsaid things… but really, what's there to say? We hate each other. We had sex, hot sex, now we pretend it didn't happen… again. Then go back to hating each other? Does that even work?

"Hey, Max. Let's make what happened here like a raising of a white flag. We'll still have a strong dislike for each other, but maybe we can take it easy. My middle finger was starting to cramp up for a few weeks there."

"Okay. Truce." We shake on it.

"Never again, Max. Remember. We plead temporary insanity here."

Max winks and nods. He walks out the door, closing it quietly. I flop on my bed, covering my face and I turn and scream into my pillow still asking myself out loud why that just happened and why I allowed it and why… I enjoyed it.

My momentary lapse in judgment is buried in the back of my mind. This is now what I call "The Max Situation." It creeps in though. I try not to let it but when that damn band of his plays and I see him on that stage sweating and playing that guitar with such passion, sometimes I need to kind of cross my legs… tightly.

Then he does something that reminds me that I don't like him one bit. For example, he'll make a sexual hand gesture towards me when no one is looking and my comeback? The middle finger. What else do I have? Gone are the days of my witty comebacks and sass. It's like I've been stripped of it. I don't even see much of him nowadays anyway. Max is either sleeping or rehearsing with the band or playing here. He's only been to the beach a few times since our encounter and even then he naps or I have my face planted in the pages of my favorite celebrity gossip magazine.

That's fine. Makes my life easier. I get tired sometimes of the back and forth between us. Lately there hasn't been a lot of that.

Another night at Jax and I'm pretty sure now there's a stool at the bar with my name etched in it. I'm with Harlow. Dickcop is working the door so she's sitting with me gazing at the door and they make googly eyes at each other making me incredibly nauseous.

"Will you two knock it off? You're with each other every day and every night. Don't you get tired of seeing his ugly mug 24/7?"

She giggles. "Look at him, Wills. I mean seriously. Would you get tired of looking at that?"

I stick my finger in my throat making a gagging noise.

She nudges my arm.

"Okay, yes, he is sort of easy on the eyes. I'll give him that much." I can't believe I just admitted that.

I bite on the straw of my drink and sip when I feel a tap on my shoulder.

"Excuse me, but you look like you could use a fresh drink. Mind if I buy one for you?"

I turn with ease towards a voice that sounds like warm, gooey chocolate. And the eyes I meet are the same color of the confectionary I'm thinking about.

I give my best "Willow" smirk and tell him sure.

He signals for Porter to give me whatever it is I'm drinking. Porter gives me the evil eyes when he hands it to me and I know he's just trying to act the role of the over-protective cousin.

"Thank you, bartender," I say cockily and he sticks his tongue out at me. I spin on my stool and thank the stranger for the drink.

He extends his hand and introduces himself. "I'm Jace." I take his hand.

"Willow."

His eyes grow wide. "Willow. What a beautiful name for a beautiful girl."

I motion to Harlow. "And this is my friend Harlow." He takes her hand and shakes it.

"Another beautiful name for another beautiful girl. I have to come here more often."

And like this guy is a magnet, the stupid cop is behind him like a tree.

He clears his throat.

Jace turns around and looks up 'cause if he didn't he'd be staring right at Dickcop's chest.

With his strong booming voice he asks, "Everything okay over here, ladies. Are you in need of assistance?"

"Oh, my God, are you kidding me? This isn't a routine traffic stop, Cruz. The guy bought me a drink."

Cracking his knuckles and staring at Jace, he sizes him up and says, "I'm not concerned if he bought *you* a drink, Willow." He drapes his arm around Harlow's shoulders and she leans into him. He kisses her temple and asks her if she's okay.

She looks at him adoringly. "I'm fine, babe. This is Jace, he bought Willow a drink."

Cruz looks suspicious of Jace but lets it go.

He gives Harlow a quick kiss and comes nose to nose with Jace.

"Fine. I've got my eye on you, buddy. No funny stuff. That's my fiancée."

Not wanting to give my new friend a bad impression of me, I refrain from making any snide comments.

Harlow slips off the stool and excuses herself and follows Cruz to the door of the bar. She tells me she'll be back but when I look at this hot guy in front of me I tell her not to hurry. Maybe this is the distraction I need when I see Max enter onto the stage with the band. My eyes go to the stage but then travel to the big brown eyes next to me.

"So, Willow, you here for the summer or do you live in Sandy Cove?"

"No. Just a summer girl. I teach during the year so I come down here and stay at my family's home. I'm from Princeton. And you?"

"Pennsylvania. I'm in grad school now so I live in the city. I'm here on and off, crashing at a friend's house whenever I can."

"Grad school. Very impressive. For what, may I ask?"

"I'm in the MBA program at Wharton. Almost done too. So, a teacher? What do you teach?"

"Middle school Spanish."

He smiles and nods approvingly. "Spanish?

Really?"

"Si, señor."

Jace leans in close to me and to my ear. I can smell his fantastic cologne and it's making my mouth water.

"Eres una chica muy sexy y hermosa."

Translation: You are a very sexy and beautiful girl. Yeah, okay, that's a line I've heard before but when he says it slowly and seductively in Spanish, my panties almost fall off my body even without me shimmying them down my legs. I turn to him and cross my long, tanned legs in front of him. I touch my knee and draw circles around the cap.

"Usted es un hombre muy sexy y guapo."

He licks his bottom lip. The tip of his tongue peeks out and it's hot.

"Gracias."

"Well, you are sexy and handsome and I speak the truth. Even in Spanish."

The band starts to play and he reaches for my hand and asks me if I want to dance. I oblige and follow his lead to the dance floor. I look behind me to see Harlow and Cruz watching and Har gives me an excited thumbs up and Cruz makes 'V' with his fingers and licks the air between them quickly. He's so gross.

Jace and I get into a good rhythm and bump and grind on the sticky floor. It's hot but this guy is even hotter. His hands are on my hips and he leads them to the same beat as his. I have my arms raised above my head and I sway and my back rubs up against his front. Which I must say is impressively protruding outwards.

Hot damn. We may have a winner. The dry spell may be over.

We continue to get closer and closer — our bodies rubbing against one another and his face buried in my neck. Even if my feet kill me in my heels, I pay them no mind because this guy makes me forget my impending blister.

I wrap my arms around his neck and hang my head back so he can kiss his way up my neck. The pounding of the music, the sea of sweaty bodies surrounding us and his lips driving me crazy. He lifts his head and kisses me. It's not a bold move, it's actually very smooth and slow, but when he kisses me it's neither.

I like the feel of his lips on mine. It's nice. He smells really good too. I like a guy who can smell like cologne and salt air. It's a good combo. The music stops and people around us hoot and holler for Max's band. Jace and I pull our lips away from each other. Before we know it, it's last call and Jace asks if I want some water. I'm parched so I follow him up to the bar and Porter gives us two waters. As we sip and cool off, the band makes their way to the bar and stands diagonal from us. I can see Max and the two other members whose names I forget all the time. I only see him look up at me once then he signals Porter for a beer. My attention goes back to Jace. We chat up about what goes on in Sandy Cove in the summer and I fill him in on a few things. Cruz and Harlow come over to us and tell us they're leaving. Cruz eyes Jace up again and Harlow gives him a tug and gives me a wink.

When they leave, Jace leans in and gives me a soft kiss on the lips. When he pulls away he asks me if I want to take a walk on the beach. I nod and excuse myself to the ladies room so I can check my boobs for sweat and freshen up downstairs... just in case. You never know.

Jace remains at the bar and I hurry to the bathroom. I check myself. I run my fingers through my hair and dip into a stall to check under the girls. They are a little damp but it's nothing the night air can't dry up. I look good actually. My tan looks good and I stick a little bit of tinted lip gloss on. I spray myself with a little purse-sized perfume I have and I thank God no one is in here because I give myself a pep talk.

Okay, señorita. Here you go. Give it your all and make this guy beg for it. You can do it.

I take a deep breath in, close my eyes, and pop them open and head out the door. I walk to the bar and I don't see Jace. I look to my left and to my right. I walk over to the group of tables in the corner and he's not there. I walk back over to the bar where it's just about empty and I notice Porter is crouching down doing something so I lean over and pull at his shirt.

"P, did you see where my date went? To the men's room, maybe?"

He stands up and shakes his head. "Um... He, um... you know what, I'm not getting involved. I want no part of this game you two have going on." I look at him like he's a psych patient.

"What the hell are you talking about, Porter.

Seriously."

"You and Max. Leave each other alone with the games and shit."

I ball my hands into fists and slam my purse on the top of the bar. Hard.

"What in the fucking hell are you talking about?" I grab him by the front of his shirt when he doesn't tell me.

"Where's Max?" I ask through gritted teeth.

He points to the back door of Jax and I let go of my death grip on him and grab my purse. I storm out back where I know he parks his car when Porter or Cruz doesn't give him a ride home. I noticed his car was gone before I left for Jax earlier so I know he's out there.

I push open the large steel door with force and hunt down his car through the back parking lot. It's dark but it's like I have secret nighttime vision so I can seek it out. I spot it a few feet away from the back door and hurry my pace. The trunk to his car is open and I come to the back of it to see him putting his shit in the trunk. He raises his head but doesn't see me. I smack him in the head with my purse.

"Ow! What the hell?" He grabs his head and I push at his chest.

"What did you do? What did you say?"

Still rubbing his head all he does his shrug at me and continues to add another piece of equipment into his trunk, ignoring my assault.

"I'm talking to you, short stuff. You better start flapping your good for nothing gums or else. What did you say to Jace?"

Max laughs. "Jace? What kind of name was that anyway?"

I see red. I breathe fire. I rage in anger.

"Listen, I may have told him you used to have a dick, okay?"

I shake my head not even comprehending what he just said. I blink a few times and rub my finger in my ear.

"Say… say that again? A dick? You told him I *used* to have one?"

"Yep. He was trouble. I could tell. Guys like that are the ones you need to stay away from, Wills. I did you a favor. Like pink shirt guy."

I slam his trunk down and bang my hand on the top of it.

"A dick! A dick! Are you some kind of maniac? So is this paybacks from a few weeks ago with that girl? I thought we were past this crap." He chuckles and has no idea what a big mistake that really was. Max grabs my wrist before my hand has a chance to collide with his face. He gives me a warning look that makes me flush and as he keeps his fingers on my pulse points, my breathing becomes even more rapid than when I started to yell at him. My other hand comes up to smack him and he's so damn quick I'm too late. He catches it then catches my lips and kisses me hard and demanding. He leans me against the back of his trunk and all my defenses are down. Down and out and I relax in his kiss even if it's rough.

Bloody hell.

He lets go of my hands while his lips are still

on me and he grabs my face to cradle it as he kisses me. When he pulls away I'm breathless and confused so I sneak attack him with a nice slap. I'm really good at that. He looks at me and just glares. Before I know it he's lifting me over his shoulder and walking me away from his car to a spot beyond a few more cars. I fight at him. I punch his back and kick my feet. He smacks me on my ass and tells me to behave, that he just wants to talk.

When we reach our destination, a brick wall, he sits me down and I'm so angry I could stroke out right here.

He puts his hands on my shoulders and backs me up against the wall.

I try to protest his restraint on me. It doesn't work.

"If you'd shut the hell up I want to apologize but I think I have a solution to our little problem."

I really don't want to listen to anything he has to say.

"You ruined my night. Haven't you said and done enough?"

He captures me again with a kiss and this time he's relentless. I know he's doing it to shut me up and as bad as I want to push him away, I don't, I just grab onto his ripped up t-shirt and give it right back to him.

He slides his hands up and down my body, feeling the tops of my legs and finding his way to the inside of my skirt. He slides my panties to the side and enters me with his fingers.

I tear my lips from him. "Oh God. What the

hell are you doing to me?"

He kisses my neck and whispers in my ear, "Making you feel good. You want to feel good? You want me to make you feel good?" All I can do is nod. I swallow hard and let him continue.

"I have a proposition for you, Willow. Last time we were together we know we both enjoyed it. Why should we torture ourselves by denying how good we make each other feel? Even though I'm sorry for getting rid of that guy tonight, I'm really not *that* sorry."

He's not making sense, but what he's doing with his fingers does.

Through shaky breathing I ask him, "What... what are you talking about?"

Max licks my salty skin and dips his tongue in the hollow of my throat and I'm pretty sure I'm about to fall apart.

"I mean a deal. We enjoy each other. Maybe we should *continue* to enjoy each other. We can hook up with other people and we can have fun with other people but the sex, that part is reserved for us. We just give in to what we both want. It's never just assumed when we hook up with people that we are going to... you know."

"Score. Get lucky. Get some."

He laughs. "Yeah."

He's giving me choices? He wants me to only have sex with him? So the pros would be that if I don't hook up and/or take it any further with someone who would be a potential candidate then I get to have sex with Max and allow him to make me feel like I'm feeling right now.

His fingers are like magic wands. I swear it.

And the cons: I have sex with Max anytime, anywhere, whenever. And keep it between us. I'm not transparent, at least I think I'm not. I don't think anyone would see through us. No one would catch on.

Right?

"So you want to use each other when we need to? If we don't get lucky with other people, we get lucky with each other? Am I right?"

He grabs my hair and pulls at it slightly making me look directly at him.

Forceful. I'm into it.

"Yes. Exactly what I mean. It's not for a relationship. There will be no jealousy, or torturing, or romance. It's strictly this and nothing else. You despise me as I do you. Are you game, Willow?"

Am I game?

As he gives me one of his infamous orgasms and I shake beneath him I realize in all the years that I've been having sex with people no one has ever made every nerve in my body stand on edge. And in the good way. Nerves — yes, Max gets on them, under them, he makes me crazy and makes me feel so good at the same time. His lips are amazing and I could get used to this. I could really get used to this.

So I could have him anytime I wanted. In my bed, in his bed, in a car, against a brick wall. That's the deal. Sounds a bit contrite to me, but then again, I'm me.

I could contemplate this in my mind over and

over again, but I am a woman who takes control and thinks before she acts… well, maybe not all the time.

Max looks at me with lust and want in his eyes and he can tell I'm trying to weigh this decision. He takes his hand from my panties and cups my face and kisses me again and I see flashes of light as I close my eyes so tight and moan into his mouth.

As I feel like my body is not mine at this moment, I bite his bottom lip sealing the deal and tell him yes.

"Yes. Let's do this. No strings attached. Just to get off. No attachments, nothing more."

A look of satisfaction flashes on his face and his eyes give me a silent agreement.

"Okay, good. So we know the rules. Now let's get this deal off the ground."

CHAPTER 6

Kinky Stuff
Max~

In the closet in her room. (cramped but it worked)

In the closet in my room. (even more cramped but it worked)

In the storage room at Jax after hours.

My car.

Her car.

On the beach when we knew everyone went to bed.

And a few other places I can't think of right now.

No one suspects because she plays the part of "The Bitch" really well towards me. Constantly degrading me for my musical skills, my beach volleyball skills, my cooking skills. We're the same people we have always been. The people who have such a distinct distaste for each other it's scary. The difference is we really seem to get along when we're naked. And as the days go by we find ourselves like this more and more.

I'm becoming more familiar with that gleam in her eye. The smoky look she gives on a night we are all at home just playing board games solidifies her wanton need to have me when she wants it and I'm not fighting it. Trust me. Having Willow Taylor in every sexual position known to man is not something you fight. Bottom line: You. Don't. Fight. Off. Willow. Taylor.

End of sentence. Why would I anyway? She's fucking phenomenal in bed. Her middle name should be sex.

I'm pretty sure if I looked at her birth certificate it would say it.

We are pretty under the radar with our little covert operation. Sneaking around is actually kind of hot. A head nod is all it takes or a widening of the eyes from across the room. A silent signal telling me, 'Oh, it's on.' But I will admit being with her, it's becoming somewhat of an addiction. The times I'm not banging her against a wall, I'm thinking of banging her against a wall. It's insane.

I'm not, by any means, saying this happens every day. I don't have time for that. I sort of wish I had all the time for that. I'm trying really hard to get this damn band off the ground. I know I can't do what I have to do. I want to do what I WANT to do. I want to play music for the rest of my life. It's in my soul. I bleed it. I don't want to be stuck behind a desk all day in some stuffy office. When I travel the world I don't want it to be in some executive board room in some foreign country. I want to *see* the foreign country. I want to play in a stadium in a foreign country then I want to go explore it. I want to feel the culture and experience that firsthand. I know that being an engineer may bring me the same opportunities, but not really. I know I have some hefty student loans to pay back and for what? I guess doing what you really want comes with a price. A hefty price tag, if you will.

I scored gifted in school at a young age, and my dad saw this as an opportunity to maybe try to shape me into some kind of mogul. This went above the dad cheering on his son and encouraging him to be his best. My pop keeps harping on me to put out resumes to the top firms around but I asked him to give me the summer to enjoy before I really have to get out into the real world.

Sometimes I believe my father thinks he's the bureaucracy of my life. Ruling and deciding what's best for me. But he really doesn't know me. I know he wants better for me than what he had. My pop didn't do too badly. He owns his own garage and has since I was little. I never went without. We always had but never asked.

My mom ran off with the CEO of some car parts manufacturer after she was introduced to him at a parts conference in Cleveland she and my dad went to. I guess Pop figured being a car repairman wasn't good enough for her. He thought the rich CEOs who ran major conglomerates were the ones who mattered. The ones with power. He thought you had to have power to win people over. I think you have to have the smarts and a good heart to win them over. The man my mom ran off with had power. When Mom visits it's mostly to see my ailing grandfather and she'll ask me to lunch, but for the most part it's an exchange of fake pleasantries and to find out if I need any money. But that's okay. I don't have Mommy issues. I'm fine with it all.

Tonight is all about fun with Willow and me. It's raining. Everyone wants to go to a movie. I'm horny, and according to the text I got from Willow a few hours ago, so is she. Okay, so game on motherfuckers. Willow came down with a 'migraine' and I told everyone I needed to get some writing done. The guys in the band want some new lyrics. If all goes according to plan, I'll be inspired to write some really bitching ones.

No one questions us. Willow put on a great act of taking off all her makeup and keeping her room freezing and dark. Typical setting for migraine sufferers. Before she leaves Willow, Thea comes to me with all her sweetness.

"Max, I know you hate her but Willow really isn't feeling good at all. She worries me. Can you just call a truce for a few hours and check on her for me. We won't be out too late."

Here's an angel right here on earth. Not my type, but nonetheless, Thea Thornton is beautiful, sweet, and thoughtful.

"Of course. I heard she wasn't feeling well. I'll check on her but if you come home and there's a high heel stuck in my eye like that dude in *Single White Female*, I'm holding you responsible." I wink at her and she kisses my cheek.

"Hey, Thea. What time will you be home exactly?" She shrugs and thank God doesn't see the real reason for my question.

"Um, well the movie we're seeing isn't playing in Sandy Cove so we have to go to the next town over so I guess we'll be home around eleven."

Hot damn! That gives me three hours to make Willow Taylor my own personal playground.

"What is this a picnic or are we fucking?" I laugh at Willow. Such a smart mouth.

I currently have her in the middle of my bed. Nude. The woman could care less about clothes around me. In the center I have a tray with three items on it.

A squeezable container of vanilla infused honey, chocolate sundae sauce, and a jar of peanut butter. I sit across from her, cock hard and out on display because, come on, I have a naked girl with the tits of a porn star in front of me.

I'm a dude.

"Relax. I thought we'd try and spice things up a bit. My back still hurts from the steps of the empty stairwell at the mini-mall yesterday."

"Oh, you're telling me. I think I have permanent indents in my ass from the treads on the stairs."

Like I said, anywhere, anytime.

She adjusts herself on the bed. Her hands are resting on the edge of the tray as she points to each object.

"So what's with the toppings? You plan on making me a human sundae?" She cocks her brow and smiles.

So damn sexy.

"Nope. That would be very clichéd, now wouldn't it?"

"Pretty much."

"That's not why I have brought you here to my lair of sex. Have you ever been restrained?"

"Um, like tied up? No. Not sure I'm in to bondage."

I shake my head. "No, neither am I, but I heard that a little restraint with a little touch of one of the four major food groups can heighten sexual pleasure."

She looks at me skeptically.

"Do you trust me, Wills?"

She nods. "Okay. So I have these two neckties my dad bought me in case I go on stupid interviews. Never even took them out of the boxes."

"And you want to tie me up. I get that part but what are you going to do with the rest of the stuff?" For a second she looks so innocent when she asks me and I begin to think that maybe she's not as experienced as I thought she was.

"Willow, let me ask you a question. When you've slept with someone, has it just been a romp in the sack with maybe multiple orgasms and some cuddling after? Nothing kinky or out of the ordinary?"

She waves a dismissive hand towards me.

"Oh, please. I've… well, this one time…" She

looks as though she's trying to think of a scenario she's been involved in.

Not working for her.

"So the answer is no, and it's cool. I don't judge."

She gets flustered. "Okay, smart ass, just get to the point."

Her cheeks are a hot shade of pink and I lean in and kiss her mouth. She accepts my tongue and I make her dizzy. I can tell from the way she looks when I tear my mouth from hers.

"Lay back." She obeys like a goddamn child. She falls gracefully into the pillows I have on my bed behind her. I close my eyes and take a breath in. The naked sight of her makes everything in my body go tense but in a good way. My neck muscles twitch and so do my hands because Right now I want to rub that spot between her legs and bury my face in it for the first time. But all in good time.

I grab each tie and fasten her wrists with them to the wrought iron bed frame.

"This too tight?"

She answers so faintly, "No."

"Okay, good. Now I'm going to coat your body with the item of your choice and I'm going to lick each drop off of you. You'll keep your eyes closed or I'll be forced to use one of my tube socks as a blindfold. Got me?"

"Ew. Not your socks." I cover her body with my own. I have her caged in with my arms and I stare right into her eyes. I rub my dick over her center and she bucks up her hips. I take my one hand and with a little force, lower her hips.

"Down, girl," I say all breathy.

My lips linger over hers and she bites her lip to stifle whatever pent up sexual frustration she has going on.

"Fuck my socks, Willow. Which one do you want? Honey, chocolate, or peanut butter?"

She doesn't answer. Her face contorts into something I'm not sure of.

So I inch my hand down to her center and slip a finger into her. I coax it in and out at a painfully slow pace.

She winces and arches her neck back.

"Don't get used to this right now, baby. I'm not finger fucking you. You're not coming that way. Like I said I'm going to drizzle whatever on you and lick it off. On your gorgeous tits and flat stomach. I'm going to dip my tongue in your belly button and lick whatever drips inside it. Then I'm going to cover your sweet pussy with my mouth and I'm going to lick you up and down and suck on you so much that that pretty pussy is going to come all over my face."

She lets out a cry. I withdraw my finger from her.

"You understand?" Her breathing is heavy and I feel it on my own lips because hers are so damn close to mine.

"Honey," she whispers out. I lick at her lips but don't kiss her.

"Good choice."

I take the bottle and rip off the cap with my teeth. I begin to drizzle it first over that dirty mouth of hers. She goes to lick her lips as a moan escapes her.

"Ah, ah, ah. No you don't, you bad girl. You need to save that for me." I dart my tongue out and slowly lick the seam of her lips. The honey coating my tongue and she wiggles her legs under me.

I slurp the honey into my mouth and tell her to hold still. She obeys… again.

I continue my quest to lick the contents of the bottle off her mouth. After my mission is completed, I snake my tongue between her sinful lips. I lick the inside and take in any of the honey that has seeped inside. Her mouth hangs open and I watch. I watch her reactions. I watch the way her eyes are shut so tightly with anticipation of the next part of her body I'll do this to. Her neck. God, I love her long neck. Just the fine tip of the honey bottle traces along her neckline and I squeeze just the right amount out. I take her chin while her eyes are still tightly shut and tip it back a bit, then I lick. And I suck gingerly. Her sexy as fuck tits are next. I dribble the honey in a circle around those gorgeous erect pink nipples and I salivate quickly as I do so because all I want is my mouth around them. I alternate light suction and soft sampling of her honey coated skin.

"Oh, shit, Max. That's… oh God, so so good."

That's the stuff I want to hear.

I concentrate next on her stomach and belly button. As the sticky substance coats her skin, my lips work their magic, making her break out in goosebumps and causing her to shiver. My mouth is hot on her skin but the intensity makes her shake. I like that.

I strain my eyes up to look at her face and it's flushed and tanned and beautiful. I straddle her and when I reach her deep belly button, I dart out my tongue and do what I promised. I suck out the honey and switch to dipping my tongue inside and she yells out.

"Oh God. I may come if you keep doing that. Max, please."

I let out a hearty, deep chuckle. "Oh, no you don't. Beg for it, Willow. Beg for where you want my mouth to go next. Fucking beg me."

She tries to break out of the ties but it's not happening. Her eyes pop open and she raises her head off the pillow.

She just stares with the heat of hell in her eyes. I know what she wants, where she wants me to go.

I stop what I'm doing. Her eyes are open and I put down the bottle of honey.

She looks at me shocked.

"What… what are you doing? Why'd you stop?"

My face looks unbothered and I shrug.

"You didn't do what you were told."

"Seriously? Jesus, Max. I'm dying over here." She looks frustrated.

Nice.

I smack her on her ass playfully. She lets out a yelp.

"Ah, you like that. We'll save that for another day but I'll put it in the mental bank." I rub her ass after I say it. She coos.

Fucking hot.

I kiss the cheek of her ass and breathe onto her hot skin.

"Tell me where you want me to lick next, Willow. Say it, baby." I am as hard as a diamond right now and if I don't get her off soon, I'm going to get off without even being inside her.

She lets out a sigh.

I take the tip of one of my fingers and place it on her clit. I press down and she gasps for air.

"Oh, there. I want it there."

Well, that was easy.

"You want me to lick here?" I pour a little honey on the tip of my finger and rub it all over her clit. The sounds that come from her mouth are so lascivious that it's driving me out of my mind.

"Willow. Answer me."

"Uh, hm." Her answer is almost inaudible but I know what she wants.

I take the honey and drip it on her pussy.

"Ahh…" she whimpers.

And that's when I go for it. I angle my head in between her legs and waste no time burying my face in her. My whole mouth covers her and I suck on her. Madly.

She blissfully cries out and I hear the sound of her trying to release her hands from the light restraints. The iron bangs against the wall, but it's no use.

I don't even need the honey to taste what her sweetness really is. Willow tastes amazing without it. I lavish in her heat and try and steady her legs as I lap at her and make her so crazy. My pace picks up as she struggles more and more and I know I'm driving her insane. She's making me insane and I need her to come so hard on my mouth because I need to get inside her and finish the deed. My greediness is taking over and I need to feel her around me. Her hips buck up and meet my mouth each time I flick my tongue. Faster and faster I go and then in a moment of exploding electricity, she rolls her narrow hips and fucks my face. She comes so hard and so fast that I place my mouth on her and suck on her as if my life depends on it.

I look up and see her thrash her head back and forth and watch her mouth hang open as sounds come out that drive me towards insanity.

When she comes down from her orgasm, I quickly reach for a condom and roll it on without missing a beat.

I drive into her with force and she wraps those long legs around me. I grab under her ass and rotate my hips and then pound into her wet, soft core.

I let go of her legs and reach my hands out to play with her nipples.

As I continue to fuck her, I speak, "You like me fucking you like this. You see what you do to me, Willow. You feel what you do to my dick?"

"Yes, oh fuck, Max, yes. Harder."

I answer her with a question. "Harder? You want it harder?. I'll give it to you harder." And I do. I'm relentless. I don't waver. I fuck her so hard, I'm lightheaded.

"Max, I'm going to go again. Faster. Do it faster."

I shake as I watch her come again and I love to watch her come. I follow her cue. My eyes snap shut and a few more pumps and I release while still feeling her clench all around me.

What words can I possibly say about what just went down? Besides me going down on her, this was all for her. Who am I kidding? I enjoyed it just as much as she did.

We are sticky. We are sated, and we are high on each other.

I pull off and dispose of the condom, and then I release her hands from the ties. She just lies there trying to still catch her breath. She perches herself up on her elbows after a few minutes and the glow on her face isn't just her golden-tanned skin, it's satisfaction.

"Why didn't you warn me it would be like that?"

I laugh as I lay next to her. I smooth her hair away from her face and she looks over at me.

"I didn't know it was going to be like that."

Willow smiles. "That was really good. Like really, really good."

I fall back onto the pillows and breathe out. My heart still beating out of my chest.

"Yeah, it was. Really, really good." I take her wrists in my hands and rub them.

"You okay?"

She nods as she looks in my eyes then quickly pulls her hands away, looking a little embarrassed but I'm not going to address it.

"I'm… I'm fine."

I'm just going to go with her saying she's fine.

"Are you always kinky like that?" I rub my face and look up at the ceiling.

"I can be. You liked it?"

I turn to look at her but she's looking at the exact spot on the ceiling I just was.

"Yeah. It was fun and exciting and interesting."

"Good. 'Cause I have other plans for us." She looks at me with ample eyes.

"You do?"

"Yeah. A shower 'cause we are so sticky I think we won't be able to get off of these sheets."

She lets out a hearty laugh and it's really cute and sexy. A heady combo that I think I like to hear.

Now to scratch another thing off my mental 'what-to-do-with-Willow' list.

Fuck her in the shower.

I met a random girl at Jax tonight. She stayed after and we had a drink at the bar. Porter closed so he let us hang for a while. I walked her out and we made out near her car. It was nice and she was hot, but it went no further than some tongue action and some over-the-bra boobie touching. No problem. She gave me her number and told me she'd be staying for the next week. I tucked the number inside the pocket of my jeans, and then on my way home I ripped it up and threw it out the window.

I pull up well after two and the houses seem

dark. No one came to Jax tonight, which is fine. They hear me play all the time. When I get inside the house, Cruz is awake and working on some paper for school. Only the light from his laptop glows throughout the room.

"What's up, man? You're out late. You score or something?"

I shake my head appearing to be a little disappointed but I'm not really.

"Oh, yeah. I think her name was Amber. She gave me her number. She'll be here all week. We just kissed."

Cruz looks up at me with a sorry look on his face.

"Dude, you are in a serious sex dry spell. Not that I know what that's like but I can imagine it sucks."

Cruz has never had that problem. Not that I am either and I hate lying to him, but I have to keep Willow and me to just Willow and me. I try and keep up the façade that I'm scoring left and right with every hot girl who looks in my direction. Truth is, when I do meet a girl, it seems like the same old, same old. Bar girls. Drunk girls. Girls who only see me playing my guitar — only wanting me because I play in a rock band. They want to be able to say to their friends that they fucked someone in a band. I'm not a teenager. It sorta gets old after a while.

I really can't believe those words just came out of my mouth.

"Eh, you know how it is. Not like I haven't gotten any. I just chose to do it discreetly and not outside on a deck at dawn."

He points his pencil at me.

"Hey, now. That happened a long time ago. A very long time ago and I'm not the same person I was back then. I'm getting married for Christ's sake. Harlow's the only one I'd want to fuck on a deck now. Even when we're old and gray I'd have no problem bending her over a railing and giving it to her."

I let out a laugh.

"Same mouth on you though."

Cruz shrugs. "Some things just don't change."

"Cruz, can I ask you something?"

He's focusing back to his laptop and not at me but tells me, "Sure, fire away."

I sit in a chair across from him not sure exactly what I want to ask him or how to ask the question rather.

"I guess I just had a girl question."

He furrows his brows at me as he peeks around from his laptop.

"A girl question? What kind of a girl question? If it's about girlie stuff like gifts or flowers and shit like that, talk to Harlow. If you want tips on how to properly go down on a girl then I'm your man." He pauses and thinks about what he said just then.

"Come to think of it, if you want to know about that, Harlow would be able to answer that too."

I throw a pillow at him.

"That's. Gross."

Cruz throws the pillow back in my direction,

hitting me in the chest and I catch it like a football.

"But, seriously, what kind of question?"

A million questions run through my head. Mostly about being with one girl. I want to tell him what Willow and I are up to but we solely swore to keep it to ourselves. We discussed it again during one of our romps why we are doing it. We decided that we do enough judging of other people and we don't want to be judged either. Willow is doing a great job dealing with Cruz and Harlow's not-so-upcoming nuptials but she's listening to her and looking through those bride magazines with her when they're on the beach. She swore to Harlow she would give it her best try and she's actually doing it.

"Well, I guess since I've never been in a real serious relationship and you were never going to be until you met Harlow, what changed it all for you?"

He closes the lid to his laptop and places it on the table beside him. Cruz swings his legs around, feet planted on the floor, and leans his elbows on his knees.

"It's not *what* changed it all for me, it's *who* changed it all for me. Har did that. I was this immature idiot, just fucking anything that had long legs and was up for a good time. I drank a lot. I didn't care about anyone or anything else but myself. But you know that already. Then this girl... fuck, this girl walked into my life and, damn, did she turn it upside down. She made me see there was more to me than I ever expected there could be. I fell in love with her because she made me believe there was more to life than what I was doing and there was more to *me*. Once I realized it, I knew I never wanted to spend another day of my life apart from her."

It's funny, really. The people you least expect to change are the ones who do, in fact, change. Never in my life would I ever expect Cruz to talk and feel the way he does. I guess that's how it happens. I believe in finding it. I can be a romantic, I just haven't found the person like Cruz has to make me feel that way.

I don't have a response to Cruz's confession I just listen and he never questions why I'm asking. He doesn't grill me. Why would he anyway?

It's a shitty day out today so I decided to stay in and write some lyrics. Porter is working because people tend to be permanent fixtures on a bar stool on rainy days at a beach resort. Thea is home working and Cruz and Harlow decided to drive home for the day to see Harlow's sister's baby, Avery, who is their Godchild as well. And I have zero idea where Willow is. We got into an argument the other day while we had game night with the crew. She lost Pictionary for her team because she can't draw for shit and Harlow and Thea had no idea what she was drawing. I said it looked like a leprechaun's dick and she started to bash me — telling me not to talk about *myself* that way. Then I came back at her telling her that her tan was spotty and her boobs looked like a twelve-year-old boy's in the top she was wearing.

It went on and on. Finally, we needed to be separated and put into our respective corners like five year olds.

We haven't talked since... or anything else for that matter.

As I sit on my bed listening to the rain outside, my song notebook is out and about a dozen and a half crinkled up papers from lyrics gone bad surround me. I hear a knock at my door.

"Come in." I don't look up from my notebook. I'm concentrating but I have some serious writer's block that no amount of beer or vagina will help.

Speaking of vagina...

"Hey."

Willow.

I look up briefly at her then immediately back to my book.

"What do you want? If it's my dick, I'm not in the mood."

She makes some kind of annoyed sound then shuts the door.

"No, it's not your dick, dummy. Not this time anyway. I have a favor to ask."

I bite on the eraser of my pencil and tap it on my lip as I sit back against my headboard and fold my arms over my chest. I look up at her. The woman doesn't even know how to look like shit. Her hair is wavy today, probably from the rain and humidity. She has a pink raincoat on and shorts... short shorts on with rain boots and, to be perfectly honest, it makes my dick twitch.

Damn the bitch.

"Favor? You need a favor?" I grin cockily. "I

can't wait to hear this one."

She takes off her dampened jacket and hangs it on a hook behind my door. Not even asking if that's okay. Whatever.

She has on a tiny t-shirt that accentuates the positives and it's not the 'normal Willow' look if I must say. Usually it's skirts and tanks or a killer bikini. This is 'casual Willow.'

So sue me for getting a boner. She's hot. I can't help it.

She leans against the wall, bending one of her knees and resting her foot flat against the wall. She tucks her hands behind her and holds herself up this way.

"It's not actually a favor for me, but for my dad."

I look at her confused. "I've never met your dad. Why would he need a favor from me?"

Uninvited, she pushes off the wall and sits on the edge of my bed. She picks up some of the crinkled papers, opens them and reads what's on the pages.

"Lyrics? Why did you crumple them up?" Frustrated because of my writer's block, I snatch it from her hands and toss it on the floor.

She grabs another one and reads it.

"Why do you keep doing this to them? They don't half suck."

"Mind your business, princess."

She peers up at me through her long lashes and her head tilts as once again she reads another.

I searched for you for such a long time
hoping you weren't just a dream.

That when I'd wake up
you'd be waiting for me.
You were something unexpected.
I had no idea I wanted you
but when I finally woke up-

She reads what I wrote and puts down the paper looking annoyed.

"Like I said, it doesn't half suck."

When she read it out loud it actually doesn't sound that bad.

But she doesn't get it.

"You don't get it, Willow."

"What don't I get, Max?"

"Writer's block. Everything I put down on paper sucks. Every strum on the guitar sucks."

Willow casually reaches out and grabs the pencil from my hands. She snatches my lyric book from under me and I'm just not fast enough to stop her.

She flips through it — reading what I've written — and starts to jot things down in it. I reach out for the pencil but she smacks my hand.

I run my hands through my hair and just sit back and let her do whatever it is she's doing. After a while and a few erase marks, she hands it back to me.

I read what she wrote, changing up the words I wrote and making them into some kind of carousel of mixed emotions. Centering the focus on what the words actually mean. She wrote frustration, tragedy and anguish and turned them into poetry.

She has feelings in the words she wrote.

Willow stirs up the emotions that the lyrics speak.

Willow just surprised the shit out of me.

As she sits and waits for me to respond to what she wrote, I hear her getting restless. She makes sounds and sighs and she keeps moving on my bed.

I hum a tune in my head that would very well match up with the words.

Willow stands up and places her hands on her sexy hips.

"Jesus, Max. Say something, for fuck's sake."

I shrug half-heartedly.

She stutters, "Wha... what the... what the hell is that?!" I laugh at her.

"What do you mean? I didn't say anything."

She yells, "Exactly!"

She flies over the bed and tries to snatch the lyric book from me. I keep a firm grip on the top of her head as she tries to claw at me. I roll off the bed and she chases me around the room. I hop back on the bed and dangle the book in front of her, teasing her. I jump up and down waving it around.

"You want this? Is this little book what you want? Not used to not getting your way, princess?"

"You little shit. If you didn't like it, why'd you let me write things down?"

I laugh. "I didn't let you do anything. You took it from me and wrote. You're bat-shit crazy."

"You little shit. Give me that."

"Come get it."

Wrong choice of words because those long

legs of hers allows her to leap onto the bed and tackle me. She straddles her hips and pins me to the bed — still trying to grab the book — but my cat-like reflexes are too much for her. I'm like a ninja. Fast, agile, and smooth.

Not smooth enough…

She does something I would have never expected her to do.

She kisses me.

Her head dips and her lips land on mine.

It's not a soft kiss either. It's the kind that could bring a man to his knees. Like me.

Hot and lustful. Needy and greedy. So I drop the book and grab onto the back of her neck. I weave my hands through her hair and flip her over so I'm on top of her. I roll my hips around, inviting her in for more. She feels my hard-as-a-rock cock through my shorts. I know she does because she lets out a sigh. We lick at each other and bite at each other's lips. Every time she licks at my bottom lip my pants grow tighter and tighter. Her hands grab at my ass, claw at my back and make their way up the back of my neck and into my hair.

Then I feel it. Not her boobs, not the warmth between her legs, but a bang on my head.

Somewhere between the groping and kissing she somehow got a hold of the book and smacked me in the head with it. Hard.

I sit up and touch my head.

"Ugh, you brat. What the hell was that for?"

She wiggles her way from under me and stands up adjusting her shorts and shirt, then in her own Willow-esque way, she runs her fingernails through her tousled hair like a comb.

"You don't mess with 'the bitch,' Max. Remember that. I have."

"What do you mean?"

She steps a little forward towards the bed. Her eyes send me a pained look.

"You don't think I know what you call me. How you refer to me? I know I'm what I am, but it doesn't help when you overhear conversations where your name isn't said, but your pet name is. I'm 'the bitch.' That's what you refer to me as and it's fine." She backs away and breaks her eye contact with me.

"Willow, I didn't mean…"

A tight-lipped smile appears on her face. "Yes, you did, Max."

I get up off the bed and go towards her, the notebook in my hand.

I let out a breath and tell her the truth.

"Okay, so yes, I refer to you as that and… I'm sorry, but you don't make it easy for me, Willow. You don't make anything easy for me either."

She says nothing. No witty comeback, no cursing at me, no smacking me around. Just a blank, unreadable stare.

So unlike her. Maybe she's sick.

"I know," she barely says it, but she does.

She is sick.

I'm not going to push her buttons. I'm not going to stir the shit pot. I'm picking and choosing my battles carefully. She looks a little off so I shake it off and ask, "So this all started because you wanted to ask me a favor for your dad, right?"

She snaps her fingers as she remembers in the first place why she's here.

"Oh, yes. Well, my dad and mother rent this gigantic house in the Hamptons the week of the fourth and on the actual fourth they throw this gorgeous party on the beach with about a hundred people. It's amazing usually. Last year I missed it and my dad asked me to go this year. Porter is coming as well."

She's rambling.

Please, God, make her stop.

"Okay, Willow. I get it. It's an amazing party for rich people. Noted. What does this have to do with me?"

"Daddy hired a band for the party but they backed out at the last minute, so I told them about you and your band and he wants to hire you for the party."

I rub my forehead in confusion.

"But, Wills, aren't they swanky people who would rather hear crooners than rock and roll? I mean we do a ton of covers that we twist into our own sound but I'm not sure we could pull off some classy stuff."

She points at me and winks.

"Ah, see that's where you're wrong. These people love to party and the band wouldn't be playing until nighttime and they would all be more than half-cocked in the ass anyway. They all just love to dance and have a good time. During the day he has a D.J."

Sitting on the edge of my bed, I lean on my knees shaking my head. Doubt clouds my mind.

"I'm not sure it's going to fly. We play some really hardcore tunes. Like head banging shit."

She sits next to me.

"Listen, I've heard you guys turn some songs from the 80s and 90s into some really cool stuff. Things I've never heard before that I love now. I go back and listen to the originals and, in my opinion, they're not even as good as you guys. Besides…"

She stays quiet… not finishing her sentence.

The tone of my voice is high pitched. "Besides… what?"

"He said he'll pay you guys $3,000. If you play for two hours with a twenty-minute break in between."

I jump up. My eyes bug out of my damn head.

"Did you say three grand? That's like… that's a grand for each of us. You can't be serious, *he* can't be serious."

"Dead as Lincoln serious. He asked me what you guys were worth and I gave him a price and he shrugged and said okay."

This is where my racing mind stops and the puzzle that is Willow Taylor is again placed before me.

"You… you told your dad we were good enough to be paid that kind of money. I mean, Christ, that's a lot… I mean you told him we were worth that?"

"Max, you irritate me like a fungal infection but you're talented. When I see something good, and original, something that exudes talent, I'll admit it. Contrary to popular belief of *some* people, I'm not always a bitch." She elbows me at the bitch part.

"Okay. I'll call the guys and we'll start to put some stuff together."

"You don't have much time. We leave in three days. My parents want you guys to be their guests as well so we are going to leave at the ass-crack of dawn on the fourth and stay overnight."

I disagree with her. "No way, Willow. We are professionals. No way are we hanging out at the daytime party as well."

She stands up and grabs her raincoat and starts to put it on.

"Nonsense. They would never want that anyway. They treat their staff at our house like family, not like the hired help. Porter is coming and so are Thea and Harlow. Cruz has to work at Jax and he told her to go because all of their parents are coming anyway."

That makes me feel slightly better knowing that our friends will be there as well.

And, like I said, I am picking and choosing wisely. Battles with Willow Taylor come with great consequences.

"Okay. You win."

She goes for the door handle and as she opens it she turns quickly around to me.

"I always do."

"Hey, Wills. No one's home. Want to… you know, as a thank you for getting us the gig."

CHAPTER 7

His Voice Hurts My Heart
Willow~

The house my parents rent in the Hamptons is amazing. It's even bigger than my house in Princeton. Eight bathrooms, eight bedrooms, a pool and a spa, and a small putting green on the west side of the house. Right on the beach. It's amazing. I wish they'd buy it but they would never get enough time away from work to really enjoy it. That's why they let all of us use the Sandy Cove homes — my mom and my aunt Addy, Porter's mom, never use the homes that my grandfather left them. My parents like Europe or the Keys. My aunt and uncle go with them most of the time. The week they rent this is a way to celebrate the summer with their friends and co-workers.

When we arrived, I introduced Max and his other bandmates, Alex and Drew, to my parents and Max couldn't have been more appreciative because I finally remembered their names. My dad was so happy to oblige and Max reassured him that they would make him a happy man with the entertainment. Daddy asked Max about a dozen questions regarding the business. I have a little secret that Daddy wanted me to keep from Max because he would be nervous if he knew but there's a friend of his who is in the music business and he's coming to the party. Daddy told him all about the band and they are anxious to hear them play.

Daddy took the boys along with Porter and Uncle Paul, Porter's dad, for a ride in the golf cart around the estate. The guests aren't here yet so Mother, Aunt Addy, Harlow, Thea and I are sitting on one of the decks of the house sipping on mojitos my mom made.

The party staff is busy putting up tents and setting up tables. They assemble a stage for Max's band and a spot for the D.J. Dozens upon dozens of lights are strung between the tents. Tables are set up and decorated in blue and white striped linens with red, shiny centerpieces that adorn the middle of the tables. Everything looks pristine and clean. Sharp and classy. Just like my parents.

The mid-afternoon sun shines brightly on the beach and the party is in full swing. I'd say there's about a hundred people here. Close to it at least. Daddy shows me off like I'm his prized possession. I am actually. I'm Daddy's pride and joy. I know some people here but not everyone so Daddy introduces me. Some even speak Spanish so we carry on conversations after Daddy tells them I am a Spanish teacher. Max and Porter and the other guys in the band are playing water polo and Harlow and Thea are sipping away drinks on the over-sized lounge chairs near the pool. I excuse myself from Daddy's guests and he kisses my temple and I go to the girls. I plop down next to Harlow.

"Ugh. If I had to say hello to one more person and have them ask me a dozen and a half questions I think my head would have exploded."

"My heads going to explode any second now," Thea mumbles between sips of her drink.

"Why?" She's staring at the pool. I have no idea why she looks so pained. It's just Max and the guys playing in the pool with a few girls. No biggie.

"They're just playing water polo, Thea."

"Who are those girls?" Harlow asks.

I point to the one in the white bikini who is currently hanging on my cousin like an appendage.

"That's Skylar Smith. Daughter of Harry and Dina Smith. They own a chain of steak houses in New York. Mega rich."

"And the one near Max?"

I didn't even see the one who is now in front of Max. He is behind her and running his hands up and down her shoulders and showing her how to play the game. She's a little too close. No, actually she's a lot too close.

Wait, what am I saying?

"I have no idea who that is but I'm about to find out."

The girl currently hanging on Max is thin, with long auburn hair. She looks Brazilian. Not sure if my parents even know anyone Brazilian. I don't think they do actually.

I stand up, ridding myself of my bathing suit cover-up, over-sized hat, and heels.

"And where are you going?" Harlow peeks up at me from under her own hat.

"Going to find out who that bitch is."

I leave those two and saunter down the large steps that lead into the pool. Swaying my hips and, for the love of God, I have no idea why I'm moving like I'm on some kind of catwalk.

Fuck it.

Totally.

I make my way down into the pool. The cool water hits my warm body, sending a chill down my spine. I casually drift over to the guys.

"What's everyone up to over here?"

Porter, laughing along with Skylar Smith, greets me. "Hey, Wills. What's going on?"

I raise my body up a little from the water, pushing out the girls in my coral colored bikini top trimmed in gold.

"Oh, I was just so hot that I needed to take a dip. Skylar, nice to see you."

I nod to Skylar, who is an even bigger bitch than I am.

"Willow. Porter, show me how you make that muscle move again." She lowers her sunglasses and hangs onto Porter's arm as he flexes and I want to puke right in this pool. Can she be more audacious?

I turn to Max and the Brazilian.

"Max. Having fun?" He doesn't even hear me because Miss Oh-My-God-Her-Tits-Are-So-Fake-And-Huge is monopolizing all his time. They laugh and splash and carry on.

I stick out my hand to introduce myself.

"I don't think we've been properly introduced. I'm Willow Taylor. This is my parents' party."

Yep, that came out bitchy.

Brazilian big tits takes my hand.

"Oh, my. I had no idea. Hello, Willow, I'm Cora."

Not recognizing her I bite my inside lip and ask again.

"I apologize, Cora, but are you friends of my parents? Do you work for the PR firm?"

She smiles sweetly.

"No. I'm Gary Carpenter's daughter. He's a music promoter and he's friends with your dad."

Max takes my elbow and pulls me gently towards him.

"Wills, Cora's dad asked about us. He said he was really looking forward to meeting us and hearing us perform tonight. Cora said he may want to talk to us about some things if he likes what he hears. Can you believe it, Willow? This could be our shot!"

Yes, I know it could be his shot and I wanted to be the one to tell him. That did not go as planned.

I act dumb. I have no idea why. He just seems so excited and I don't want him thinking I kept it from him to be a bitch.

My face falls from disappointment and something else that I can't quite decipher, but as soon as I feel it, I remember who I am.

I raise my chin and look towards Cora but my words are at Max.

"Wow… that, that sounds… amazing." I know the words come out a little flat and my tone may not be as enthusiastic as it would have been if I were the one who told Max.

Max leaves my side and goes back to where Cora stands in the water.

He's all smiles and so is she. They float around in the water and just laugh and begin splashing each other.

I call out to them. "Well, Cora. It was a pleasure meeting you. I'm sure I'll see you later."

She continues to laugh as her boobs bounce around from her incisive cackling.

"Oh, you too, Willow. Thank you again for having me. I'm thrilled to be here."

Fuck, she's actually nice. I can tell when someone is being genuine.

I hate her.

I give an even-lipped smile.

"Max, I'll see you later."

Still gazing at Miss Nicey Pants, he tells me, "Okay, Wills. See ya later."

I exit the pool, go to where Harlow and Thea are still on the lounge chairs and grab a towel from them. A waiter comes by with a few drinks on his tray and I grab two of them off of it. Not knowing really what they are, I down them. One, two.

Yikes. Those were strong.

I delicately wipe the corners of my mouth and notice Thea and Harlow looking at me — wide-eyed and full of questioning looks.

Harlow shakes her head, clearly confused.

"Um, what the hell was that? You need to control yourself with the drinking today, Willow. This is your parents' party. Pace yourself."

I wrap the towel even tighter around me. Plopping down beside Harlow, I let out a rush of air from my lungs.

"I'm fine. I was just thirsty." Cue the eye roll from both of my best friends.

"No, really. I'm fine. Both of you stop looking at me like that." I brush off my annoyance and change the subject immediately before they suspect that my sudden attitude is nothing more than the effects of heat and thirst. I'm not even sure why I feel like a jealous, jilted lover over here. I mean, Max is not my boyfriend, he's my… Well, I don't have to spell it out. We are what we are.

I turn to Harlow. "So, the meathead you're engaged to couldn't get off work?"

Eye roll.

"No, sadly. He's been working his ass off between school and bouncing at two places in Sandy Cove. He applied for a few police officer jobs in between Princeton and Sandy Cove."

I scrunch up my face. "Why the hell would he do that?"

"Because he knows that I live for going to Sandy Cove for the summer. It's going to be a long time before we get married and he told me he'd rather commute than not see me at all. He doesn't think an hour-long commute is bad as long as I'm happy."

He makes me want to projectile vomit, but he does make her happy, so be it.

"Well, too bad. I was looking forward to busting his balls or lack thereof."

Mother and Annabelle Hannum stroll over to us.

"Hello, girls. Enjoying the day?"

"Hi, Mother, hi Annabelle."

"Thank you for having us, Tessa. This is so beautiful." Harlow smiles up at Mother and her mom. Annabelle goes over to sit on the lounge with Har.

"Honey, I'm so sorry Cruz couldn't come. That boy works so hard. I give him so much credit."

"I know, Mom. He does work really hard. I miss him. I'll see him tomorrow. It's good to spend some time apart."

My mother sighs. "Oh, I only wish my Willow would find someone like Cruz. Someone who loves her and respects her. A hard worker and a family man just like her dad."

I laugh out loud. Maybe a little too boldly.

"Me, find someone like Cruz? Oh, please. Like a guy whose muscles are bigger than his brain. I swear that man has so many tattoos I bet the ink sunk into his bloodstream and dissolved some of his brain cells."

Mother gives me a hard look. "Willow, that's

enough."

Harlow waves her hand at her. "Tessa, it's fine. I'm used to it."

"No, Harlow. I didn't raise my daughter to talk about others that way. Cruz is a good person. Anyone who was willing to stay by someone's bedside for weeks upon end while in a coma and fighting and doing everything possible to get her love back again, in my book, is someone to be respected."

"Mother, I…" As I try to tell her that I'm just kidding as usual, she stops me.

"Harlow, did you know that Bill and I have been married for twenty-six years?" Harlow shakes her head no.

"Did you know that we met in high school?" Harlow shakes her head yes.

"He was going to become a doctor but realized that it meant long hours away from me and if we got married we knew we wanted a family and he didn't want to miss a single moment of that child's life. He sacrificed a lot for us and gave up his dream because he loved me that much." Mother grabs Harlow's hand and holds it in hers.

"Harlow, when we find a man who is willing and able to sacrifice so much for us and love us with so much passion, we need to hold on to those because they are the good guys. I have a good guy. You found yourself a good guy. Don't allow anyone else to tell you anything different." Her eyes go to mine and I feel the heat of embarrassment creep up my neck.

"Now, girls. It's almost sundown and that

means the real party will begin shortly. You girls know which room you're in, right?"

"Yes, Tessa. Thank you, again. We'll be going up shortly to freshen up and change."

"You're welcome, Harlow." Mother turns in my direction.

"I'm looking forward to hearing your friend's band play tonight."

Without another word she walks away and I'm left with the feeling that, once again, quite possibly, I should have kept my mouth shut.

The day has turned into night. Waves of people align the many levels of decks surrounding the house. There are still people in the pool. Many of them with drinks in hand and bags with changes of clothes for nighttime. The lights the party planners put up are lit and cast a soft glow across the landscape of the area. The mist from the ocean is seen through the lights and the air is thick with humidity; the atmosphere euphoric. I changed into an above the knee cobalt blue sundress. The strapless dress is comfortable and I paired it with hoop earrings and my compass necklace that my dad gave me, and, of course, some heels.

I walk around saying hello to new guests who weren't able to come during the day. I see that the stage is all set up for the band. I haven't seen Max since my time not so well spent with him and the Brazilian babe in the pool but I see her and, yep, she's with Max by the side of the stage. He's playing with his amp and he's showing her his guitar. I'm watching like a stalker as they laugh and he gets behind her and shows her how to strum it. She looks like a model and he looks like an ant. They look ridiculous together. Then I see it. A kiss. A kiss between the two of them. A soft one. It's quick but I see it happen. I swallow the lump in my throat. I blame the pollen in the air. I turn away and find Harlow and Thea standing behind me.

"Wow, she's gorgeous. I hope Max gets her number. He needs a good woman."

I sniff and take Harlow's drink out of her hand and take a few sips.

"Why do you think he needs a good woman?"

Harlow leans against the deck's rail as she looks out where Max and Cora stand.

"I don't know. Maybe because he's a passionate person and needs to take that passion out on something else besides a guitar."

Oh, if she only knew.

This angers me and it really shouldn't because it's not like Harlow knows that anything is going on between Max and me.

"Yeah, well… maybe," I say it quietly and, for the most part, quiet enough that only I can hear it and also to let myself know that what Max and I do with our time is nothing more than sex. He can kiss who he wants. He can have fun with whomever he wants. I'm just the plaything to him and he's mine. Not in the literal sense but I use him just as much as he uses me.

Cora gives Max a kiss on the cheek before he grabs his guitar and makes his way towards the stage.

The band takes the stage and I see my dad go to the microphone first. When everyone sees him they applaud.

He waves his hands, signaling for everyone to settle down. So many people love my daddy.

"Thank you, everyone, for coming tonight. My wife Tessa and I are so pleased you all could join us. Tonight I have a special treat. My beautiful daughter Willow…" Daddy searches for me in the crowd through the bright lights of the stage. "Willow, honey. You out there?" I wave back at him and to the guests, pageant like.

"Ah, there she is. My pride and joy. Well, when our original band cancelled on us at the last minute, my beautiful daughter convinced me to have her friend's band play. Even though I was unsure at first, my daughter told me they were well worth the price of admission. And I trust her with my whole heart. So, without further ado, let's hear it for The Band."

People seem confused at first, and no one claps, but then my dad fixes it.

"No, for real. The band's name is 'The Band.' Let's hear it for them." The guests laugh and then the applauding begins.

I see Max shake my dad's hand and reach for the microphone. Thea, Harlow and I have a perfect view of them. Being on one of the higher decks gives us a great vantage point. An absolutely perfect view.

"Hey, everyone. Thanks so much for the warm welcome. We are The Band."

The first strum of the guitar begins the

cheering from my girls and me.

They play with heart. With soul. With… passion, just like Harlow said.

Max's voice weaves like silk. He plays with such vibrancy and smoothness.

I can't help but smile. I beam actually. I look to see Daddy and Mother dance amongst their guests and everyone looks to be having a great time. The girls and I sway. Thea and I twist each other around and dip each other. Poor Har's legs still aren't what they used to be so she just laughs at us while she watches.

Just as promised, Max delivers. The songs they play are such an eclectic mixture of genres that some of the songs the crowd is very unaware that they are heavy metal tunes. It's impressive.

When they finish their set, the guests go clap crazy.

"Wow, thanks, everyone. We are going to take a short break but we'll be back very soon."

Max gives the crowd a wave and exits the stage. I turn to Harlow and Thea. "I'm going to go down and talk to Max. I'll be back." They nod and I make my way down the steps and through the crowd. Porter stops me halfway.

"Hey, Wills. How awesome were they?" Porter has something hanging on him. Oh, it's just Skylar Smith.

"Hello, Skylar." She ignores me. I want in the worst way to flip her the bird. She can go shove off.

"Yeah, P. They were incredible. I'm going to go talk to Max. I'll see you guys later."

Before I have a chance to step away from them, Skylar opens her fat mouth.

"I think Max may be a little busy right now. You probably should wait." Her painted fingernail points down where the stage is.

And her red nail isn't the only thing that makes me see red.

Max is shaking hands with a gray-haired gentleman who I am assuming is Cora's father. I see her hands toss between him and Max. Her other hand rests comfortably in the crook of Max's elbow. The two men shake hands and exchange some sort of babble. I watch them like I'm watching something on a big screen. In a theater, maybe. Some kind of show rather than the one I just saw on that stage.

Cora's dad pulls out a card and hands it to Max. The look on Max's face is one of surprise as the gray-haired man continues to talk. Max hangs on his every word and they vigorously shake hands when the conversation ceases. When Cora's dad walks away, Max just stares at the card. He looks up at Cora and she throws her arms around his neck. Slowly, she pulls her face around from his neck and their faces are inches apart and then they kiss. But it's not the kiss I saw earlier. This one has much life to it. It has attraction and want behind it.

He weaves his hand into the back of her hair and his other arm wraps around her waist, pulling her in even closer. Hell, what's he doing? Checking her for cavities, he's so deep in her mouth. It goes on and on and it looks like a horror movie that you don't want to watch but you can't help not to.

I turn away and furiously make my way through the thick crowd to the beach. I grab a bottle of something off one of the make-shift bars. I walk down to the beach, tripping on the sand because it's so soft and I'm in a hurry. When I reach my destination — far enough away from the party — I sit on the dune and shiver. Not because of the air because it's warm and muggy, but for reasons I am trying to figure out. And for the first time in my life I have to figure something out on my own. I need to stop what has started and let the softening that may have entered my heart become hard again. But I don't know if I can.

Drinking alone is not fun. Watching fireworks bursting above your head alone on the Fourth of July is not how you should watch them. They're supposed to be watched with someone else. This is no fun. I want my stomach to stop churning. I want my head to stop thinking.

As I take a swig from the bottle — very un-ladylike of me — I can hear the band playing and the laughter of the partygoers. I lay back after the buzz of the vodka kicks in. I look into the now empty sky and just look at the stars and hear the rush of the waves as they crash on the shoreline.

I think I fall asleep but I'm slowly awakened when I hear the sound of my name being called out.

I groan and cover my face with my hands, full of sand.

"Jesus, Willow. Where the hell have you been? Your parents called the cops and everything."

I look through the fingers that cover my eyes and see Max standing above me.

"Ugh… call off the search party and leave me alone."

I hear him make a call.

"Harlow, it's Max. I found her. Over by the dunes. Tell her parents I'll have her back. No, she's okay. I see an almost empty bottle of vodka next to her so I think she may be drunk. No, let me handle it. No, you don't have to come all the way down here, Har. It's a lot of walking for you. Yes, tell Mr. Taylor she's fine and he can to go on to bed."

"You want to tell me why you've been out here all this time by yourself?"

"What the hell time is it?"

"Two. Last time I saw you was right after I talked to Gary Carpenter. I saw you on the steps but you turned away before I could reach you. I would have come after you but I needed to get back on stage."

I sit up a little on my elbows and push my tangled hair out of my face. I stare out into the black, endless ocean.

"Where's Cora?"

"What? That's what you're asking me? Where's Cora? We've been looking everywhere for you."

I puff out the frustrating air that's building in my lungs. "We've been? Don't you mean my parents and my friends?"

Max plops down next to me and grabs the bottle of vodka that I just reached out my hand to take. He throws it away from us.

"No, I mean me too. Porter, your dad. We just seemed to skip the dune. Your dad figured you wouldn't have gone out here at night."

"Well, guess he was wrong. So you didn't answer my question."

"Question?"

"Yeah, where's Cora?"

"Why the hell do you care where Cora is? She went home."

"Why?" I snap.

"'Cause she went home, that's why. You're being weird. What's your deal?"

I try and stand up quickly but I'm off balance. So I fall, gracefully, I might add. I fall on Max and he whines.

"Dammit, Willow. Where do you think you're going?"

I want to kiss him but decide against it. I roll off of Max and stand up, this time slowly and more carefully. I wrap my hands around my arms because of the chill in the air. I rub them up and down trying to cause friction.

Max sees this and stands up and begins to rub my bare arms for me. I don't want him touching me.

But I do.

"You're freezing, Wills. Let's go back to the house." I pull away from him abruptly, turning my body away from his.

"Did you get her number?" The words come

out harsh and even if I didn't have some alcohol raging through my bloodstream, I'd still say it the way I do.

"What's with you, Willow? You sound like a goddamn jealous girlfriend."

My face is damp and I'm thinking it's the sea mist that has coated my face, but it's not. It's tears.

The last time I cried was when Harlow was leaving for England, then when she told me she was engaged and pretty much told me I was a shitty friend.

But I don't cry.

Willow Taylor doesn't cry. Often.

Especially over a boy. A stupid boy. And he will never know.

My coldness returns because I can't let him know that his affection towards Cora has reduced me to tears.

Pointing at myself, I turn towards Max.

"Me? A jealous girlfriend? Doubtful. I'm not your girlfriend. I'm not really even your friend. I'm your fuck buddy, Max. We use each other for fucking sex when the mood strikes and that's about it. So don't think any more about why I'm asking you questions about Cora."

Max runs his hand through his hair, clearly frustrated by my outburst.

"Then why the hell are you yelling at me like this? We've been getting along for the most part. This weekend has been great. And, as usual, you're confusing me."

I calm myself down and maybe I am getting

carried away. I know my voice is hardened and I have to try to turn this conversation around. I maneuver around it and change my story up.

"Because I've known that Mr. Carpenter was going to be here and he wanted to hear you guys. I'm mad because I'm the one who wanted to tell you. Not Cora."

His expression is slack.

"How did you know Cora told me?"

Wrapping my arms around my waist, shivering I tell him, "I saw Cora introduce you to him and I kind of just guessed. That's why I'm mad. It's nothing else."

By the look on his face I'm pretty sure he accepts that answer. Part of it is true in a way. Maybe not the whole truth but jealously is not part of who I am and accepting that I may be slightly jealous, that, in itself, is hard for me to take. Nothing usually bothers me but I do know this: ever since we started this little deal between the two of us, I've found jealousy creeping into my life. I've never had anything to be jealous about. I'm pretty and smart and rich. What else would I possibly have to be jealous about? Oddly enough my answer rests with the current situation.

"Oh, okay. Well I'm sorry you didn't get the chance to do it first. Like I said, I wanted to talk with you but then you disappeared. And, by the way, your dad, he's a pretty terrific guy."

The corner of my mouth goes up in a smile. It's not forced but it's because with what Max says about my dad, I have to agree.

"Yeah. He's a great guy. He was really excited

to tell me about Mr. Carpenter wanting to talk to you guys."

Max's grin grows wide and his eyes dance in the moonlight. He looks anxious to tell me something in a good way.

"Speaking of that. I have something to tell you."

I squish my eyebrows together. I have to stop doing that. I'm way too young for frown lines and Botox.

"What? What's going on?"

He steps closer to me and braces my shoulders forcing my body to face his.

"The Band is going on tour."

Now I know I'm going to need Botox because my face is so contorted right now I know there's going to be lines all over the place.

"A tour? I'm confused. With who?"

"Mr. Carpenter is a promoter for this up and coming band that is going on a month-long tour of the East Coast and they need an opening act." He stands up straight, proud as a peacock, and folds his arms across his chest.

"And he wants The Band to open for them. Six shows a week, ten cities, and lots and lots of promotion and doors opening up for us."

Astonished, but happy, I have questions for him.

"Wow. That's really great. You guys are pretty good. Guess I'm not surprised. When do you leave?"

Max looks up to the sky and blinks a few times. Clearly excited but pained for some reason.

He's not answering me.

"Max? I asked when you're leaving."

"The day after tomorrow. I won't be back in Sandy Cove for the rest of the summer."

That's when I feel something I don't think I've ever felt before.

An ache in a spot unfamiliar to me and that spot is in my heart.

As I sit on the large chaise lounge outside on the deck of the house, I look out onto the beach and stare at the crashing waves. The sky is pink and the sun is about to rise. No, I haven't slept yet and it's not by choice. I just can't.

I sip on my coffee and enjoy the sounds of just the water and the seagulls flying across the ocean. The tents are still erected but everything else looks cleaned up for the most part. I didn't notice after I came up from the beach in the middle of the night.

After Max told me he leaves tomorrow for a month-long tour with an up and coming new band, who, according to Mr. Carpenter, will be the next big thing, there wasn't much more to say. I congratulated Max. I made some bullshit excuse that I had a pretty bad headache based on the alcohol I consumed so I needed to go to bed. That didn't happen. I did go to bed. I tossed and turned and finally just came downstairs and made some coffee and I've been here ever since.

He leaves tomorrow. Scattered cities, on a tour bus, different venues almost every night. That's going to be his life for a month. Mine will be in

Sandy Cove. Days at the beach and nights either at Jax or partying at the houses. No Max. Which means we may have to have the talk. The talk about how maybe our deal needs to end. There's no way a good looking guy like Max who is going to be on tour in a different city almost every night is going to be able to withhold from sex with groupies. And there will be groupies. I'm not stupid. I watch the entertainment news shows on TV and read all the trash mags. I know what goes on.

Realizations are the worst. This is something I'm coming to find. I don't like them. I don't like realizing I could be a jealous person. I hate realizing that things bother me when maybe they shouldn't. And I do not particularly like that feeling I had last night. I clutched my chest. I felt like I couldn't breathe. That's why I made up the story about my headache. I needed to get away. I couldn't stand there in front of Max anymore. I have to just move on and think about how it was fun while it lasted. Sex was fun and great with Max but it's done. It was a brilliant idea at the time.

Not so much now.

As I curl up my knees to my chest and breathe in the scent of my coffee and the salt air, I feel a hand on my shoulder. I look to my right and see Daddy standing there smiling. I smile back and he sits at the edge of the chaise.

"So you missed a good party last night, darling daughter."

His tone is a mixture of fact and sternness.

"I'm sorry, Daddy. I needed some time to myself."

He grabs my cup of coffee and sips from it.

"Since when do you need time to yourself and at a party, nonetheless?"

I sigh. I don't want to tell him the truth and I don't want to lie either. So honesty isn't a choice for me either way.

"It's complicated, Daddy. Just know I'm fine, but it's not anything I want to really talk about."

My tone is even. Non-emotional.

"And since when don't you tell me everything? I understand a girl needs to keep some things to herself but, sweetie, you tell me everything and it was just so odd for you to disappear like that. We were worried sick. Whatever it is you don't want to talk about, next time let us know that you need some space. Don't make me send out a search party for you. I don't think I was ever so nervous."

I'm the worst daughter in the world. I really am. I'm ashamed because this new emotion of mine — jealousy — has made my dad upset with me and he is the last person I would ever want upset with me.

I grab his hand and hold it.

"Daddy, I am so sorry. I didn't mean to upset you or make you worry. I'm just going through some girlie stuff and I just... I can't say."

His voice dips and he speaks in a quiet tone.

"I... understand. I just... I thought you could tell me anything and say anything to me without judgment or persecution. Especially from me,

Willow. If you're hurting, I'm hurting. If you're happy, I'm happy. No matter what and I'm not begging you to tell me what's wrong, I just worry because you've never said to me before you didn't want to talk to *me* about something."

He looks hurt. I panic. I can't have the one man I can always depend on be hurt — by me. I tell him enough that he needs to know.

"Daddy, no. It's… um… it's about a boy. I think I have feelings for someone and it's not reciprocated so…"

He chuckles a bit and breathes out a sigh of relief.

"A guy. Whew. I thought it was serious. You again worried me, daughter."

"But it is serious, Daddy. I've never had to deal with this before. This feeling. I'm not a fan of it."

Daddy pats the spot next to him, beckoning me to get a little closer. I snuggle into my daddy's side as we look out at the sun rising into the warm July sky. He kisses my temple and pulls me by my shoulder closer to him.

"My darling, Willow. Some feelings we have that we're not familiar with are all a part of growing up. Some feelings don't feel right. Others feel great. It's part of the process. It's part of becoming an adult and accepting the feelings that we're not used to. And if love is one of those, Willow, listen to your dad when I say this. Let it in. Accept it. Adore it. Cherish it. You'll never regret it. Even if it doesn't work out the way you want it, don't let that waver your feelings. Love can be amazing. Look at your mom and me."

Damn these eyes for filling up with this strange water again.

And the words I say barely come out.

"It scares me."

"Love?" he asks.

I nod.

"Oh, Willow. That's normal but don't let fear stop you from the way you feel. Embrace it and live with love in your heart."

I look up at him and take in his profile. So strong and handsome. Gray and dark brown hair, creases around his eyes and mouth and he's just comforting. His face comforts me and brings me peace.

"Will you promise me, Willow? Will you promise me that you will listen to what I'm saying and remember it?"

A grave expression crosses his face when he says it and his demeanor is serious.

"Yes, Daddy. I will. Anything for you."

I'm in my room packing up to go home when Thea and Harlow come storming in.

"So you want to explain?"

I glance up at them for a second. Both of them standing there, hands on their narrowed hips. All four eyes shooting fire my way.

"About what?"

"Why you were missing for hours last night?" Harlow's voice is laced with anger.

"I didn't feel like staying at the party anymore."

She counters my response.

"And you couldn't tell anyone that you were not staying? You had to go down to the beach and get drunk and not just go to your room?"

Damn, she's good.

I close my suitcase fiercely.

"I don't owe anyone an explanation, Harlow. Let's just go. My dad's driver is ready to take us back." I can tell by the look on her face that my voice cuts her like glass.

I fling my suitcase off the bed and roll it past them and out the door.

Once the massive SUV is packed, I stand in the driveway of the house, and I watch silently as Max thanks my parents for everything.

"Mr. and Mrs. Taylor, I can't thank you enough for having us play at your party. It was truly an honor. Mr. Taylor, thank you for giving me the opportunity to meet Mr. Carpenter. I still can't believe this is all happening."

Daddy extends his hand to meet Max's and they shake. Daddy brings Max in for half a hug.

"Max, I am so happy and excited for you. I wish you only great success."

"Thank you, sir. I'm going to work very hard. And thank you for the talks and the advice about my future. I appreciate it."

Then I notice Daddy do something that mystifies me.

Daddy pulls Max in — his hand on Max's shoulder — and he leans close to his ear. Max listens intently. The conversation isn't a long one but whatever Daddy is saying to him, Max hangs on his every word. Max's eyes travel up and meet mine for a second and then his chin drops and he continues to listen. Then the moment is over.

Porter hugs my parents, as do Thea and Harlow. Now it's my time to say bye to my parents.

I go to Mother.

"Everything was wonderful, Mother. Thank you for having all of us and I'll see you in a few weeks for your birthday."

She hugs me tight and rocks me in her arms.

"I'll miss you, my sweet girl. Have fun and be careful." I didn't get the third degree from her about missing last night. I'm an adult and she didn't ask many questions. I guess Daddy filled her in.

I go to my dad. He takes my hands and holds out my arms and shakes his head.

"My sweet, beautiful girl. Remember what we talked about and never forget it." He's sweating a lot and I curse this damn sun.

"I won't, Daddy. You better go inside. This heat looks like it's getting to you. And I won't forget. I love you, Daddy."

He brings me into his arms and cradles me there.

"I love you, Willow."

We break apart and climb into the car. I sit between Harlow and Thea in the back and Max and Porter climb into the middle row. Max's band drove separately with their equipment. As the car pulls away, I look out the back window and watch the two people who have showed me undeniable love wave goodbye. My eyes fill with tears. Not because of Max or because I'm leaving them, but because I do have love in my heart and the fact that I appreciate so much that they are the ones who put that love there.

The drive back was quiet, at least for me. Max just went on and on about the tour to Porter telling him every detail. I wish I had remembered my earphones so I could drown out the conversation. So after enduring an hour-long spiel of tour details, I lash out.

"Max, could you maybe shut up for a bit. You'll have to repeat the whole thing to Cruz when we get back." I'm annoyed and it shows on my face and in my tone.

Turning around, he looks at me and rolls his eyes then turns back around and Porter looks at me with a glare in his eye.

"Hell, I'll be happy that you two will be separated for a while. I could sure use a break from you two always arguing."

I extend my middle finger to Porter.

"Don't worry about him telling Cruz the whole thing. I called him this morning and filled him in." Harlow smiles and I turn my upper lip up in a scowl.

Of course she told the big, tatted dummy. Harlow nudges me and asks me quietly, "What is up with you? Why are you so miserable? This is a big deal for Max. I know he's not your favorite person but you had a lot to do with why he's getting ready to do what he's about to do."

"I'm fine. I'm PMS-ing. Leave me be."

She sticks her tongue out at me and I ignore her and rest my head against the seat. Closing my eyes I wish for sleep for the rest of the trip, but it never comes.

Once we get back to the house and unpack, I stay quiet. Everyone wants to do dinner at the house for Max. They want to bar-b-que and hang out since he's leaving. I want to crawl into bed. But I can't. Everyone will see through me. I can't have that. So, what do I need to do? Suck it up, well, as best as I can.

Max invited a few people over he knows — guys and girls. Cruz and Porter man the grill. The girls and I make a few side dishes to go along with the dogs and burgers. As I stand at the counter in the kitchen and slice cucumbers I pick one up and look at it. Then I look out the door to see Max standing there chatting it up with a few people filling them in on the tour.

"Well, my large green friend, looks like it's just you and me for a while."

Now I'm totally kidding but I guess it's just a way for me to find humor in all of this. Plus, it's the same size as Max. And that part, I'm not kidding.

Cruz walks in and asks for another platter for more food. I hand it to him without looking at him or speaking. He thanks me and begins to walk away. But then turns to me.

"What's up with you? No Dickcop reference? No making fun of my shirt? No rude comment of my muffled tan?" I don't look up at him. I keep slicing away at the cucumbers.

"Um… I'm not used to being ignored by you. Not even a fuck off?" he adds.

I shake my head no. I'm not in the mood. I can sense his presence even if I keep my eyes pinned to my task. Cruz slaps his hand on the counter, startling me.

"Listen up. You don't feel like talking, fine. Then I will." I raise my eyes and the knife up and just hold it up for him to see, looking at him like, *don't tempt me, asshole.*

"That's not going to work, Willow. I'm a Marine. I think I can take you in a knife fight."

I look at him smugly and put the knife down and lean on the counter.

"If you think you can hide it any longer then you're dead wrong, Willow. You don't think I know but I do. I see it without seeing it. I hear you when you think I don't. If you're in love with him then tell him before he goes off on this tour and fucks everything with two legs. This isn't about you two fucking around anymore. I see the way you look at him when you think no one else is watching, I'm the one who can see."

I forcefully throw the chopped cucumbers in a bowl.

I scoff at him. "You have no idea what the hell you're talking about."

I keep my eyes down and wipe the counter.

Cruz leans over and is practically right in my face.

"Don't lie to me, Willow, 'cause I do know what I'm talking about because the way you look at Max is the same way I looked at Harlow before I told her I thought I was falling in love with her. I know the look, so deny all you want."

I go to the refrigerator and grab a water. Twisting the cap off, I throw it at him.

He catches it and smiles coolly at me.

"It's not like that at all," I say softly.

"Then how is it?"

"I'm not talking about this stuff with you, asshat."

"Listen, you want to talk about it, I swear on my life I won't say anything to anyone. Not even Harlow and you know I tell that woman everything. But for your sake, I'll be willing to withhold information from the woman I love and suffer the consequences later if need be."

He's not going to let up and when I look at the sincerity on Cruz's face I know maybe later I'll regret it, but he makes sense. He did feel like I did and as much as he is a total moron, he's marrying my best friend and he sacrificed so much to win her love, so what do I do? I can't stand him. Well... maybe a little.

"We had sex the night you and Har got engaged. Neither one of us remembered it. We made a pact that we would forget it and pretend it didn't happen. Then we hooked up again and I don't know why. And then we started to cock or vagina block each other and we were striking out left and right so we decided just to use each other for sex. We could hook up with other people but we leave the sex out of it and save it for just each other."

I have zero idea why I just blurted all of that out. I'm turning into some kind of talk show guest or something.

He backs away from me slightly and sits on the stool at the counter facing me.

"I see. It's kind of what I figured. I knew the same cat couldn't be coming around our house all the time if no one was feeding it."

"Ugh… I do not sound like a fucking cat." Frustrated, I try to walk away but Cruz is quick and he stops me while chuckling.

"Okay, I'm sorry. Really."

For some reason I calm down a little and clutch the water bottle tightly in my hand rather than his balls.

"So then you started to have feelings for him and you have for a long time. Maybe even before you guys did it. You told me last year at the bar that you may or may not be in love with someone. Was that Max? Do you remember saying it? You were a little tipsy but you did say it."

I question myself. Did I? Did I feel like I may have loved him back then? Did I have feelings for him even that long ago?

"No… I don't know. Maybe? I don't… I can't talk about this with you."

"Yeah, you can."

"Why do you care anyway?"

"Because I have been where you have been. I don't know to what extent, but I'm pretty sure I'm spot on." Wanting to end this conversation because, truthfully, I don't even know why I started it and with Cruz of all people. I really must be seriously fucked up to have stooped to this level.

"Look, he's leaving. I'm ending whatever it was we were doing. I'd rather it happen that way and get on with my life. He doesn't feel any more towards me except for getting in my pants. I'll save myself the humiliation."

Cruz shrugs. "How do you know?"

"How do I know what?"

"How do you know he doesn't feel the same unless you say something to him? What would be so bad if you told him you were starting to have feelings for him?"

I laugh because I know how it would go and things would never be the same.

"Yeah, it would be bad because he doesn't feel the same way. Things would be awkward from here on out and I don't want that because I know me… I'd be the one making things awkward."

"Why's that?"

Frustrated, I blurt out, "Because I've never been rejected by anyone, you big dumbass. I'm not sure how I could deal with rejection like that."

"Oh, my God. Really? You want to really know what rejection feels like? Have the person you love and adore most in life not know you. Not love you or remember they loved you and you loved them. Imagine my hell from *that* rejection. You were there. You saw it. I took chance after chance trying to make her remember what I couldn't forget. You don't know if you're in love with him and you won't tell him you *might* love him for fear of rejection. Well, honey, let me tell you, rejection is all part of it. The game. Love. It's a crapshoot and the only way you'll ever know if it's real is unless you find out for yourself."

The bastard has a point.

I really hate that.

The room stays silent. Cruz grabs the platter he came for in the first place. He starts to walk away.

"Willow?"

Annoyed by him making sense and giving me a reason to hate him anymore I answer rudely, of course, "What?"

"I would never say anything. Not even to talk about it with Max. It's not my place. This has to be between the two of you. I just wanted you to know that, okay."

"Good, because I'd hate to have to castrate you and put your dick in the new smoothie blender we bought for the house. I'd feel really bad for Harlow if she had to use a dildo for the rest of her life."

His eyes grow wide because he knows I'm not joking.

He nods. "Noted." He salutes me and walks out the door.

Fuck me in the ear. Can I do this? Can I tell him how I feel? Being afraid isn't an option for me. Fear doesn't reside in my brain. Neither does rejection.

This is a battle I need to fight internally and I'm just afraid if I don't win this, I may miss out on something.

I keep my distance from Max. I mainly sit with the girls and chat. Craw is here. No Ally. They are apparently 'having problems.' I have my own so I just listen to Harlow and him overly discuss it.

Porter stands on one of the tables and asks someone to turn down the blaring music.

"Attention, please. Friends of Max, we are here tonight to send the little man with the big voice away for what will be the beginning of a whole new world of possibilities for him and The Band." Porter looks directly at Max.

"Max. When I first met you, you were this punk-ass kid who wore worn out black Converse and blue streaks in your hair. You were intelligent and talented. You had music in your soul and the heart of someone who knew that a man was not measured by how much money was in his back pocket but by the amount of friends he had. That, my man, makes you a rich man. And by the looks of it tonight, you're fucking loaded, dude."

Everyone laughs and Cruz grasps Max's shoulder and shakes him.

"Now everyone lift your glasses and toast good luck to our friend, Max Vincent. May your journey be one of greatness, wisdom, and prosperity. And lots of girls."

I don't laugh. Cruz looks at me and winks. I take a sip from my cup and excuse myself.

I can't tell him.

I go to my room and shut the door. I hear the music coming from outside and I just lie on my bed and twirl my hair.

What was I even thinking when I

contemplated telling Max I'm having feelings for him. I'm an idiot.

Someone knocks on my door and I know it's one of the girls coming to find me.

"Come in," I whine.

It's Max. My stomach drops in my belly and I scramble to sit up in my bed. I push my hair behind my ears. He sits on the edge of my bed looking adorable in his worn out AC/DC t-shirt. It does not help my situation because it's the t-shirt I always wind up sticking on if I'm at his room after we do it — if we do it in a bed.

"Hey, Wills. I was wondering where you ran off to. You okay?"

I nod. "Oh, yeah. I'm fine. A little headache, that's all. What's up?"

"Nothing. I just didn't see you outside and the girls said you came inside. Are you coming back out? People are starting to leave."

My heart is beating so fast because I need to get this out. I need to tell him and I get my nerve. I can do this. I can tell him. I can let him know all the strange things that are going through my head. I can tell him what I thought of him the first time I saw him. I can tell him what it felt like to hear him sing on stage for the first time. I can tell him how he gets on my nerves and I want to strangle him because I care so much about him.

I can do this and I can take the good or the bad. I'm not 'the bitch.' I can love. I really think I can love.

At the same time we speak over each other.

"Max, I need to talk to you."

"Cora is coming to help me pack."

I know what I heard so I ask before I throw up.

"Cora?"

He smiles. Fuck me, he fucking smiles.

"Yeah. She knows what I need to take on the road so she's stopping over to help."

My heart drops into my stomach but I need to keep a straight face. I can't let my disappointment show. I have to play this cool. She's just coming to help.

"Cool. She should know what you need. I'm sure her dad fills her in on all of that. I'm glad you have someone to help you."

The corners of his mouth raise up. "Yeah. She's really nice."

I hop off the bed and clear my throat. "Well, guess you better get a move on. Can you tell the girls I'm going to bed because of my headache?"

Max reaches the door handle and holds it before exiting.

"Sure, Wills. Feel better and, um… I'll see you tomorrow."

I just give him a tight-lipped smile and a short wave bye because at this point it's the only thing I have the strength to do.

CHAPTER 8

The Unexpected
Max~

I hardly slept a wink. How could I have?
Knowing what I'm about to do. I'm more excited
than I've ever been in my life. The last day hasn't
been easy though. Telling my dad what I was
doing didn't go well at first until I really made
him see what I'm all about. How music affects my
life. How it owns me. It's my favorite part of life.
It enhances me. It makes me feel more alive than
the air I breathe. Music to me is infinite and
endless. It's my energy. I think the way I told him
how passionate I was about music. How
passionate I am about life. Then I told him how
much money I was making and, well, that made a
huge difference. He's going to try to see us play
when we are in Dayton. He's not far from there
but far enough that he would have to travel
somewhat.

Then there's leaving here. Sandy Cove. My

summer is over here. I won't be back till the week before Labor Day. I've been coming here for three summers. There's been good times and bad ones. Some *really* bad times. But I focus on the good. I have to. It's who I am. But this is harder than I thought. Saying goodbye is not easy.

I'm a hugger. Always have been. I'm just an affectionate guy so when I see Harlow and Thea standing by the tour bus as the roadies load all of our shit in it, I swallow a lump that's formed in my throat. I go over to Cruz first, trying to temporarily delay my goodbye to the girls.

We bro hug. I look like an Oompa Loompa next to him and he looks like Shaq.

"Listen, little man. You do us proud. I know you will. And don't let your already too big of a head get any bigger."

I let out a laugh. It's mixed with humor and anxiousness.

"I promise. And don't go get any bright ideas and get married without me."

"No worries there. You have to play at the wedding so, no, we'll wait for you."

The big goof gives me another hug and ruffles my hair.

Porter's goodbye is next.

Another friend of mine who towers over me, and again I feel like an ant. It's my curse I suppose.

He grasps my hand sideways and pulls me in for a hug but it's quicker than Cruz's.

"I'm not getting all mushy with you like that one with the vagina. I'll just say this to you. Go for it, man. Give 'em hell. I know you'll do great." He cups my shoulder then pushes me away. I stumble and Harlow and Thea — all teary — come up to me and I hold out both my arms and motion for them to come on in. They grab on to me and I pull them towards my body and give them both an equal squeeze.

"No more tears. I'll miss you guys too. Have fun. Make sure that the house doesn't get too messy. You know me and my cleaning fetish."

I kiss each of them on top of their heads.

Harlow looks up at me with her big blue eyes with the streaks of red washed through them.

"We know you'll do great. Please call us and check in or you know we'll worry."

"I will, Har. I promise."

Thea wipes her eyes and hugs me around my waist.

"I'll miss you so much, Max. You're like the peacekeeper. It's not going to be the same without you here."

"I'll miss all of you too, Thea, and I will call you guys and it will be like I'm here. I can give pep talks from the road and diffuse any bombs if need be."

"Well if you're leaving and Willow is here then there won't be any." When Thea says that I realize she's not out here. Willow's not here.

"Um… speak of the devil, where is she?"

The girls pull away from me and dry their tears.

"I think she's still upstairs. Not sure why. Want me to go get her, Max?"

"It's okay, Har. I'll go. I have a few minutes."

The tour crew is still loading the stuff in the bus and checking everything in from a clipboard so I run up the wooden steps to the girls' side of the house. I walk in calling her name.

"Wills? You in here?" No answer. I walk down the hallway to the bedrooms and knock on her door. No answer so I open it and walk in. She's on her little balcony that faces the docks. Her blonde hair is blowing in the air and I see her arms wrapped around her middle. Her painted fingernails rest on both her narrow hips. I slide the door open and walk out to her. She turns her head to the side slowly then turns back to look out onto the water. I move to stand next to her and lean on the railing of the balcony.

"All ready to go?" she asks.

"Yep. The tour crew is loading the bus. Everyone is outside. I couldn't find you. Why are you in here?"

She sighs. "Just thinking."

I clear my throat. "About what?"

"Stuff. Things. Life."

Her voice is soft. Not what I'm used to. She's dressed in small jean shorts and a t-shirt. She's not wearing makeup and her hair is wavy and undone. I'm pretty sure Willow is even more beautiful when she's not dressed all ritzy and polished. Her natural beauty outweighs the debutant style she frequently possesses.

Silence blankets the air and I'm not sure what to say or how we leave things and I have to admit, it was another reason why I couldn't sleep last night.

"Willow, listen…" She turns to me and cuts me off before I have a chance to say anything.

"No, Max. I need to say something to you. Our deal is off and it's not because I'm upset or angry. It's because it wouldn't make any sense to continue it if you're going on tour. We can't expect one another to, you know… do without. There's going to be thousands of screaming fans and girls all over the place. Plus, I… um, I wouldn't want to deprive myself of… you know. It's not fair to either of us. Do you agree?"

This is what was going through my mind last night. Sex with Willow was becoming addicting. I craved it. I could kiss a girl at the bar then think about how I couldn't wait to find Willow and fuck her. It's so wrong to even think like that. Maybe I'm not normal. Maybe in my mind it is normal because it's the deal we made. Almost everyday for weeks straight I was inside her. I could kiss her and grab her hair and have my way, any way with her. And it was fun. It was exciting and off the charts hot. But she's ending it and I'm guessing it's the right thing to do.

"And there's Cora, too."

"Cora?" I question.

She shrugs and moves her blowing hair away from her face. She tucks some strands behind her ear and looks at me.

"Yeah, Cora. I'm not stupid, Max. Her father is running the tour. I'm sure she'll be around. I *know* she'll be around."

She's right. Cora will be around. She told me

last night when she was helping me pack. She does the accounting for the tour and she said she will be there for a few dates. We have a lot in common. She's very easy to talk to. She's intelligent, funny, full of life, and knows the business. She's in love with music like I am. There's so much I know about her in such a short time, but also more than I think I want to know as well.

When Willow says she knows Cora will be around, she says it with vigor. Not cockiness, but very matter-of-fact.

"Yeah, she'll be around sometimes."

She deliberately raises her eyebrows at me and the corner of her mouth turns up.

"I'm sure she will be. All the more reason to put the brakes on this. It was…"

"Fun," I say before she has some kind of comeback. If any at all.

Willow turns and leans her back on the wooden rail. I stay the way I am and I look out onto the bay for the last time for at least a while. I see her through my peripheral vision as her gaze wanders to nothing. I have no idea what she's thinking. What she's feeling. It's so impassive and confusing. I want to ask her but I think I know it's just that she'll miss the sex. It's really all it ever was to her anyway. Willow's a sexual person. She'll miss the convenience but she won't have a problem finding someone to fill in the gap. I'm sure of it. I let her off the hook by telling her what I think she wants to hear.

"Yeah, Wills. You're right. Better to just end

it. I mean it was just sex." She opens her mouth to say something but stops herself from going any further.

This is the part that has to end but the more time we've spent together the more I'm starting to like the bitch she really isn't. Maybe it's good we're getting away from each other. Maybe we can muster up a friendship with the distance.

"But what would you say to talking while I'm on the road. It would be cool to hear a familiar voice. You know… like being at home. Just 'cause we won't be doing you know what anymore, maybe we can just… talk."

She rolls her lips together and inhales, letting out a controlled breath after a moment.

"That sounds good. Max, I hope whatever happens that you'll be happy. I mean it. Whether it's the thousands of screaming fans, or playing your music for them, or even if you find out it's Cora who might make you happy, let it happen. Be happy."

Willow Taylor getting all deep on me holds me in my stance. It doesn't allow me to move or think. It stuns me. There's a surprise always around the corner where she's concerned.

I allow myself to push up off the rail and with much caution I approach her. I wrap my arms around her back. I rest my chin on her shoulder. I don't expect her to hug me back. I don't expect her to say anything to me. Maybe one of her infamous 'fuck off's' but nothing comes. She just allows me to rest my body on hers and engulf her with a hug because there's zero chance that she'd do it first and I'm not leaving us like this.

"I will be happy, Wills."

I pull away from her. There's reluctance behind it but I have to. I hear the bus horn going off signaling me to get my ass moving.

She stands with her back still to me. Words for me are lost. I don't know what to do or say. Agreeing to talk and be friends has raised the stakes between Willow and me. It's an unusual situation between us and I'm not just talking about our little deal. I'm talking all around. We were the worst of enemies who became more than that. I can't even say we were friends when the whole thing began but I think we could get to the point of friendship. I don't want to come back to the same old, same old. Us fighting, mouthing harsh comments and insults towards one another. It's run its course.

"I gotta go. If you want I'll email you the tour schedule. We are in Florida first and we make our way up the coast. Last stop is some festival in Vermont."

Making her way to the door to her bedroom I hear her mumble, "Yeah… email."

"Hey, we can Skype too. I think that would be so cool to be able to see you… I mean, um… everyone. Can we make a different kind of pact that at least once a week we can talk? It would be weird not to see you everyday."

Jesus, what am I saying?

But I mean it. I see her everyday, now I won't and it feels weird. It's going to be weird.

She nods and agrees with talking via laptop.

No words, just recognizing that this will be the agreement. It's odd for Willow Taylor not to speak. She has the biggest mouth I know.

I go to her and place my hand on her shoulder, and she turns around and I'm faced with the most unexpected thing that I think has ever happened. Willow turns around and grabs handfuls of my shirt and pulls me to her soft, wanting lips. She kisses me, and it's just not a kiss that breathes lust but it breathes the fire of passion, of meaning. It makes my hair stand on end and leaves the skin beneath electrified. The soft motion of her mouth with mine, the scent of her hair and the taste of her tongue dancing inside my mouth, spins me into oblivion. There's more to this kiss. I feel it in my bones. I feel it in my soul. She kisses me like we are music. We are the rhythm joining together with the notes and the melody. I grasp the back of her head and thread my fingers in her hair softly. I deepen the kiss and I reach the point where I swim in this moment so deep that I don't want to come to the surface… and that's when she pulls away and I know I'm fucked.

I'm so fucking fucked.

She holds her lips with her long, slender fingers. Her eyes find mine and I'm still lost in whatever that was. I can't even ask her because I can't even speak. It wasn't the normal wanton kiss that happens between us when we just use each other. No, oh no, this was something else.

"Willow…" She holds up her hand to stop me.

"Let's just leave it at that, Max."

I walk past her slowly as I hear the

relentlessness of the bus's horn and slide open the door to her room. I turn around and she's already back to leaning on the rail. Her body turned to the calm waters. The sun shines down on her bare, bronzed shoulders and the wind picks up and blows her hair around again. It's the last time I'll see her in person for a while and after that kiss, my head and something else right at this very moment doesn't want it to be the last time. It's not the right time to analyze what that kiss was. Maybe it was a goodbye kiss. A proper send off. The end of whatever we were to each other. Was it a blessing for me to go and see where it goes with Cora? What was that? I'll tell you what it was. The unexpected.

"I'll miss you, Willow." Not being so sure she can hear me, I say it as I walk out the door. I leave her with my brain consisting of mush and my lips already feeling some sort of loss.

Most of all… a lot to think about.

CHAPTER 9

Six Degrees of Loneliness
Willow~

"Wills? Earth to Wills? It's your turn to pick out of the hat."

My mind has been wandering all night and when Harlow snaps me out of my daze, I feel a little discombobulated.

"Huh? The answer is five." Everyone starts to snort and laugh and I have no idea what I just said that's so funny.

Porter throws a pillow at me.

"What the hell, P?"

"Five. The answer is five? Really, Willow. We're playing charades for Christ's sake. The answer is 'Titanic'. Weren't you paying attention?"

No, actually I wasn't. I haven't been. All night. For the last ten days. I'm pathetic. If I'm on the beach during the day, all I do is read and keep to myself. No beach volleyball, no games. I just read my magazines. I'm not really partaking in any conversations. I'm kind of in my own world. On the nights we go to Jax, it's like something is missing. I check to see if I forgot my purse, or an earring. I even check if my shoes match which is so unlike me. It's like I'm not living in my own brain. I know what's missing, but I can't keep allowing myself to be caught up in something that isn't really anything.

I make zero sense.

And add in the kiss. That's enough to scramble a brain. Even if you're the one who has done said scrambling.

I try to give Porter my best excuse for *not* paying attention to the stupid game on stupid game night.

"Yeah, I was paying attention. Five is the number of idiots here trying to figure out that it's stupid Jack hanging on the stupid door in the middle of a freezing cold ocean. It doesn't take a genius to figure who the five of you are."

My sudden outburst gets nothing but silence and stares.

"Jeez. Someone must be having the red dot special this week."

I glare at Porter, who snorts after he says it and I watch him take a long drink from his beer bottle. He eyes me and I just give him the one-finger salute.

Craw is here — sans his pain in the ass girlfriend because she flat out refuses to hang with us. Well, fuck her and her British arse. I'm keeping my cool because he's like a little brother to me and he's hardly been here this summer. Now we have even teams for this stupid game. We all pulled names out of a hat and I got Craw. Porter got Harlow and Cruz got Thea.

We draw our categories for charades the same way. It's my turn but I'm suddenly distracted when Craw asks about Max.

"Anyone heard from Mr. Rock and Roll?"

"I have. He's texted me," Cruz answers Craw.

"Where is he?"

"When the tour first started, he was in Jacksonville, now he's in Atlanta. Next is Charleston, then I forget where else."

"North Carolina, West Virginia, D.C., Philadelphia, Dayton, Boston, then Vermont."

Yeah, I blurt it all out. And five sets of eyes look my way. Most confused, except for Cruz.

"How do you know all of that?" Harlow asks.

"He emailed me his schedule."

Now that really confuses her. More than usual.

I shrug and throw her off by using Cruz as a decoy of sorts.

"He emailed you too, right, meathead?" I motion to him.

He looks at me wearily and draws out his answer until the dumbass catches on.

"Uh… yeah. No big deal, right. Just as long as some of us has his schedule."

Good save, dummy.

Not only do I have Max's schedule but he kept his promise and we video chat. More than he told me he was going to. I didn't hear from him for the first few days. I knew he had to settle in. I know he had meetings with the booking agent, the tour manager, and some of the promoters. I know this from Porter. Max must have filled him in on some stuff.

The first video chat happened when he first arrived in Florida. It was late. I heard the chimes going off on my laptop and I thought I was dreaming. When I clicked on the chat icon on the screen and saw his face it was the happiest I had been in days.

Our conversation was short. He wanted to check in. He was tired and it was well past three when he called. He looked tired too. He told me that their rehearsals were starting the day after and the day after that then their first show was the night after.

I didn't expect to hear from him on the rehearsal days but I did. He texted me first to see if I was home. One night I was at Jax with everyone. When I got the text I found myself hauling ass out of there and hailed a cab home.

I told another white lie to the gang. A sudden migraine came over me and, of course, I get the twenty questions from my second mother, Harlow. She probably thinks I have a tumor or something awful like that.

I recall running up the wooden steps of

the house, straight to my room and plopping on my bed with the laptop. Our conversation was light. He was still very tired but said rehearsals went really well and the band they are opening for was super talented and cool. He was nervous about his first show but I told him just to pretend he was playing at Jax but in front of a few thousand more people.

I think I made him more nervous by saying that.

As our chats continued over the course of the following days, Max filled me in on some tour business. He explained the jobs of the people on the tour. What his schedule was going to be like and the songs they were going to be playing. It all sounded really fascinating. I found myself hanging on his every word.

He never mentioned what happened between us before he left and he hasn't mentioned Cora. I didn't bring either of those things up. The kiss lingers in my mind and I'm doing my best to put Cora in the back of it.

There haven't been any arguments or disagreements. No smart-mouthed responses to our conversations. Just simple ones. He asks how everyone is and wants to know what we all have been up to. He hasn't missed much. I told him Craw was coming over and he was surprised by that but happy.

Ever since that night, it seems like a ritual. When he gets done with a show or if he's on the tour bus he calls. It's always late when he does and I find myself either going to bed early, complaining of some sort of fabricated illness, or coming home early from a night out.

I wish for time to pass during the day. I yearn for the night and the time when I get to see his face. Tonight is no exception. I know he had a show tonight so when it grows closer to the time when he usually calls and these dipshits still want to play this stupid game I grow a little nervous. They're at my house and usually when Max calls, the girls are sleeping or they're not even home. How am I supposed to talk to him when they're all here?

Silently, I wish.

All of you, get the fuck out.

Yeah, that doesn't happen.

Porter brings me out of my haze once again. "Let's go, Willow, pick already. Christ."

I roll my eyes and dig my hand into the hat. I pull out a piece of paper and unravel it.

And laugh.

Oh, this is good. Too good.

I got cop. This is just way too easy.

We always play with person, place, thing, or movie. I certainly got thing!

So I begin my act.

I make muscles. I draw stupid lines on my arms. I contort my face into something unrecognizable and walk like I have a stick up my ass and I can't put my arms down because of the bulging muscles. I pull out a pretend gun. I mimic cuffing someone too.

It doesn't take long before Harlow yells out while hysterically laughing, "It's Cruz! She's doing Cruz! Oh, my God! Willow, that's fantastic!" Everyone is laughing except for the Dickcop. He just looks confused.

Big surprise!

Then it's like a lightbulb goes on and he purses his lips.

"I don't walk like that. And what's with my arms?"

Harlow explains, "Babe, sometimes you walk like that when you feel threatened. And your arms are too big to put at your sides, flush to your body anyway."

His facial expression is priceless. Like he doesn't believe it. He playfully shoves Harlow's hand off of his shoulder and she gets up and then falls into his lap and kisses his cheek.

"Aw. Did Raphael get his wittle feewings hurt? Poor baby."

And with that. Game over. At least for Harlow and Cruz it is because in one swoop he lifts her up and over his shoulder and smacks her ass so loud we all jump and laugh.

"Oh, I'll baby you, my Turnip. Just wait till I get you in my room."

Craw holds his ears and closes his eyes as Cruz carries Harlow to his house.

"TMI, TMI, TMI."

Okay, so two down, three to go and it's

almost one. I know my phone will ding an incoming text any minute now. I could easily just tell the other three I'm going to bed with a headache, but lately I've been using that excuse a little too often. I don't know why I just don't tell them I'm chatting with Max, but I sort of like the fact that it's just him and me knowing. Like our *other* secret. I am such a straightforward person, but in this case, being that way I chose not to be.

So after the yin and yang leave, I panic when Craw goes for another beer.

Fuck my life!

I need a plan.

Think with that beautiful brain of yours, Willow. Think, dammit.

"We still have another hour before the bars close. Anyone want to go out?" I have my reasons for doing this, trust me.

Craw shrugs. "Yeah, why not. I'm hardly here. I think it's a great idea."

After Craw says he's hardly here, he looks a little sad. I don't want to waste time with my plan but I want to ask Craw what's been going on.

The new and improved Willow Taylor decides to ask. Hopefully it's a quick answer.

"And with that being said, Craw, what's up with you and Ally?"

"Nothing much. We see each other when we can. She's going to England at the end of the summer to see her brother. She's not happy I'm here. Not sure if it's because she won't come or if she's upset it takes away time from her. I'm really confused and as much as I think I love her, I'm getting tired of the babyish way she goes about things. She's younger, I get that, but when I mention Harlow she shuts down. I mean, won't talk to me or let me touch her."

I bite the inside of my mouth, feeling the blood seep out. I want to tell him to dump the bitch but I'm trying to compose myself.

"Craw, does she realize that in the end you'll choose Harlow? You always will."

Porter tilts his chin up to Craw. "Yeah, since when do you allow a girl to run your life? You should be here this summer. Not in Princeton working for your dad being a coffee fetcher and doing menial law office work like some uneducated baboon."

Thea stands up. She looks like a fire-breathing dragon. Her face is as red as the shirt I'm wearing. She looks like one of those cartoons when the cat has smoke coming out of its ears. Maybe it's the alcohol, maybe it's not but when she turns her eyes to Porter I thank God I'm not him.

She waltzes up to him. She's a good head-and-a-half shorter than him but lifts her chin so all eyes are on Porter.

"Menial law office work? Coffee fetcher? Uneducated baboon? You do realize, Porter, that I do those things for Mr. Hannum. I'm his assistant. I also do more than that. Do I get him coffee sometimes? Yep, but I do when

I'm getting my own. Do I do office work? Yep, I do but it's so much more than that. And I'm educated." She's pointing in his chest and he's backing up with every poke. She's mad and Thea Thornton doesn't get mad. That's all saved up for me. I look to Craw and we both cringe. My cousin said the wrong choice of words.

"Thea, I didn't…" Porter tries to speak, Thea interrupts.

"Yes, you did. You disrespected what I do for a living. I didn't grow up like all of you." She motions her hand around to all of us. "I've had to work since I was sixteen years old. I put myself through school. I did it all by myself. So if you don't have any respect for me or what I do for a living, you can kiss my ass, Porter. You're no better than me."

Porter's face is emotionless. His eyes are blank and I see him swallow so hard his throat bobs up and down.

This is so not how I wanted this night to go. I have my phone in my hand and it starts to go off. It's Max sending me a text.

Max: *Hey, just got back on the bus. Shows over. Can you chat?*

I don't respond because I'm too engrossed in the whole Thea/Porter debacle right now.

"I worked my ass off for years to have this job. I earned it not because I grew up with Harlow but on merit alone. I graduated with honors and was actually offered several higher paying jobs than what Mr. Hannum's practice was offering. I knew Mr. Hannum would be a good teacher because someday, when I save enough money, I will go to law school. I will be a lawyer and not what you call a coffee fetcher. Next time you want to put someone's profession down, Porter, think first before you speak. Asshole."

She turns away from him.

"I'm going for a walk." Her voice cracks and she grabs her jacket and walks out the door.

I want to run after her but I get a second text from Max.

Max: *Wills, you there? Are you out with everyone or are you with… never mind.*

Crap. He thinks I'm with a guy.

"Porter, you better go after her and apologize your ass off."

His eyes look remorseful. Don't blame him. He should feel like shit.

"Want me to go with you, P?"

Craw asks and I pray Porter says yes.

"No, man. I owe her an apology on my own."

Dammit.

Porter runs his hand through his hair and groans.

"I didn't mean it the way I said it and, Craw, I'm sorry. I didn't mean to put what you're doing down. I just miss you being here in the summer and I just don't want you to do something you'll regret. Family first, pal. The

ones you love should always come first."
Porter clears his threat and in almost a
whisper he says, "Speaking of which, I better
go talk to Thea."

Porter walks out and our mouths are so
wide open we could probably catch flies.

Craw raises his eyebrows to me and I
complacently look at him.

"Yeah, he kinda loves her, doesn't he?" I
smile.

"Pretty much. He's been dropping hints for
years."

Craw counteracts. "Yeah, and she has
too. They need to do something about that."

I smile and nod, agreeing with him.

"So what do you say? Want to head to
Jax?"

Two texts later, Max thinking I'm with
some guy, and I know I can't go. I have to talk
to Max.

"Nah, I changed my mind. Those two just
destroyed my buzz." I fake yawn. "Sorry.
Raincheck." He looks disappointed but like I
said, I *need* to talk to Max.

"Yeah. I'm going to walk down. I know a
few people who are there. I'll be back. I have
my key."

I smile at him and wave as he walks out
the door.

I send Max a quick text.

Me: *I'm here, I'm here. Sorry. Was
defusing a bomb.*

I press send and in an instant he texts

back.

Max: *Bomb? Who? What? When? How?*

I laugh.

Me: *Thea and Porter. I'll explain. Give me five minutes.*

He responds with a 'K'.

I rush to the bathroom. I fix my hair, brush my teeth and slip into my tank and pajama shorts. I fuss over myself.

I fuss over myself for Max.

Unbelievable.

I grab my fully powered-up laptop and get snuggled in my bed. I press Max's contact on the laptop and it begins to ring.

The smile I have on my face is permanent and his face isn't even on the screen yet.

He answers. At first he looks pixelated from the connection but as he moves his laptop about, his face becomes clearer.

"Hey. There we go. So what the hell happened with Thea and Porter?"

"Hey. Porter stuck his big foot in his mouth and Thea shot back at him. She even called him an asshole."

Max's eyes get big and I laugh. Thea can't even say crap without blushing. I don't think she's ever said penis or vagina out loud.

"Wow. I can't believe it."

"That they fought?"

"No, that she said asshole." I let out a good, hearty laugh.

"Ah, I could have used that laugh earlier tonight. Ugh."

"What's wrong? Not a good show?"

Max makes a sour face.

"Eh, could have been better. The crowd didn't like us. They just wanted the main event. We even got beer thrown on us."

"Well, at least you can now say that you sucked so bad you got a beer shower from an audience. That way when you guys are big with a record contract and not opening for anyone, you can say, yeah we sucked once."

He squeezes his eyes and shakes his head.

"Yeah, I guess. I just want to move on from it. Tell me what you guys did today."

He adjusts himself and lies down on his bed placing his laptop on his chest. I get into the same position.

"Today? Craw came for the weekend. We beached it. He, Porter, and Cruz went fishing later on and then we bar-b-qued and stayed in and played charades."

Max lets out a sigh. "Sounds like heaven to me."

"You're not missing anything, Max. It's the same old, same old."

He shakes his head, disagreeing. His voice is soft.

"You're wrong, Wills. I'm missing… a lot." He smiles at me, megawatt-like and it speeds up my heart.

I ask him more stuff about the upcoming cities he'll be in. He tells me how they practice everyday for a few hours and how there's not a lot of downtime. He fits in food and some working out between sound checks and rehearsals. He said he has no idea what the beaches of Florida look like. I fill him in on that. I've been to that state for vacations more times than I can count.

When Max speaks of the tour, he sounds like he's having the time of his life. He's doing what he loves to do, but there's some kind of affliction in his voice that tells me that maybe he's homesick for Sandy Cove. I can't blame him. I would be too.

Max is yawning which triggers me to yawn and we both realize that it's well past three a.m.

"Hey, why don't I let you go? You look really tired and I know you have a long day tomorrow. Atlanta, right?"

"Yep. Not that I'll see much of it. I'll only be there for two days."

"Make the most of it and try not to get another beer shower, okay." I wink. He smirks playfully.

"I'll try my best."

"Go get some sleep, Max."

"Same time tomorrow, Wills?"

I bite my lip and feel my stomach flip-flop. Another unfamiliar feeling I'm experiencing.

"You got it."

"Nite, Willow."

"Goodnight, Max."

His face disappears from the screen and I feel the same loss I used to feel when he pulled out from inside me or after we did the deed, he would leave from wherever we just were.

Just when I think everyday is just like the next — which it actually is — the nights I talk to Max puts to rest the monotony of those same old beach-by-day, bar-by-night aspects. He makes me laugh. He makes me smile. There's a comfort there that makes me excited just from the sheer anticipation of knowing I'll be talking to him.

God, I've never felt like this. I mean over a guy. I'm not the flippity-flop, butterflies-in-the-belly girl. I've dated A LOT but never felt this way from just talking to someone. I have no idea what sort of pull he has over me. I mean, a few months ago I couldn't even look in his direction without wanting to rip his balls off. Now… it's a different story. Maybe I'm growing up. Maybe I'm maturing. Maybe it's just Max.

I lie here in one of the same positions I'm usually in when I talk to him. Pillows are gathered behind my head. Laptop is placed either on top of a pillow on my lap or I'm lying on my side with the laptop strategically placed beside me on the bed. This is the position I'm in tonight.

"Favorite movie?"

"*The Goonies.*"

He looks surprised.

I laugh. "What? Is that so hard to

believe?"

"Well, for you… kinda. I would have taken you for *The Notebook* or some girly shit like that."

I roll my eyes. "Just because I'm a connoisseur of cosmetics and designer fashion and I have a deep concern for nail care does not mean I like all things girlie. I guess I'm a sucker for pirates and droopy-eyed malformed giants who like to say, 'Hey, you guys!' Do you know I love watching hockey with my dad? Huge Rangers fan right here, and I love rock and roll. Like classic rock." I shrug when I see the look of astonishment on his face.

I shrug. "What can I say? I'm full of surprises, aren't I?"

Max shakes his head back and forth. "Yep, you sure are. So what kind of classic rock do you like?"

I purse my lips together as I ponder the question.

"Let's see… Aerosmith, The Eagles, Fleetwood Mac, The Kinks, The Pretenders. Don't tell anyone I have a mad girl crush on Chrissie Hynde." Max makes the sign for sealing his lips and throwing my secret away.

"Oh, and my favorite is AC/DC. I love 'Shook Me All Night Long.' I could listen to that song on repeat all day."

"Wow, Wills. Crazy. No wonder you like The Band. We play a lot of the cover songs for those bands."

And maybe, just maybe, that's just another reason the flippity-flops and butterflies are going on hard core in my belly and down below. Dear Lord, I need to change the subject before I spontaneously combust. I adjust my seating on my bed and tuck a strand of hair behind my ear. Clearing my throat I ask him, "Um… write anything new lately?"

Max reads me lyrics he wrote. Not for the tour but because he jotted something down when he had an idea.

"What do you think? Too cheesy?"

I pop a gummy bear in my mouth and shake my head.

"No, not at all. I think they're deep but not cheesy." I chomp on another and he furrows his brows.

"What the hell are you chewing on like a rabbit?"

"Gummy bears," I say and laugh.

"God, I'd kill for one. All they have on this bus is healthy, green shit. Salads and quinoa, and grasses and shit. I want candy."

I sing the tune.

"I want can-dy. I want can-dy."

"Bow-Wow-Wow. Love that song." Max hums along with me as I sing the only three words I know from the song. He disappears from the screen for a second.

"Max? Where'd you go?"

He's back in a flash and he readjusts his laptop and straps his guitar around him and starts to strum the tune of the song. It's slow. Unlike the real version of the song. It's an old song. Probably from before we were even born. I just watch him. I'm mesmerized by the way his fingers hit the strings. Each sound that comes out is better than the last and this is from his acoustic guitar, not his electric. His talent is absolutely amazing. Then he sings the words. The only three words from the song each of us knows. Slowly.

And I feel a tingle. An ache. Right between my legs and I hold my knees together. I wiggle around trying to dull the ache but nothing helps. I realize that three weeks have gone by. I haven't hooked up. I haven't had sex, and I haven't had an orgasm. When you're getting it on practically on a daily basis, then it ends, it sure doesn't help.

I close my eyes not even realizing I'm doing it. My breathing changes. It's deeper now and my eyes and legs are closed so tight I swear his voice could make me come. I fucking swear it. Every stroke of his guitar makes me fantasize that he's stroking my skin. My breasts, between my legs. I dart out my tongue and lick my bottom lip from one end to the other. My hand travels down between my legs and I just press my fingers against my clit. I'm trying to help it go away, but this is not the solution.

"Fuck," Max says it long and drawn out. His voice is low and gravelly.

I pop open my eyes and I see him staring at me. I feel panic in my chest and I can't speak.

"Willow, are you touching yourself?" His voice is still low but he asks in such a sexy way that even though I feel a blush creep up my cheeks, I don't lie.

"Yes," I whisper out.

"Do it again."

"Do what again?" I ask.

"Touch yourself. Make yourself come and let me watch."

I gasp. I actually gasp.

"No way! Are you nuts?"

His face is impassive.

"No… no, I'm not nuts. I'm serious. I haven't had sex in weeks. This you are already aware of."

I clear my throat. "No, this I am *not* aware of."

"Trust me. I haven't."

"What about Cora?"

His face twists in confusion.

"Cora? I haven't seen Cora."

"Oh," I say quietly.

"I want to watch you come, Willow. I need it. Please. I need to as well." His voice has never sounded more erotic. So deep and so full of lust.

I groan then think about the fact that he's in very closed quarters.

"How the hell are you going to pull that off on a tour bus without anyone seeing you?"

He shrugs. "I'm on the top bunk. I have a curtain that surrounds the whole entire bed and it's past three in the morning so everyone is sleeping."

I cover my eyes with my hands, not sure this is such a good idea.

"How do you know they're all sleeping?"

"'Cause I can hear all of them snoring like Curly from *The Three Stooges*." I snicker.

"Oh, my God. Are we really going to do this?" I think I have time to weigh my decision before Max answers but that's not the way it goes.

"Yeah, we're really doing this. Pull down your pants and adjust the camera where it needs to be."

Fuck, if that just didn't make me wet. How can I be so submissive to him? To one person? Especially Max. What is happening to me? What is this man doing to me?

There's not a moment of hesitation and I do it. I slide off my little boy shorts and move the laptop right in front of where I know Max wants it. My knees fall to the side and I'm open to him.

"Holy, fuck," he mumbles out.

Even all the times we've had sex, been naked, he's gone down on me, and vice versa, I don't think I've ever felt more vulnerable and more sexy in my life. I can feel the heat in my face, the wetness in my center, and all of my inhibitions fade away because he's looking at me in such an intense way.

I see his throat bob up and down and he swipes at his forehead. His tongue rolls over his bottom lip and he sucks in his lip for a second.

"What's next?" I ask with a seductive tone in my voice.

"Touch yourself, Willow."

I bring two of my fingers to my mouth and suck on them. I hum as I do it and I hear some sound come out of Max's mouth. Whatever it was, it was hot. He's more turned on than an oven.

I slide my now wet fingers down my chest, stopping at my tank for a second and popping out my nipple. I roll it between my slick fingers and squeeze a little. Just like Max used to do. I continue following the path of my body with my fingers and I stop at my center.

"Where would you like them to go now?" I wiggle my fingers to him on the screen.

"Where I wish my tongue was," he answers and I swear to the heavens I could explode right now just from the thought of it. It's been there, plenty of times.

As soon as I touch myself, my hips buck up.

"Oh God," I moan out slowly.

"Rub it in circles, Willow. Let me see it."

On command, I do what he asks. Round and round my fingers go. My eyes solely fixed on Max as I do. I see him squirm around and I know where his hand just went.

Down his pants.

"Willow, you have the prettiest pussy I have ever seen. Keep doing that. Rub your fucking clit faster. Don't fucking stop."

Jesus, Max is so good at dirty talk. Always has been. And so I concede and do as I'm told and I have zero problem with it because it feels so damn good.

"Faster, Wills, faster."

His laptop shakes and I can tell he's pulling at his dick.

"Let me see you, Max. I know what you're doing. I want to see it."

His laptop goes sideways and appears to have fallen off of his chest. There looks like there's technical difficulties but then he recovers.

"Sorry, was pulling down my pants." I snicker in a fun way.

"I showed you mine, now you show me yours." He wiggles his eyebrows and turns the monitor towards his crotch.

Oh, there's my old friend.

"Sweet Lord."

If I haven't said it before, Max is huge. I mean like porn-star huge. I'd pretty much do anything right now for it to be here in the flesh. And there's a lot of flesh there.

He starts to stroke it. Up and down. The head is red and swollen and looks good enough to lick. The tip glistens and I shake my head. Max notices.

His breath is unsteady as he speaks, "What's wrong? Don't like it?"

My head moves back and forth and I smile.

"On the contrary. I wish it was here, right now. In me."

Max bellows out a sound. "Uhh… I wish it was too." His breathing hitches, his face takes on another form and he pumps away with his hand. The screen shakes and moves and makes me a little seasick but I'm so turned on right now I could care fucking less.

"Does that turn you on? Thinking about fucking me, Max. Being inside me? Making me come? Make me come, Max. Do it. I'm so close."

His pace increases and muffled sounds come from the back of his throat.

This is something I have never done before and by far it's the hottest.

I rub myself to the same rhythm as Max and I watch the erotic expression on his face. The faster I rub my swollen self, the faster he beats his dick.

Our eyes never waver from each other. It's intense, so intense. My fingers are so wet they slide all over and I can feel the rumble in my lower belly signaling my impending orgasm. And I know the look on Max's face. I've seen it dozens of times. It's burned in my memory.

"I'm falling, Max. Here I go. I'm coming. Oh God… Max. Oh, shit!"

And I do. I fall apart. At the seams. I close my eyes as I do. I'm floating. My whole body is a buzz. I've never gotten high but I imagine that this is what it feels like.

When my eyes flutter open I watch Max. Profoundly.

My fingers are still slick and placed between my legs.

And I watch. I watch something so lascivious. I think if he doesn't finish soon, I'll be ready again. I'm like a dude.

Seriously.

"Here we go, Wills. Fuuuccckkkk…"

And there we go.

Max's eyes roll back into his head and his body jerks and he looks like he's having a damn seizure.

Whoa. That was kinky.

As Max cleans up, I pull my panties back up then pull my covers up to my chest. I snuggle in and when Max appears again he looks a little uncomfortable.

He doesn't meet my eyes and I wonder if maybe someone heard him.

"Are you okay? Did someone hear you?" He clears his throat and shakes his head no.

"Nah. I'm fine." But he's not.

Maybe that was weird to him because he's seeing Cora and he feels like maybe he cheated on her in a way. Maybe it wasn't as big of a turn on for him as it was for me. I'm not an insecure person and I'm not sure why I run these questions through my head.

"Listen, if you feel weird about all that, it's fine. It's cool. We don't…"

He stops me. "No, Wills. I'm fine."

"Then what's with the face like you're a shy school girl?"

He runs his hand over his short hair. His face is complacent.

"It's just… I just never… I've never done anything like that before and I've been around the block a few times on the old tricycle. But that? That was the single most seductive, steamy, raw sexual thing I have ever done."

I wink and run my finger across my lip.

"Well, I'll admit, I feel the same way. I thought it freaked you out in a bad way."

Max flashes his fantastic smile at me.

"The complete opposite. I don't think I was ever more comfortable with anything in my life."

"Agreed and that's so strange for me to think that way, but… it really was, wasn't it?" Max grins.

"Yeah, it was."

I'm so tired from my orgasm and I feel my eyes start to flutter closed.

Sleepily, as I snuggle down more in my comforter and pillows, I ask him, "Where are you over the next couple of days?"

He yawns. "D.C. the next two nights. We're on our way there now."

"Yeah… then Philly, right?"

He yawns again. "Yeah… close to home."

I match his yawn. "Yes, you will be. So close to home. To Sandy Cove."

My eyes close but I'm still awake. Twilight is what I call it. The time right before you're about to fall into sleep.

"I miss you, Willow."

"Miss you too, Max."

All of our words are said so lazily and before I know it, I'm dead to the world.

You know how girlfriends tell each other everything? Yeah, well, I'm not like that and I want to tell the girls so bad about Max's and my porn-style Skype chat. But I keep it to myself. These two aren't dummies though. As hard as I try to get this plastered smile off my face, they're catching on and as we sit here at our favorite boardwalk breakfast place I wait for the Spanish inquisition.

"So what gives? Did you overdose on meds or something?"

I stick a fork full of French toast in my mouth. I wipe the corner of my mouth.

"I have no idea what you're talking about, Har."

She looks at Thea and then both look straight back to me in sync.

"Cut the crap. There's a guy. We know it. Who is it? Why haven't you brought him around? Where'd you meet?"

I look at both of them like they're bat-shit crazy. I don't want them to know. I don't want them to know how much I like Max, how strong my feelings are for him. That I miss him. And I don't know why. Would it be so bad?

If Max didn't feel the same? Yep, it pretty much would be a disaster. I don't know rejection. I don't know how I would accept it. My life has been a blessed one. I have had everything I have ever wanted in my life. Clothes, cars, jewelry, exotic vacations. I'm rich. It comes with the territory. I was accepted to the college of my choice. My job as a teacher — bam! Nailed it without the history of my social status or my parents' social status. It was done on my own merit. Christ, I graduated summa cum laude.

Everything has come easy for me, except rejection.

These two will drive me nuts with questions so I give them a little tease.

"Okay fine. You two pain in the asses will never leave me alone. I'm not giving you too much info so deal." I point my fork at each of them.

"He's not around. He travels for work. He's very smart and he's hot. I met him at Jax. That's it. Don't ask another question 'cause I won't answer it. You're both lucky I gave you that much info."

They look surprisingly satisfied.

"Okay. When you're ready, you'll let us know."

Harlow just freaked me out. Her response was not what I expected. Far, far from it. It was very nonchalant. Very unlike my dear friend here. But I let it go.

My phone buzzes with a text and I look at it on the seat in the booth. It's Max.

Max: *How long of a ride is it from Sandy Cove to Philly?*

Me: *Maybe two hours? Less, possibly. Why? What's up?*

I wait. The girls chat about something to each other so I sit and wait.

The ding sounds.

Max: *I have tickets for everyone for the Philly show for this Wednesday night. Can you guys make the trip?*

I look at the girls and casually ask, "Max just texted me. He has tickets for all of us for the Philadelphia show for Wednesday. Can you guys go?" Thea looks sad. "I'm leaving tonight. Work tomorrow. Won't be back till Friday."

"Can't you take a sick day?" I ask annoyed.

"No, I can't, Willow. I save my days and I always save my vacation till the end of the summer."

I roll my eyes. "Harlow, it's your dad's practicc. Don't you have any pull with this?" She laughs sarcastically.

"Yeah, no, Willow. That's my dad's business. I don't get involved in his business."

My phone dings again.

Max: *Wills? Can you guys come? Did you*

talk to everyone? Where are you? Who are you with?

The thing about texts are they sometimes are taken out of context. Max seems anxious with his.

Me: *I'm with Thea and Harlow at breakfast. Why do you seem so wound up?*

Harlow asks, "What's he saying?"

"He's asking who can come."

He answers back.

Max: *I'm fine. I am anxious because I want you guys to come to my show. My dad can't make the Dayton show but he can make the Philly one and I want him to meet you.*

Whoa. Me? My heart flutters at that.

Right away he shoots me another text.

Max: *Sorry. I meant all of you.*

Then my heart falls into my stomach.

But that's okay.

Harlow gets a text from Cruz.

"Max must have texted Cruz. He's off so we can go. Porter can't get off work. So the three of us can go." She bounces in her seat.

Oh, great. In a car for two hours with those two. Lucky me. They'll be making out at every stop sign and stop light.

"Wonderful." My voice, yeah, less than enthusiastic.

Harlow gives an eye roll.

I text Max back.

Me: *I'm coming with Harlow and Cruz. Guess I'll be seeing you in a few days :)*

Max: *AWESOME! Can't wait!*
And a smile is on my face.
I'm going to see Max in a few days.
I feel those silly, girlie butterflies in my lower belly and I like them. As much as I would try to push them away I can't.

CHAPTER 10

My Blessing and My Curse
Max~

My fingers hurt. So does my back. Exhaustion is now a part of my repertoire. This tour has been the greatest experience of my life, but it can burn you out just as much as it can raise your spirits so high.

The rehearsals can be brutal. Each venue we play has a different stage, a different lighting system, a different angle. We have to grow accustomed to each place. If we screw up a key or a chorus, it's back to square one.

Mr. Carpenter is coming to the show tonight. He came to the Jacksonville show and afterwards told us how impressed he was with our performance. That was our first one and I think over a month later, we have improved greatly.

We are so used to playing places that hold a few hundred people. Not thousands. We're in Philadelphia. The Wells Fargo Center seats 19,500 people and tonight's show is sold out. Not because of us, of course, but still, it's a sold out crowd.

Cruz, Harlow, and Willow are coming tonight. I'm really excited to see them. Oh, and so is my dad. I haven't seen him in months and he's never seen me play so my nerves are on overdrive because I've been trying to get him to understand how music is my muse in life. There's nothing more I want than to make music until I die. I hope he sees how much it really means to me. If music for some reason doesn't work out in my life, I have my Plan B. I have a degree and I could always fall back on engineering if need be. But I don't want the need be. I want this. I want music.

I'm so damn nervous and I have to calm down. I pace in front of the tour bus. I sweat, my hands shake. I need to relax. Having Skype sex with Willow the other night was a tension breaker but I should have had it with her last night. I'm wound up so freaking tight. I need the next best thing.

I call her.

I dial and she picks up on the first ring.

"Hey, rock and roll. What's up? How are you?"

"Nervous." I spat out. No sense keeping how I'm feeling at bay.

"Why? This isn't your first show. You can do it in your sleep."

Just the sound of her voice eases me. Relaxes all my senses like a drug would. Never in a million years would I have thought Willow Taylor would be the one person to ease any worries I would have.

The world is made up of so many fuckcd up things. Good or bad. Things that come along that we least expect. Things that we would never expect to help us or change us. This girl — she's a thing. A good thing.

"I know. It's just that you guys are coming and my dad is going to be hearing me play for the first time ever."

"Huh? He's never heard you play? Didn't the man raise you practically on his own?"

I think about how I hid it from him. All he wanted was for me to use my talents in other ways. My brain talent. Full scholarships, grants, awards adorned my dad's living room wall. He wanted more for me in life than he had. I can't forget the look of disappointment on his face when I told him how I wanted to play music and not be an engineer. It was like I crushed his world. But, in retrospect, he crushed mine by being disappointed.

I'm surprised he's coming tonight. But I'll take it and I'll prove to him how much it means to me.

I answer Willow with the short version of the story.

"No. He's never heard me play. He's not crazy about what I'm doing. You know he wanted me to do something with my degree. I just need to see if this works out first. The music. I have to really prove myself to him. That's really why I'm nervous."

Willow lets out a breath and I hear her lips

smack together.

"Max, the only person you need to prove something to is yourself. You are talented and smart and if your dad can't see that then I think he's crazy. Just wait till he sees you on that stage. How electric you are. How mesmerizing. Music lives in your soul, Max. It's what you were born to do."

Her words make me smile and make me want to cry as well. I don't cry but my emotions are running on a track. Going round and round. She speaks so softly and in such a positive way. I really can't believe I'm speaking of Willow Taylor.

"Yeah, you think so?"

She lets out a little laugh. "Yeah, I *know* so."

There's silence on both our ends until I hear her clear her throat.

"Now stop being your normal pain in the ass self and go get ready for your show. I'll see you in a few hours."

"Okay… Hey, Wills?"

"Yeah?"

"Thanks."

"No problem, shorty."

She had to get that dig in, didn't she?

Okay, so the Wells Fargo Center is pretty awesome. Great staff and the place is packed. The buzz is that people who went to the last show in D.C. to see the main attraction wanted to see more of us so some drove up. Ain't that a kick in the ass?

The lights dim as we take the stage. The roar of the crowd lingers. The smell of sweat and beer and girls' perfume surrounds me and for a split second I feel like I'm back at Jax. I feel like I'm home. Maybe it's because I know my friends are here. Maybe not. Doesn't matter 'cause I'm about to shred.

We sound tight tonight. The energy is amazing and my fingers glide so effortlessly on the fret board that sometimes I don't even realize how hard I'm hitting it. I can't wipe this stupid smile off my face. I jump onto the platform where the background keyboard player is and keep up my pace along with his rhythm. He plays the keys and I hit every note, strong and clean.

Our set is amazing. The crowd is wild and intense and for the first time I can hear our names being chanted. When we finish the last note of the last song, I'm a little disappointed because I am so high on this right now, I don't think I want to come down.

The cheering I hear says, "More, more, more." We were told to run off stage if this happens and, if time allows, we can go back on and do another song.

But this has never happened.

That was until now.

When we thank the crowd and run off the stage, Mr. Carpenter is there and greets us. He shakes our hands vigorously and has the biggest smile on his face.

"Well, what are you guys waiting for? Go give them more. That's what they're asking for."

Holy shit.

We go back out onto the now darkened stage. We huddle around for a second and decide to sing something that we just play on a whim during rehearsal, but we have perfected it, so it comes easy to us all.

When it ends, the crowd goes crazy. I am dripping in sweat. The tips of my fingers bleed and the permanent grin on my face won't be gone anytime soon. Nothing can destroy the mood I'm in. The guys and I hug and congratulate each other. We automatically go to the green room they have set up for us. I grab a few waters and down them. I'm handed a fresh towel from one of the roadies and wipe my hair and my face off with it. So many people tell us how great we were. Mr. Carpenter makes his way through the crowded room and comes right to me.

"Max, that was unbelievable. Great song. Such a great song. Love the arrangement. I'm telling you, son, you guys are going to go places. I have big plans for you. Big plans."

I shake his hand back.

"Thank you so much, Mr. Carpenter. I'm so stoked you enjoyed the show. This is… it's just amazing." I'm at a loss for words. When the door to the green room opens again — even if I wanted to speak more — I can't because who walks in steals my words.

She walks in.

Willow.

I've been with a lot of chicks. Gorgeous ones. Short ones, tall ones, dark-haired ones, red-heads, big tits, small ones, but for some reason, when I see this girl walk through the door my heart literally bangs against my chest.

It's her smile. It beams. There's an aura around her that makes her glow. Like she's walking in front of the sun and the light from it surrounds her and illuminates her. Head turner is a phrase that doesn't do her justice. Stunner doesn't either. She's just a life force that stops you in your tracks and when I see her spot me all I want to do is run up to her and kiss her — hard. But I can't. Cruz and Harlow are with her and I just have to keep what I'm feeling to myself.

When she sees me there's a look in her eyes that, for a split second, makes me think she's feeling the same way. But then when Cruz steps in front of her to get to me from across the room, the momentary spell is broken.

The big guy comes right up to me and picks me up in a hug. He bounces me like I'm some kind of doll but I don't mind. He's an idiot and my best friend.

"Holy shit, dude. That was amazing, unbelievable, impressive. I can't believe we were watching you in a venue like this. I can't even hear right now. My ears are clogged from the music. Damn, that was cool."

He finally sets me down after Harlow smacks his arm. "Thanks, man. So glad you liked it." Harlow shoves Cruz aside and gives me a huge hug. Tears are in her eyes.

"Max, oh God, that was… I can't even talk right now. I'm so proud of you. When you're rich and famous and you win a Grammy, I can say I know you." Harlow is the sweetest girl. She's so genuine and has become such a good friend.

"Thanks, Har. I'm so glad you guys made the trip. It means a lot to me."

Behind her is Willow, who is now fiddling with a strand of her hair. She looks despondent as she chews on the side of her lip. I go to her because she takes one step towards me but retreats.

Oh God, I want to grab her and hold her. Why can't I? Why shouldn't I? Because she only sees me as someone who gets her off, that's why. And I'm conflicted because even though she does that to me as well, I'm starting to feel something more than something sexual.

I'm fucked. I seriously may be fucked.

"Hey, Willow." I give her what seems like an awkward hug. Her hair touches my cheek and I smell her flowery scent when my face is in the crook of her neck. I close my eyes and for a moment, I want this hug to be more, to last longer.

She reciprocates the hug but it's in the same manner as mine. It's not a tight hug. It's more of a friendly tap. I look up finally and peek over her shoulder to see Mr. Taylor standing there.

I pull away, so surprised to see him.

"Oh, wow. Mr. Taylor. You're here, too?"

My eyes meet Willow's for a second and my breath hitches when we connect. She looks away towards where Harlow is standing and she steps aside so her dad is more visible to me.

Mr. Taylor takes my hand and shakes it while

patting me with his other hand on my shoulder.

"Max, that was a great show. I'm so impressed, son. Hope you don't mind me tagging along. Gary got me a ticket."

"Of course not, sir. I wouldn't be here if it wasn't for you…" My eyes go towards Willow. "And Willow."

She hears what I say to her dad and a small smile appears on her face.

I realize my dad isn't with them. I turn and ask the gang if they have seen him. All of their seats were supposed to be together.

"Did you see my dad? His seat was with you guys."

They all eye each other and their faces have peculiar looks to them.

I don't get it.

"Um… yeah. He sat with us. We all introduced ourselves." Cruz looks a little uncomfortable when he tells me.

I shrug. "So where is he?"

Cruz thumbs out to the outside of the green room door.

"He didn't want to come in but told me to tell you he's outside waiting for you."

Why wouldn't he want to come in? I don't get it.

"Okay. I'm going to go talk to him. You guys going to hang out for a while before you have to get back to Sandy Cove?"

Mr. Taylor speaks up.

"Well, I wanted to take you, your band members and these knuckleheads out to dinner."

He motions to Cruz, Harlow, and Willow. "Can you do that? I booked myself and them a room for the night so no one had to drive back late."

Mr. Taylor is awesome.

"Oh, wow. That's really nice of you, Mr. Taylor. Would it be okay if I asked my dad to tag along? I haven't seen him in months."

Mr. Taylor doesn't hesitate. "Of course it's okay. It would be my pleasure to have him join us."

I thank him and tell them I'll be right back. I head out the door towards the long hallway. I look both ways and see my dad down by where the restrooms are located.

"Dad," I yell and walk briskly towards him.

He turns and smiles at me, holding his arms out for me.

We hug and pat each other on the backs.

We pull away and he's smiling at me but it's not his typical smile.

"It's good to see you, Max. You look good."

"So do you, Dad. I'm so glad you made it. How'd you like the show?"

"I enjoyed it." His answer is flat.

I'm not even convinced he means that.

"But what did you think of the music and my playing and all the lyrics? I wrote some of the originals."

He has an apathetic look on his face and he shrugs.

"You know me, Max. I'm not much of a music man. I mean you looked like you were having fun. It looks like a good hobby to have."

"Hobby?" I question. "This, Dad… this is not just a hobby. This is my life." I look down at my raw, calloused fingers and snort in annoyance. "I just played a sold out show in front of over 19,000 people."

He squints and leans his head to the side. "Eh, well, technically you warmed up the audience for the main act. *You* didn't sell out that crowd, son. They did."

I can't fathom why he isn't giving me credit for what I just did tonight or what I have been doing for the past month. Actually, what I've been doing for the past few years. I try to smooth this out not wanting to argue with him or maybe take what he's saying out of context. But I know what he's saying. He doesn't believe in me.

"Dad,I know you've never heard me play but they wanted an encore. The audience wanted *us* to play an encore. They just don't do that unless they really enjoyed what you did. Do you or can you understand that?"

He looks down at his shoes and shuffles a foot, never responding to my question. He leans the side of his body against the wall and I step in front of him when he says nothing. I shield him with my body so my back is to the hallway where people linger and lean in because I need to get through to this man how much music means to me.

"This isn't a hobby, Dad. This is my life. This is what I want to do with it. The way I want to live my life. It's my future. It's all that matters to me."

His face reddens and he looks infuriated. He speaks through his teeth at me and spews his distaste for what I just said.

"This is NOT your future, Max. Your future is written on a piece of paper that shows that you are not a musician, you are an engineer. That's what you spent four years achieving. Christ, son, you know what someone who has your degree starts out making a year? Have you even researched it? Gone on an interview?"

I shake my head and try to keep my heart from coming out of my throat.

"Eighty thousand dollars a year, Max. Fucking $80,000. I've been working my whole goddamn life and I still haven't reached that amount. I'm fifty-two years old and I fix cars for a living. I smell like grease and car exhaust all day. I didn't have the opportunities you have, Max. You're twenty-four. You have the world by the balls and you want to throw it all away for what?" He motions down the hall and to the musicians who stand around with their guitars strung around their bodies.

My voice automatically rises in anger. "I'm not throwing shit away, Dad. I never wanted to be what you wanted me to be. I never wanted to disappoint you because it made you so happy when I excelled at school and won the scholarships. School came easy for me but being what it says on that stupid piece of paper doesn't mean the same to me as music does. Why don't you get that? Why can't you understand that and just be happy for me?"

He hits my chest with his finger and it's done so harshly it knocks me back and off balance.

"Because you won't make it. You aren't good enough," he says it so nonchalantly — like what he was saying wouldn't affect me.

I swat his hand away and I feel a lump in my throat. I want to vomit and I want to cry. But I'm a man. I don't cry. I won't cry. Not over him, not over him not believing in me.

My dad doesn't believe in me.

"Fuck you," I spew at him and in an instant he has me by the shirt and thrown against the wall with great force.

He shakes me and yells, "Who the fuck do you think you're talking to, boy? I'm your father, you un-talented little asshole."

I hear a voice yelling, 'Hey' a few times and the sound of it grows closer and closer.

"Get your hands off of him."

I turn my blazing eyes away from my father and see Willow stalking down the hall towards us. My dad looks at her as she pulls at his arm to get him off of me. He automatically lets go of me and I'm so hyped up I have a hard time catching my breath.

"That's your son. How could you say those things to him?"

My dad turns to her.

Smugly, he says, "What do you know about it, sweetheart? You're right, he is *my* son and I can say whatever the hell I want. You don't know him so keep that pretty mouth of yours shut."

With my heart hurting and my head spinning, I

still manage to have enough strength to grab my old man by the shirt and turn him towards the wall and jack him up.

"Don't you dare fucking talk to her like that."

Willow grabs my hand and pries me off of him. I stumble back a few steps and try to catch my breath.

She looks over to me and holds up her hand.

"Max, I can take care of myself. Calm down." I place my hands on my knees and bend over. My breathing is shallow and I feel like I just ran a marathon.

"You're wrong, Mr. Vincent. I *do* know him. More than you do. I know how talented he is and smart he is. I know how caring he is and what a good friend he knows how to be."

Willow Taylor stands up to my father like she has a set of gonads the size of Texas. She doesn't hesitate to get right in his face. Nose to nose.

Her voice is even-toned but stern and she's even more beautiful when she's angry.

"You don't know anything about him. You didn't even know his talents until a few years ago. How do you not know this about your own child? All you care about is money and power. I have it and came from it and to tell you the truth, it's not all that. Doing what makes you most happy is. If you don't want your son to be happy, then you don't deserve to have him as a son. *He* deserves better than you."

My dad's eyes are on fire. With each staggered breath he takes, his shoulders raise up and down. His fists are balled and if I didn't know my father

222

to not be a violent man, I'd bet he'd hit her. That's how angry he looks. I don't want this. I've always had an okay relationship with my dad. He practically raised me by himself. But I can't forget his words. I'll never forget his words.

I'm not good enough.

I also won't forget hers.

He doesn't protest what Willow says. He just smooths out his shirt and wipes the sweat on his brow.

He's all I have but now that I know how he *really* feels about me, I'm not sure I even care.

"Look, Dad. You either accept that this is my dream, or you don't. Me being an engineer was your dream but I'm an adult and I can make my own decisions. I love you, but if you can't let me live my dream then…"

He smiles artificially and tilts his chin up in my direction.

"Then what?"

I bite the inside of my mouth so hard, the coppery taste of blood is almighty in my mouth.

"Then I can't have you in my life. You don't believe in me. How can I have someone in my life — especially a parent — who doesn't think I'm good enough?"

The expression on his face is fruitless. He looks up to the ceiling and snickers.

"Think about what you're saying, son. You have a mother who doesn't give two shits about you. All you have is me. You'll have nothing."

Willow steps in front of me like a shield and eyes up my father.

"That's not true, Mr. Vincent. He'll have me. I'll be there for him, and trust me, I'm enough."

Wow.

She steps beside me and crosses her arms.

"Remember what you just said to me, Max. Don't come knocking on my door if you strike out with this whole thing. I won't be there."

I give him a curt nod. "Don't worry on both counts. I won't call you and I won't fail."

And with that my dad walks away down the long, dark corridor and towards the exit.

My dad just walked out of my life.

I pull at my hair and lean against the wall, closing my eyes tightly — so tight that I see flashes of light behind my eyelids. I can't catch my breath. I literally can't breathe.

After I moment, I feel a smack on my arm.

"Okay. That's all the time you get for the I-feel-sorry-for-myself. Go clean up and let's get shit-faced."

This girl always knows the right things to say.

The image of my father telling me I'm not good enough is slowly disappearing at the bottom of this wine glass I drink from. I've never drank wine, but I have to say, it's damn good. Mr. Taylor comes to Philadelphia for business sometimes so he knows the good places to go to eat. He takes us to this restaurant called *Vetri*. An Italian place that has such a homey, old-world feeling to it. The wine flows like water and the food comes out in troughs. Cruz, Harlow, Willow, Mr. Taylor and I sit back and stuff our faces. The guys from the band hooked up with some groupies and decided to go to a few local bars in the city.

We laugh as Mr. Taylor tells us stories about Willow and Harlow when they were younger and the trouble they'd get into. The one story that has us in hysterics is when they were sixteen they tried to sneak out of Willow's room to go to a party. Willow's room is so high up and they couldn't sneak out downstairs because of the alarm system. The two of them decided to tie bed sheets together and lower each other down to the main floor. It didn't go as planned and when Willow was being lowered down by Harlow, her grip slipped and the both of them went down landing in a few hydrangea bushes. But that wasn't the kicker. The kicker was that there was a bee's nest in one of them and they were running around the grandiose front yard of the Taylor home — setting off the sprinkler system for some reason and looking like escaped mental patients swatting at bees and dodging water from the powerful sprinklers.

We all laugh so hard at the visual. Mr. Taylor has tears coming out of his eyes from laughing and Harlow's head is down and her shoulders are shaking so hard from her fits of laughter.

"Not my Turnip. No way she was sneaking out of the house to go see a boy."

Harlow and Willow look at each other and blurt out at the same time, "Billy Rogers." Then the laughing begins again.

"Oh, Cruz, trust me, Harlow was an angel. It

was all my princess's influence."

Willow's mouth hangs open.

"Daddy! How could you say that?" she says half kidding, half serious.

He grasps her shoulder and pulls her to him. He kisses the side of her head then ruffles her hair.

"Oh, Willow. You think I don't know that you were no angel? Even though you're my princess doesn't mean I don't know what a troublemaker you could be. I'd be a fool if I didn't know."

He laughs when he says it. He turns to Cruz and me.

"She gives you guys a run for your money, right, guys?"

Oh God, how do we both answer this? I know Cruz will have no trouble saying yes, she's a pain in the ass and maybe a few months ago I would have, but I speak up.

"Nah. Not really. I mean she's got a mouth on her, but I think the thing I like best about her is how brutally honest she is. You don't come across many people like that. It's… I don't know, refreshing."

The table goes silent. I look up and everyone is staring at me. I finish my glass of wine and I blame the fermented grapes on my sudden honesty.

I probably should lay off the wine.

Mr. Taylor clears his throat.

"You know when you're a parent you try your best at making sure your child has a good foundation. You make sure they're polite and attentive, and your job is to make sure they know right from wrong. The one thing you don't have control over is their personality. I know what a good person my daughter is. She's a strong-willed, independent woman with a good heart. I know she's no angel but I also know that she would give the shirt off her back for the ones she loves. I like to think I had something to do with that. Me and her mother, of course."

My eyes travel to Willow and I see a single tear drift down her cheek and her skin glows in an illuminating blush.

"I'm very proud of the woman she has become."

Tonight of all nights I realize how a parent is supposed to feel about their child and it makes me sad. For me. And I know how lucky Willow is to have this man stand by her and everything he says is true. She is all those things.

Willow wipes her cheek and I so badly wanted to do that for her. To touch her skin and hold her face in my hands. But I don't and that's my mistake.

My back is to the entrance of the restaurant and when I look at everyone at the table, especially Willow, I'm not sure why her expression looks pained. I feel a presence at my back and Mr. Taylor stands up.

"Cora. Hello, dear. Good to see you." He reaches out and kisses her cheek.

I stand up abruptly and turn around to see her.

"Hi, everyone." She waves and I go and hug her.

"Hey, Cora. Good to see you. What are you doing here?"

"My dad told me you were here and I didn't get a chance to see you after the show. I was with the promoters and some winners of backstage passes who wanted to meet the guys from the other band. I hope I'm not intruding."

I shake my head no because I don't want her to feel uncomfortable.

I motion to the table. "Want to join us?"

She smiles and shakes her head no.

"I'm sorry. I can't. I need to get back to the bus to grab some paperwork my father needs for the remainder of the tour. I... um, Max... I wasn't sure if you were coming back and I didn't want to miss the opportunity to see you before I head back to New York."

I've talked to her a lot through text and on the phone but haven't seen her. I do have to go back to the bus because we are leaving early for the next city in the morning so I think it's only right I go. But I do waver for a moment if it's the right choice. The wine and the whole scene with my dad swims in my head and without really thinking, I make the decision to go.

"Oh, okay. You guys don't mind if I head back, do you? We leave for Dayton at six tomorrow morning and it's been... well, it's been a long night."

Mr. Taylor and Cruz stand up.

Mr. Taylor extends his hand to shake mine.

"No, of course not, Max. I can't imagine how tired you are. I'm pretty tired myself so I'm going to head back to the hotel."

I shake his hand vigorously. "Mr. Taylor, I can't thank you enough for tonight. For everything. I'm so glad you were able to make it."

"Max, I have no doubt that your success will continue and I really enjoyed myself. Next time you come to Princeton, make sure my daughter brings you by. You hear?"

I smile at this terrific man and I wish I had a father like him. He's always in Willow's corner.

Speaking of her. Her expression is bare. Blank. She doesn't get up after Cruz hugs me goodbye and Harlow kisses my cheek. She sips her wine and wipes the corners of her mouth with her cloth napkin. I go to her and bend down to kiss her cheek. I get down to the level of her ear after I kiss her.

"Thank you for coming tonight, Wills. Thank you for… well, everything. I'll call you from Dayton."

She nods and her face is unreadable.

"You're welcome. I'll talk to you soon. Safe travels." When I step away from her, she stands, excuses herself and goes to the ladies room.

I watch her walk away and a sudden ache comes to my stomach.

Watching her walk away is hard especially when the she's the one person who you know is in your corner. I also know when she walked away she looked like she wanted to put my balls in a blender then feed it to Cora.

CHAPTER 11

Dr. Dickcop
Willow~

You'd think I'd be happy. You'd think I'd be satisfied with my life at the moment. Sometimes I'm really good at covering up how I feel. Sitting on the beach day after day. Going dancing almost every night. Relaxing. It's one of the many reasons I wanted to be a teacher. My goddamn summers off. There's no real thinking, no set schedule. If I want to sleep till noon instead of waking up at six a.m. to go hang out with a bunch of hormonal adolescents I would have gone and asked my father for a job at his P.R. firm working with One Direction groupies. But I didn't and this is what my chosen profession allows me to do. The difference? I'm not having fun. Not at all. I'm pretty sure I'm in fucking love.

Scratch that. I *know* I'm in love.

For the first time in my life I think I know what it feels like. Love. Being in it. Living with it inside you. My explanation of it: when you can't stand being away from the person. When you can't fathom that you'll be apart for another day. When you breathe you feel like you can't inhale enough oxygen in your lungs because basically you can't *breathe* without them. I can't breathe knowing he's not here. I want to, I just can't. This was so unexpected. So beyond any reasoning behind the way I feel. I just do — I feel. I need him to help me breathe. I need him to fill this tremendous void I feel because I can't see him. He's not here in the flesh. I don't get to see his heart-stopping smile or his dancing brown eyes. I don't get to hear his voice when he sings or watch his skillful hands when he plays. I don't get to see any of it. And why is that? Because the night of the show in Philadelphia he chose Cora. Granted, left with her and I have no idea what went on when they got back to that tour bus, but I'm an all assuming type person so I assume he fucked her silly style. And again, I'm assuming.

I had to excuse myself from dinner and go to the ladies room to try to compose myself and that's when it first hit me. The fact that I couldn't breathe. That's how I knew I was in love. That's how I knew I was in love with Max.

Fucking Max Vincent who annoys the ever-living shit out of me. Sometimes he annoys me so bad I feel like my throat closes. The one who is so smart he recites questions straight from the game show *Jeopardy.* He's short and chews with his mouth open for fuck's sake. He has a distasteful wardrobe and he only has one pair of sneakers. Chuck Taylor's. So worn down they don't even look black anymore. More like an unpolished gray.

So why would I, Willow Taylor, be in love with someone like that?

Because it's the way it's supposed to be. I'm supposed to love him. I think it's always been that way.

Over the last few years I've learned a lot from my friends. Especially Cruz and Harlow. What have I learned? Well, for starters, you absolutely, without a doubt cannot help who you fall in love with. It's a natural progression of things on a list in our lives that we cannot control. I can't control my mouth. That's part of who I am. I have to have pink or purple nail polish on my nails at all times. That's just another part. I can't live without gummy bears. If they ceased to exist, so would I.

Falling in love with someone who you thought was the bane of your existence, well just add it to the list.

Oh, and the other thing I can't control, he doesn't feel the same about me. If he did, there's no way he would have gone off with Cora.

And after I stood by him and defended him when his piece of shit father berated him in front of me. I thought there was a moment there afterwards where we connected in a way that maybe he felt something for me. At the time I knew I felt something for him but I wasn't sure it was love.

But he walked away.

That night when I went back to my hotel, I shared a room with Harlow and Cruz. Thank the sweet, sweet Lord they kept it classy and just spooned each other in their bed. If I had to be a witness to their sexual escapades when they thought I would be asleep, my throat would be slit right now.

I tossed and turned in bed all night. The old Willow — the one who didn't give a shit —would have cut Max off at the ankles. No more texts, no more Skype chats about what our favorite things are, and no more webcam sex. But when I was tossing and turning and thinking about how much I was in love with him, I knew I couldn't go without seeing his face on the screen or hearing his voice or even a receiving a simple text. Just the ding and his name popping up on my phone screen sent waves of excitement through me. I mean, Christ almighty. It's words on a screen. But they are from Max, and that's all that matters.

So I haven't cut off communication to him. If we don't video chat, we talk on the phone from wherever he is. I didn't ask him about the night with Cora, I haven't asked him about any other girl he has met or been with. Not sure I could handle that so it's better I don't ask. And he offers no further info on the subject either.

Good.

On this perfect day in August when the sun is at its best and the waters of the Atlantic are somewhat at their warmest, I wish I were any place than here. I wish I was with Max.

My trashy romance novels that I never get to read during the school year because of time consuming lesson plans and online master's courses do nothing for me. They don't transport me to a place where they used to. I read a paragraph about some woman getting fucked against a wall and it literally does nothing for me. It used to make me squeeze my thighs together like a vice but I've lived that... with Max. Our chemistry does not compare to those in the fictional world. But the more I talk to him and we develop a friendship, the more I believe that it's more than sexual chemistry and maybe one day when this tour is over and I dig my balls back out from wherever they are hiding, I'll tell him that it's more than sex with us. There's more to us.

I throw down my book in frustration and let out an aggravated sigh. I tip my wide- brimmed beach hat over my face and cross my arms over my chest. I pout. Yeah, I pout like a baby because I'm frustrated.

I feel something thrown at my face and it stirs me from my toddler-like state.

"Okay, enough. What's with this piss-poor attitude, Willow? All you do is mope and sigh. You don't even insult people the way you used to."

Porter threw a beach towel at my head and he stands above my chair yelling at me in some attempt to get answers. But I can't give him any. Sure, I could tell him and the rest of my friends I love Max and that we should be together, but I won't. Like I have said in the past, rejection and me are enemies. We won't work well together. I know it. So I'll spare myself the humiliation for now. I said for now.

"Nothing is wrong with me. Jesus, Porter. Can't I just enjoy the day without being ridiculed because I'm not flapping my gums or being hostile towards someone?"

He looks at me pointedly and his eyes say, *"Well, no, you can't because this isn't you and you're not yourself."*

"Well, he's right, Wills. You're not yourself and haven't been for a few weeks now. Is it because we have to go home soon? Worried about the school year starting or is there some sort of underlying issue that's making you like this?" Harlow's voice is full of concern but also has some vibrancy to it.

I stand up abruptly and begin gathering my things because I feel the back of my eyes fill with unshed tears and fuck if I let anyone see me cry. I'll glue these goddamn sunglasses to my face for the rest of my life.

"I don't know why my attitude is of anyone's concern. I'm fine. I'm fucking hoop-de-doodle-dee okay. So why don't you just go back to your perfect life, Harlow. With your hot fiancé, your constant sunny disposition and good fucking hair and leave me alone."

Her jaw drops… well, everyone's does but I waste no time in allowing someone to chastise me so I leave. Yep. I run. Up the beach, over the boardwalk and across the street towards the bay. And as I reach the other side of the boardwalk, I can't breathe. I can't take another step without losing my breath and it's not from exertion from walking too fast. It's because I'm missing something that has become a part of me and I'm becoming more and more transparent to my friends.

As I lie here on my bed and try to control my spastic breathing, a knock at my bedroom door temporarily pulls me from what I think is the beginning or the end of a full blown panic attack.

"Go away," I groan to whomever is on the other side of the door.

I roll my eyes when the door opens. Of course he'd just walk right in without an invite.

"What do you want, Cruz? Sorry if I talked to your Turnip," I air quote, "rudely. I'm not in the mood for another psychoanalysis of me."

He shakes his head. "She didn't deserve that and you know it. She's worried about you and I suck as her fiancé because I know what size stick is up your ass and I feel like I'm betraying her because I know the truth.

I glare at him and turn by body away from his face.

And I pout… again.

"Don't think I didn't notice your… how do I put this in a nice way… I really can't so I won't. Your royal bitchiness the night at dinner in Philadelphia when Cora walked in. It was all over your face that you wanted to gauge her eyes out with a salad fork. How long are you going to keep this up, Willow?"

I know he's the only one who knows about Max's and my little deal but he's not aware that

237

my feelings go past our secret humping rendezvous.

But something in me snaps and I can't hold in these feelings any longer.

"I miss him, okay. I miss him so much it's… hard to breathe." I grab at my chest and I turn to Cruz, who stands leaning with his arms crossed against the wall across from me. I'm saying this in front of Cruz. Lord, help me.

"It wasn't supposed to happen. I wasn't supposed to fall in love with him."

Cruz's face is blank as I avert my eyes to the ground and the tears that haven't fallen yet cloud my vision.

"I see. So it's not only because you were doing the tango on his face? You love him."

I sullenly look at him and I wrap my arms around myself. Holding on because that's the only thing I can do right now to comfort myself.

The air in the room isn't so uncomfortable with Cruz in it like I would expect. I just blurted out to him how I feel about Max. I fully expected him to laugh right in my face.

"Do you think he's seeing Cora?" My voice is cracking and I clear my throat to suppress my sadness. Not working.

Cruz sits on the edge of the bed across from me and sighs.

"I have no idea. Honestly. And I'm not lying because I know what sort of diabolical plan you have to suddenly make me a woman. But I will come clean and tell you he asked me a while back if you were seeing anyone."

My stomach drops for a second with the hope that maybe he cares more than I thought.

"This was before the night he left with Cora though. It was a while ago."

And that crushes that theory.

He must see my expression change because his eyes look solemn.

"I'm sorry, Willow."

I inhale strongly and lift my chin at him.

"Hey, can't win 'em all, right?"

"Wrong," he says sternly. His voice booming deep.

"What the hell does that mean? So he asked if I was seeing anyone a while ago. Big deal. It means nothing. He was probably just curious to see if I was having sex with someone."

"It means that you need to tell him how you feel. You are just assuming he's seeing Cora, but you have no real proof. Can I tell you something without you interrupting me or threatening my manhood?"

At this point I know I'm not getting rid of the big goof, so let me just allow him to spew his psychobabble. He needs to lay off the psychology courses.

So I nod.

"Promise?" He looks wary and unsure.

I roll my neck and eyes at him.

"For Christ's sake, yes. I fucking promise."

Cruz makes himself more comfortable on his spot on my bed. He adjusts that big, goofy body of his and braces his hands beside himself.

"You're a fucking wimp."

Blood enters my mouth as I swiftly bite my lip… hard.

Through gritted teeth I say, "Excuse me?"

"You heard me. You're a coward and ever since the day I met you would I never think this way about you. I'm actually disappointed."

Steam comes out of my ears and I search the room quickly for a weapon.

"There better be a point here, assface."

He smiles softly.

"Yes, there is. I always thought Harlow was the strongest person I knew. She almost died, twice, but I realize that she's a different strong. She's strong like a fighter. She fought for her life and fought for her recovery. You… you're strong in will and in your mind. I can see past all of your tough-girl-don't-mess-with-me-bullshit, Willow. It's a front. When you're scared or you feel something unfamiliar for you, you put up the wall. You put on the armor. No one can get in no matter how hard they fight you. But it's all crap. It's not really you."

I'm listening to him. But it's hard to listen to things like this being said to you and about you.

He looks at me for reassurance that he may continue — trying to read my thoughts, and honestly my only thoughts are that I want to hear what else he has to say because no one has ever said these things to me. I motion to him with my hand to continue, granting him permission.

"When Harlow got in the accident, I saw how you were. The devastation, the grief, the strength. You displayed all of that. Even through my own pain of possibly losing her, I saw the wall come down, but when you sat by her bedside while she was in the coma you told her to cut the bullshit and wake the fuck up. On more than one occasion. You were so unrelenting that the nurses were afraid of you. That was half of the real you. Half the wall came down. I saw you sit there and cry. I saw past that wall and saw a woman who was so afraid to lose her best friend. But it's okay, Willow, to be afraid. To be afraid of the unknown."

I question him. "The unknown?"

"Yeah, the unknown. You didn't know if Harlow was going to live when she almost bled to death. You didn't know if she was going to come out of that coma. Now, you sure as shit don't know how Max feels about you. It's the unknown. The things with Harlow, we had zero control over that outcome. How you feel about Max, that could be easily answered. You will be able to find out that outcome. So what's stopping you from telling him how you feel?"

Why not just hand my ass over to him. He already knows how I feel about Max, so what do I have to lose about telling him.

"I'm afraid of rejection."

Cruz scratches at his chin. "Um... okay. So you've never been rejected by anyone?"

"Anyone or anything. Guys, no, the college of my choice, no, the car of my choice, no."

His eyes go wide. "Whoa. You don't know what you're missing."

In frustration, I rub my eyes with the heel of

my hands. I don't want to feel this way anymore. The anxiety, the fear, all the feels. And I feel. I feel it all.

"Willow, I can only speak from experience. Harlow didn't choose me. That was rejection at its finest. But I didn't give up and I know I'm the last person who you would want to take advice from but we have no idea where the path will take us. It's okay to be afraid, but I think I'd feel a helluva lost worse if I didn't let the person I loved know that I loved them. I think that's more fearful. Am I making sense?"

Everything that Cruz says I let sink in like a sponge. He's right about everything. He's lived through a lot and, oh God, I can't believe I'm admitting to this, but he's someone to be admired. He never gave up hope and when he found love, he didn't give up on it. Cruz and I are a lot alike. We didn't really recognize certain feelings we had. They were all new to us but people changed us. Harlow changed him, and Max changed me. Max.

He knocked down my walls. He made me take off my armor. That's how I know I love him.

"What do I do if he doesn't feel the same? How do I handle it?"

Cruz shrugs. "I can't give you that answer. Everyone deals with rejection differently. I think you'll know what to do. But you have to take that chance, Willow."

I rise off the bed and look out the door where my balcony is. The water off the bay is so calm today. So soothing just to look at. My stomach, not so much. But I have to have some kind of faith. I have to take some kind of chance. Maybe it's just time for me to grow the fuck up.

"I never thought I'd start to need him until he wasn't here. I never thought it would be him that I wanted." I turn to Cruz and let out a small chuckle.

"Max of all people, right? Oh, the irony of it all. How weird, right?"

Cruz shakes his head and motions a hand between us. "Nah, I think this is weird. You and me, talking all deep. Now that's weird."

Cruz gets up and begins to make his way to the door. Before he leaves I need to break down a few more of the bricks of the wall.

"Where did you tell everyone you were going when you left the beach?"

"To lift."

"Oh, Lord. Why am I not surprised?" I smile.

"Hey, Dickcop." He turns around to look at me and I purse my lips.

"Thanks… for everything."

"You're welcome."

My phone rings and it's my mom. I hold up a finger for Cruz to wait a second because I want to go back down to the beach with him and apologize to Harlow for spazzing.

"Hi. Mother. How are you?"

She's crying. I can't understand what she's saying.

"Mom, calm down."

"Baby, it's Daddy. Oh God, Willow. Oh God."

"Daddy?"

CHAPTER 12

Needed
Max~

She wakes me from my sleep. She tells me her
dad is dead. She tells me she needs me through
her sobs and tears. There's no hesitation after her
call. I knew I needed to get to her. Whatever it
took. I'd take the first flight out to reach her. We
were already on the bus to Vermont. I had to wait
till we got there to grab a flight. When I called
Mr. Carpenter to tell him of Bill Taylor's death, he
told me he'd have a private plane waiting for me
at Burlington's airport to take me to where I was
needed. They would figure something out for the
festival we were supposed to be playing at. The
show wasn't for three more days so he told me not
to worry. I didn't even bat an eyelash about
missing the tour or disappointing anyone. I just
knew I couldn't disappoint her.

Willow needed me.

CHAPTER 13

Goodbyes and the Temporary Fix
Willow~

Pulmonary embolism. That's what killed my
daddy. Mother found him in their dressing room
before they left for work. He collapsed. He was
unresponsive when she tried to give him CPR.
She called the ambulance. When the EMTs got
there, she watched them work on him. She
watched them as they tried to save him. My
mother drove in the ambulance with him, holding
his hand while they did everything they could to
bring him back. She was alone when she told him
over and over again to hold on even though she
knew he was already gone. She was alone when
they pronounced him dead at the hospital.

I wasn't there for her, I wasn't with her. I
didn't hold her hand when she went through all of
it. She didn't get a chance to say goodbye. I didn't
get a chance to say goodbye.

I will never talk to my daddy again.

When I got the call, Cruz was there. I fell to

the floor when my mother said he was gone. He ran to the beach to get everyone. We all got in the car and Cruz broke every traffic law in the state of New Jersey in order to get me from Sandy Cove to Princeton. Porter just wrapped me up in his arms on the ride there and I just sobbed onto his chest. I didn't feel like I had any more tears to shed until I arrived at my house. A sea of cars were already parked along the length of my parents' driveway. When I walked in and went and found my mother, well the rest — except for us holding each other — is a blur. A stream of visitors came in and out that day. I just sat by my mother. I finally held her hand. I feel guilty that I wasn't there to hold it when she had to go through everything she went through. It's eating at me and I know it's not my fault. I know there was no way to know he was going to die and she was going to be the one who found him. But his death — the signs were there, we just didn't know. We thought it was just fatigue from working so very hard.

The dry and constant cough, the tiredness, the lightheadedness. All the things my mother told him to go get checked out. But there was never any time. He didn't make the time for himself. He was too busy making the time for other people. And when I say that, I say it because I mean mostly time for my mother and me.

How could I have not known?

I'm being strong for my mother. I'm the beacon of strength for her. I have to be. But it's natural for me to be this way.

I'm all she has now.

My friends are all here. The Hannums are here. Porter's parents. All of my parents' friends and Dad's colleagues are here. I always knew my parents were surrounded by so many people who loved and cared for them, but this outpouring is overwhelming. Do you know how many hands I have shaken or cheeks I have kissed in the last day and a half? Countless. The number is countless.

My '*thank you for coming*' speech has become colorless. Humdrum. The same old, same old. I'm almost like a robot. I take a hand or someone goes in to kiss my cheek and the unvaried speech is spoken immediately afterwards. It's appreciated. I couldn't be more impressed by the people who loved my daddy so much. I don't cry. My smile remains tight until the one person I need so much walks through the door — my dignified reserve flies out the door. All I could do was run to him and throw my arms around his neck and sob.

Max was here.

When he arrived, the gang and I were sitting out back by my parents' pool. I needed air. I sat next to Harlow and Thea on one of the oversized loungers and even though I wasn't facing the door to the yard's entrance, I sensed he was there.

When I cried in his arms, he just stroked my hair and hushed me gently in my ear, soothing me. He spoke no words. He only held me and I never felt so safe in my life.

I also never felt so afraid.

The funeral arrangements have already been

made. The church is booked, the flowers have all been ordered. I did it all with the help of my aunt Addy. I've been running on empty. I haven't been able to stop and think about anything. The visitors, the arrangements, some paperwork I needed to help my mother with, all of it has been consuming me so much so that I haven't had a chance to comprehend it all.

Tonight my mother took something her doctor prescribed for her in order to help her sleep. That was all my doing. I knew she hadn't slept really since it all happened. You could see it in her eyes. They were so dark and despondent. Dark circles surrounded them. She wasn't eating. She wasn't showering. She wasn't functioning. This was not my mother. And all with good reason. So I made the executive decision to call her doctor and have something prescribed for her. Just to take the edge off and let her rest. She needed to rest. She needed time.

After all the day's visitors left, I tuck my mother in for the night after she took one of the pills.

My friends are still here and they have been all day and night. They didn't want to leave me. I'm grateful for that.

After a few subconscious yawns from Harlow, Cruz decides it's time for them to go. I get a kiss on the cheek from Harlow and a pat on my shoulder from Cruz. I don't react or move to their exit. I can't. Thea and Craw follow reenacting what Harlow and Cruz do. Max is staying at Porter's so they both hang around for a bit longer.

I'm quiet and tired. There's not much to say. Porter asks Max a few questions about the tour. But I know it's all small talk. Porter tries to get me to engage in a conversation but I feel indifferent. Porter is playing the protective cousin/brother role. He hasn't left my side. I'm thankful.

All I can do is sit out here by the pool, under the pale moonlight and count the stars. Porter and Max have a conversation and I don't know what they're talking about or do I care. They're just voices that are taking up residence temporarily in my mind so I can't think about what's going to happen in a day. The day I bury my dad. I stare out into the endless sky and wonder if he's up there, looking down on me. Is there a heaven and are we in hell? The living. Are we the ones? Even in this August heat, I feel a chill. I shiver. Max comes behind me and drapes a pool towel over my shoulders. I'm blanketed in a bit of warmth not only from the towel but from his smile. It goes through my soul. I go back to gazing at the sky and Porter gets up to go.

"It's getting late. Wills, you should get some rest. Tomorrow is going to be a long day, honey."

I shake my head adamantly. "I'm not tired, Porter." He accepts my answer without any interrogation but with just a kiss on my forehead. I hear him ask Max if he's coming and Max tells him quietly that he's going to stick around for a bit. Porter says something else to Max, not sure I fully make out what he said to Max but I think they think I can't hear them talk about me.

Max shoves me in the rib with his elbow as I lay on the lounge.

"Scooch."

I don't look at him, I just do it. He wraps an arm around my shoulders and brings me in closer to his body. He sighs when I snuggle in.

"So what are we looking at? Constellations? Who's out tonight?" He makes a tsk sound with his mouth.

"Well, let's see. Ahh, I see my favorite I think. Orion. He's the coolest."

I stay silent. His voice now filtering through my head, taking up the much needed space so I don't have to think.

"They call him the great hunter. The story behind Orion is that he was so gigantic — so tall — that he could make his way through any sea. He was so strong. Did you know he fell in love with the Greek princess, Aurora?" I shake my head no slightly.

"She was the goddess of dawn. They fell in love and everything in their life was simplistic until he was stung by a scorpion and he fell sick and died. Aurora was heartbroken by his loss but in order to honor him, she made it so he rises in the East and the scorpion, his enemy, sets in the West. Now that's commitment."

I choke back a repressed sob.

"I didn't get a chance to say goodbye. I didn't tell him I loved him. I'll never tell him I love him again, Max."

Max kisses my temple and the warmth from his lips brings me a moment of peace.

"Love doesn't die when we do, Willow. It goes on and on for eternity. Love is eternal. Love never ends and he knew how much you loved him. He was the kind of man who just knew you did. He didn't need to hear it everyday."

Love never ends. I know what he's saying. My heart constricts in my chest because I love him and the way we lie here I can't help but to think if he is my eternal love like my parents had.

I raise my head and my eyes meet his. I hover my lips over his and I see the stars in his eyes and I kiss him. Not because of anything else but because I need to feel something. I need to feel him.

My lips claim his and he responds by kissing me back. It's not our typical kiss where it's fierce and full of lust. This kiss is tender and meaningful. I'm not sure what it means when he cradles my face and runs a tender thumb across my cheeks as he kisses me. The soft sounds that are released from him make my heart pang against my ribs. He rolls my body so I'm flush against the back of the lounge chair and deepens the kiss with his soulful lips and his warm body. My hands grasp the back of his shirt and I hold on for dear life. My eyes are closed so tightly I no longer need to look up at the night sky to see stars. I see them behind my lids.

There's something in this kiss. This isn't an ordinary Max kiss. This is him trying to rescue me from my sadness.

He pulls away from me and stands up after a few more moments. I lie here, breathless. He extends his hand for me to take.

I do and I stand. When I do he gently places his free hand on my cheek and runs a finger across my brow.

"Come on," he tells me.

"What are you doing?" My question is delayed.

"Making you forget if only for tonight."

CHAPTER 14

The Cowardly Lion Has Nothing On Me
Max~

With her feet dragging along behind me, I ask her where her room is. She mumbles, "This way" and "turn left" or "turn right past the kitchen." This place is huge. It's like a maze and her words are almost incoherent when she tells me where to go.

Her posture is saggy, her neck is bent downwards. It's so not like this woman to look this way. Her stature is usually so pristine. She carries herself like no other woman I have ever known. So smart-mouthed but demure at the same time. So beautiful and smart. She's the Molotov cocktail and I'm the receiver.

When we reach the bottom of the steps, Willow breaks from my hand and falls to the bottom step as soon as her feet touch the first.

She sits with her head in her lap and her body begins to quiver. She sobs into her hands. Seeing her in pain is wreaking havoc on my emotions. Fuck.

I sit next to her. I don't touch her. I just let her cry it out until she's ready to speak.

"She'll never see him again. She won't be able to touch him or to laugh with him. They won't hold hands ever again or dance in the kitchen to some old song on the sound system." I wipe the tears from her face.

She stutters as she speaks. Every word is strangled through her tears.

"She'll never kiss him again. She'll never tell him she loves him. I don't... I just don't know how she's going to be able to pull it off. How will she be able to do that, Max? How will she be able to bear it?"

I ease her head onto my shoulder and speak calmly to her.

"I'm hearing so much about how your mom is going to feel and I know how she's going to feel. She's going to be hurting like a motherfucker, but I want to know how you're going to feel. Has anyone asked you that question, Willow? I know they've asked how you are. I know people have told you they're sorry but have they asked you how you'll feel when all this is over? When all the food is put away and all the friends and family come by less and less as time passes. That's my question to you, Willow. What about you?"

She raises her head from my shoulder and looks at me with the saddest eyes I've ever seen anyone have.

"I... I'm going to miss him everyday of my life and I can't imagine him not being here for all the good stuff that's going to happen in my life.

I've always wanted good stuff to happen, but now I don't. Is that wrong?"

I shake my head. "Not now it's not because I think this is all too fresh for you to deal with. But you're going to have to move on and experience life because knowing your dad, if he heard you talk this way, he would never allow it."

Poor girl wipes her snotty nose on my shirt, but I don't care.

"Willow, death is a part of life. The dead want us to go on living because we are a part of the ones who are gone. They want us to live and be happy. You were your dad's bright and shining star. You always will be even if he's not here."

She sniffs a few times. "Will I ever feel the same?"

"Probably not, but I'm pretty sure you're not supposed to. I think it comes with the territory." I'm being honest with her. If I can't be honest with the one person in the entire world who demonstrates it so boldly, then who am I not to tell her the same.

She lets out a sigh and her head returns to my shoulder. After a minute or two, I swoop her up from under her long legs and carry her up the two flights of steps in the grandiose home. Even though she's taller than I am, I still have the strength to carry her because she seems so small and fragile. Inside and out.

She directs me to her bedroom and I go to her bed and lie her down in the middle of it. She's stopped crying and I do what I can to make her forget her pain.

I lie my body on top of hers and gaze at her undying beauty. She stills my heart but as soon as our lips meet, the beat of my heart begins to accelerate. The deeper I kiss her, I begin to shiver above her. My fingers gently flex into her hair. I massage her scalp with the tips. My tongue tangos with hers but it's slow and deliberate. I break our kiss and raise myself onto my knees straddling her. I take the hem of my shirt and raise it above my head. I return my lips to hers and I feel the need to feel her skin against mine. I pull away and mimic the same move on her as I had just done. Her shirt comes off with ease and I reach behind her to release the clasps on her bra. I unhook it and slide it down her soft, feminine shoulders. Her breasts are on display. The only light that shines through Willow's two large bedroom windows is the fantastic and magical moonlight. Her pink nipples stand at attention and I dip my head to take one at a time in my mouth. She moans lightly and runs her hand over my shortened hair. She holds my head in her hands as I run my tongue across the budded skin. I kiss the middle of her chest, up towards her long neck. I place gentle kisses all over it until I reach her lips again. A whimper rolls out of her mouth as I reach my hand between her legs to feel the softness that I've become familiar with. I rub her in small circles and she pulls her lips to mine to let out a breath that is so sexy and so needy I want to weep. Her wetness coats my fingers and as I insert one inside her, I can feel her insides tighten but the rest of her body is relaxed. I watch her face as

I add another finger and watch her as she falls under a spell. I increase my speed and I study her face. Every curve, the way her eyelashes curl up so high that they touch the top of her lids. Her pouty lips that I can't leave alone. I need to feel them on mine. I need to feel the heat of her mouth and the touch of her hands.

When I think I've brought her to her breaking point and that glorious moment when I get to see this face come undone beneath me just from my fingers, she stills my hand.

"No, please. Not like this. I need more from you. I need all of you." Her vulnerability is shown and she wants the intimacy of all of this. I will give her more. I'll give her all of me right now. It's what she needs. It's what I *want* to give her.

When I withdraw my fingers from her I don't hesitate. I pull off her panties. Sliding them down inch by inch over her thin, golden thighs, she wiggles a bit and her breathing becomes rapid. So is mine as I look down after I have completed my task and see this woman, naked and gorgeous before me. Her hair is splayed across the soft, billowy pillows and as I take off my shorts and kneel before her in my naked glory, I think about when I had to take a course on Shakespeare in college and the one quote that resonates in my brain.

For every beauty there is an eye somewhere to see it. For every truth there is an ear somewhere to hear it. For every love there is a heart somewhere to receive it.

And right now this woman is beauty and she is

pain. She was there for me at a time when I needed someone to be there for me. She was there when my dad told me I was nothing, but Willow believed I was and am something. Tonight, I need to be there for her in any way she needs me. My eye is here to see it. To see her truth and to see her pain. I see a woman in desperate need to forget the pain in her heart and if me making love to her is what she needs, I will do this. I don't have to. Sex is not what this is about. This is being needed and wanted. For both of us.

I slide on the condom I had in my shorts pocket and I climb towards her on the bed. My tip is placed at her entrance and I stop myself as I look down at her troubled face. It's a mixture of emotions. Wanton and heartache. The wanton part I can take care of, her heart... that needs to heal on its own.

She goes to reach for my dick and I stop her.

"No, babe. Tonight this is about you."

A lone tear drifts down her cheek and her voice cracks. "You... you don't need to do this, Max. I can't... I won't let you..." I remove her hand from my cock and enter her without her permission and in unison we both let out an exaggerated breath. For fuck's sake she feels so good. I lower my head as I ease into her a bit more and roll my hips and kiss her.

"What won't you let me do, Willow?" My voice is gravelly and a bit strangled because I'm inside her and she fits me like a glove. The euphoria sets in.

Paradise.

The tips of our noses touch and I wipe the single tear she's shed away. With my eyes never leaving hers, I see so much conflict in them and I don't want her to feel like that.

"I won't let you rescue me. I don't need to be rescued." She sobs out as I go in deeper.

Willow moans and her eyes roll back in her head and she stretches her long neck back exposing so much skin to me that I need to taste it. I need my lips and my tongue to taste this creature.

So I do.

I whisper in her ear, "I'm not here to do that, Willow. You don't need rescuing. You never have."

Her mouth finds mine and as I fuck her, slowly bringing her up to the highest of places, it feels like her soul moves through me. The feel of her body against mine. The slickness from the heat that surrounds us. I don't want this to end. This speck in time. This moment where it's just Willow and me. We're one. And as she comes around me and I follow her, falling down farther and farther, saying my name over and over again… I'm the one who becomes scared.

I collapse on her and bury my head in her neck and she soothingly strokes the skin on my back. I shut my eyes so damn tight it hurts. Her legs relax and fall from being wrapped around my waist, but at no point do either of us move. It's just the sounds of our breathing and the scent of us in the air.

I turn my head from the pillow and kiss her

cheek with tenderness.

"Are you okay?"

She nods. I roll off of her sated body and sit on the edge of the bed and I need a moment to catch my breath or still my heart or something because right now I'm dizzy and can't think straight. I've never experienced anything so intimate in my life and I'm fucking terrified of what that all was. I need to go.

As I lean up on my hands to rise off the bed, I feel her hand on my arm, stilling me from my movement.

I look down at her hand touching my skin and I close my eyes. Her touch doesn't singe but brings my skin to life. Every inch of flesh awakens.

Motherfucker.

"Stay. Please."

I need to run, but how can I say no. I can't. As afraid and confused as I am with what I just felt, I can't say no when I look at this woman. The anguish on her face is only part of the reason why I want to stay and half the reason I want to run.

After disposing of the condom, I crawl beneath the sheets and pull her from across the bed so her back is against my chest. I feel her breath. I smell her hair. I relish in the touch of her hand as she brings it around to tuck under her breasts.

"I'm so tired, Max. I'm so fucking tired." She yawns and I stroke her long, wavy hair.

"Sleep, babe. Everything will be okay. Sleep."

After a few minutes and the constant running

of thoughts in my head, Willow's breathing changes. It grows deeper and every once in a while her body involuntarily shudders and she lets out a sad moan that squeezes my heart.

I hush her. "Shh… you're okay. I'm here, Willow. I'm here."

She grabs my hand a little tighter, and then she relaxes.

"Max… Max…" I think she's dreaming now when she calls out my name so faintly but with a sound of desperation behind it.

"I'm here, Wills."

Lazily, she says four words that change it all. That change me. That change us.

"I love you, Max."

Four words. Four fucking words.

I check to see that she's fast asleep and find this as my opportunity to slip my arm out from under her. I do it gently and she just snuggles into her pillows a bit more. I put on my clothes but not my shoes. After I'm dressed, I stand over the bed and stare at her. Willow Taylor scares the shit out of me. Maybe she said the four words in her slumber and she doesn't mean it. But what we just shared — the magnetic force we just encountered — I can't be wrong because she said the words I want to tell her, but I know it would just be a recipe for disaster. We are the square peg and the round hole. Do we fit? Probably not. So why do I burn for this woman in my heart and in my soul. I have been in lust, I've never been in love and the two shall never mean the same.

So what do I do? I run. Far, far away like a

coward. I take another look at this amazing creature. My chest hurts.

I sneak out of her room and go to the pool area and call a cab.

"Yeah, I need a cab. 1027 Hawthorne Lane. Now, please."

I wait about fifteen minutes. My already worn shoes now have more holes in them because I haven't stopped pacing and I vomited once from nerves. Or because I'm such a fucking coward. I'm not like my father. At least he told me how he felt.

Love scares me. I'm so fucking scared. Why? Why am I? It's just a girl. Why be afraid? I have no explanation as I mentally debate my thoughts. But right now I can't handle it and Willow's grief is so great right now that *she* may not have even meant it.

The cab pulls up and I open the back door. I have nothing to bring with me. I only packed a small bag and I'm not going to Porter's to get it. I'll buy another fucking toothbrush.

"Where to?" the driver asks.

"The nearest airport."

CHAPTER 15

Max Vincent Who?
Willow~

This is the hardest day of my life. My daddy is gone and my life will never be the same. Make that I *will* never be the same.

He was my knight in shining armor. My hero. The first man I ever loved.

He's gone. How will I live my life without him?

Death just sucks.

I held onto my mother's hand as we made our way down the aisle of the church. The gray casket was in front of us being carried by several pallbearers. My uncle Paul, my mother's brother, my dad's best friend from when he was a kid, and Porter. I felt my mother's knees go weak with every step we took. For her being such a small woman, the weight of her grief was so large. I play with the compass necklace my parents gave me a few months ago and I remember my dad telling me it was a reminder so I would never lose my way.

I'm so afraid that I am.

The funeral was beautiful. The flowers were gorgeous, even though I hated the smell of them. Funeral flowers are unlike the type of flowers you have delivered to your home for a special occasion. They smell. Bad. They remind me of death. I guess that's why I hate them.

A choir sang his favorite hymns at the church. The sun shined through the stained glass windows and when it did it was as though a thousand rainbows were cast upon us. I like to think that was my dad. His light. His way of telling me, "It's okay, princess. Everything will be okay."

Porter did the eulogy for my dad. He spoke of his love for traveling. His love of music and how my mother was his high school sweetheart. He talked some about me and how proud he was of all my accomplishments. In the end, Porter told the church that *I* was his biggest accomplishment.

That's when I lost it. I did a pretty good job of keeping it together for my mother up until that point.

The burial — if I thought I lost it at church — this was nothing compared to when they lowered my father into the ground. I didn't know whether to throw up or run away. The ache was too much. I had this pain deep in my chest and it felt like an elephant was crushing me. I couldn't breathe at the priest's final words. Harlow was on one side of me holding my elbow and my hand and I was doing the same for my mother on the other. I placed a single rose on top of the casket before it was lowered. My hands trembled, my knees quaked. I don't know how I did it. I don't understand why I had to do it. Why was he gone? Why was my daddy gone?

Everyone I knew in the world was there. They were there to honor my daddy and were there for my mother and me. All my friends were there for me.

Except for one person.

I hired a caterer for a luncheon back at my parents' house after the funeral. It's quiet even with a hundred people here. I can't eat. Looking at food makes me want to puke. I may have eaten a half of a bagel since he died.

Harlow brings me a plate of food to eat as we sit out here by the pool. It's only the second time I've left my mother's side but she told me to go be with my friends. My aunt Addy was taking care of her.

"I don't want to eat, Harlow."

She makes a disapproving face at me.

"When's the last time you ate?"

"No clue."

She shakes her head at me and hands Porter the full plate of food because he'd never turn down seconds. He looks up at Harlow with a full mouth of food and asks, "Where's Cruz?"

She motions to the other side of the pool and I look to see him on the phone being very animated while on the phone.

She shrugs. "Must be something with his mother."

Craw takes out a cigarette, not lighting it
because he quit but when he's nervous he just
holds it in his mouth.

"It's always something with that crack head.
He must be talking to Tony about her."

Harlow sits next to me and looks at Cruz
again, who glances over to where we are and
points in our direction. When he realizes we see
him, his eyes go wide and he turns his back to us.

Thea purses her lips together and shakes her
head. "I'm not so sure he's talking to Tony. Why
would he point over here if he was talking to
Rae?"

I don't say a word but I see Cruz storm over to
us. He looks angrier than I've ever seen him. He
grabs a glass of some kind of alcohol off of a tray
from a server and downs it even before he reaches
us.

Harlow holds on to his arm as he seethes.

"Baby, take it easy. We have to drive back to
Sandy Cove tomorrow. What's wrong with you?"

Cruz bites his lip and his eyes go to mine. I
know he was talking to Max. I'm not stupid.

He grabs Harlow's head and kisses her gently
on it. "Nothing, Turnip. I'm fine. Everything's
fine."

I laugh. I let out such a hearty laugh that my
friends stare at me — looking quite scared
because I sound like the Joker from Batman. The
more I laugh, the faster the tears come out. My
head hangs back and I can feel the mascara burn
my eyes and drift down my face.

When I'm done with my freak-out moment I

motion to Cruz.

"Go ahead. Tell them. Let's address it now. I don't fucking care anymore. If I ever see him again it would be too soon."

So here are four sets of eyes traveling between Cruz and me. Harlow looks up at Cruz in a panic.

"What. Tell us what? What's going on? You guys are scaring me."

Cruz still stays silent.

I quietly tell him, "Go ahead."

He lets out such a rush of air from his lungs and pulls at his hair that it even takes me aback.

"Max is a fucking asshole," he answers.

I smile slightly. "And why is he a fucking asshole, Cruz? Tell the class." I put on my teacher voice.

"Because he's not here."

"And why isn't he here, Cruz?"

"Willow," he says through clenched teeth, not wanting to be a part of my admission.

"Cruz," I say in a sing-song tune.

Our back and forth causes Porter to yell out, "Knock it off, you two. What in the bloody hell is going on? I know he's not here but honestly I didn't even realize it until after the burial."

"I scared Max away," I say it like I say any other sentence. With no hesitation or consideration.

Confusion blankets everyone's faces.

"But why?" Harlow asks.

"You want the whole story or the Cliff's Notes version?" My smart mouth has returned.

No one answers. They are just fixated on my

face. I dig my lady balls out and don't hold anything back. These people are my family in every sense of the word. I can't keep this from them.

"Last night after we had sex I told him that I loved him. I think he thought I said it in my sleep, but I was awake, barely, but I was."

Porter drops his plate of food on the patio. The contents of Thea's drink slowly pours out of her cup but the cup is still attached to her hand. Craw's cigarette drops from his lips, and Harlow's eye glaze over. And Cruz just shakes his head. I watch it play out like a scene from a bad movie.

"I must have freaked him out because when I woke up he was gone. He didn't show up today — of all days — and we've been having sex with each other since you two got engaged. Well, technically that was the first night we did. We then sabotaged every chance we had of hooking up with other people so we decided to make a pact to only have sex with each other because we are really, really good at it. I fell in love with the little fucker. Oh, and by the way, that cat that was always hanging outside our houses at the beach, yeah… wasn't a cat."

I point to myself and Porter stands up and shouts, "I knew it. I fucking knew it! No cats make those kinds of noises." Then his face drops and he looks punch-drunk.

"Wait, wait, wait… a damn minute. You've been having… um."

I can tell why Porter can't say it. It's because

his little cousin is banging one of his best friends.

"It's sex, Porter. We are all grown-ups. You can say the word."

"Ugh. Fine. Okay. Sex. You and Max… and whatever. I don't need the play by play. But you fell in love with him?"

"Yes." I admit it out loud and I still can't believe I did. I'm usually the one who holds the emotions in but today my emotions are served to everyone on a silver platter. They can eat it up or spit it out. Can't turn back now.

Craw rests his elbows on his knees and rocks back and forth. "I just… you and Max. And you love him and you two hate each other. And you guys are having sex. You and Max. And sex." He pops the unlit cigarette back into his mouth looking quite disturbed by the whole thing.

Harlow smacks Cruz's arm several times with her purse like an old lady trying to warn of a mugger.

"And you knew this whole time. You shit. She's my best friend. How could you have not told me? What's wrong with you?" Then her eyes become very clear. Very, very clear.

"You two? Of all people? How did *my* fiancé, with whom you despise, know that my best friend was sleeping with… with his best friend and you obviously confided in him and… and you hate each other and you told him and you didn't tell me… and… and you hate each other." The girl talks a mile a minute and I see the distress in her face.

Cruz turns Harlow towards him and rubs her

arms up and down.

"Turnip, it's not what you think. I figured it out. I approached Willow about it and coaxed it out of her." He looks around at everyone.

"And I can't believe none of you saw it. Are you all blind? Didn't you all notice the times where both of them were M.I.A. and we were all looking for them... at the same time? The noises late at night? Har and I aren't that loud when we do it. My girl is a delicate flower when I bang her."

Craw covers his ears. "I do not hear this. I'm not hearing this."

Cruz gets in Craw's face, nose to nose. Future brother-in-laws.

"Grow up, asshole. I'm marrying your sister. We have sex. Lots of it. And we're going to have it with each other for the rest of our lives, so fucking deal."

Craw shuts up. Real quick.

I need to stop all of this because it's going south real quick and I don't want Harlow and Cruz getting into a fight over this.

"Har, I made him promise. I started to have feelings for Max and Cruz caught on to the way I was feeling. He guessed. I'm sorry I kept it from all of you. I don't know why we did it. I don't know why we had to keep it a secret. I think it was just exciting and thrilling and... none of it matters anymore. None of it because if you all thought I hated him before, you have no idea what I feel for him now."

I won't cry. I won't allow myself to shed a tear

over that asshole. I'm now stone.

Thea comes over and hugs me. My arms don't hug her back. I don't have the strength and I know it may seem bitchy but I don't need to be comforted. There's no comforting me today.

"I don't want to talk about any of it anymore. I want to forget him. I never want to see him again. I'm going back with you guys tomorrow to get my stuff and then I'm coming home to be with my mom. I won't be going back to Sandy Cove." I take Thea's hands off of me gently and stand up.

"I'm going to bed."

Harlow starts to cry.

"But it's only four-thirty, Willow. I don't want you to be alone. I'll come with you."

I hold my hand out to stop her.

"I love you, Harlow, but no. I need to be by myself. I haven't slept in days. I'll be ready in the morning to go back to Sandy Cove. Please make sure my mom has everything she needs and can you make sure the staff takes care of all the clean up? Can you do that for me, Harlow?" I speak almost robotic. My eyes are so heavy and my limbs feel the same way.

She nods through her tears.

Cruz calls to me as I begin to shuffle away from all of them.

"Willow, I'm sorry. I'm so sorry… for everything." He looks so pained.

I force a smile on my face and not because I don't appreciate his sentiment.

"You're not the one who has to be sorry, Cruz."

And he's not. Max doesn't really have to be sorry either. An 'I'm sorry' from him wouldn't do anything anyway. It wouldn't mean anything to me. It's just a word. A word that wouldn't make a difference no matter if he is or isn't.

My heart was already broken. But what Max Vincent did to me today — whatever pieces of my heart were still together possibly because of him — are now fractured with no hope for recovery.

CHAPTER 16

I Never Saw Myself As A Fuck Up Until Now
Max~

I fucked up. No one has to enlighten me on the subject. I did. I know I did. Yeah, I left her that night. And why? Because I'm fucking scared. I'm scared to death. When I look back on my life and think about all the crazy, fucked up shit I've been through and seen: my mom being practically nonexistent, her moving away and starting a new life with a wealthy man while my dad scraped pennies together to keep his garage open and make sure I had everything in life I needed. We almost lost our house twice during the recession and then to find all of it didn't matter anyway because he could really give a shit about me. Albeit, all of that is scary, but when someone tells you — particularly a girl — that they love you, that's the brain scrambler. The words that mix your brain up so bad they make you mush.

I can't wrap around why she would even entertain the thoughts of loving me. Comparing myself to her, I just can't do it. Smart, beautiful, funny, full of motherfucking sass, and money. The girl has it coming out of her ears. What could she possibly see in me?

I ran. I ran so far. I left her in the middle of the night like a fucking pussy. I had my very first, full-blown panic attack. I couldn't get to the airport fast enough. And what did I do when I got there? I sat there. In an empty airport at four a.m. I couldn't call Mr. Carpenter and ask for the private jet again. That would have gone over real well. "Oh, hi, Mr. Carpenter. Yeah, listen I just got done making love to a beautiful woman and she told me she loved me and I'm as scared as a three-year-old boy seeing a clown for the first time. And oh, by the way, I'm pretty sure your daughter wants to screw my brains out so can I use your jet to make a grand escape?" Sounds real good, right? That's not what happened. I waited till I got a flight into Burlington so I could do this stupid festival in Vermont then I'd be back in Sandy Cove, except going back to Sandy Cove just means I'll see Willow. Might as well say goodbye to my balls now. Maybe if she starts talking to me again I could talk her into sterilization. That has to be a safer alternative to castration of the testes, right?

I took the first flight there. When I got back on the bus the guys in the band could tell something wasn't right but never asked. I think they saw the visible anguish on my face. I didn't want to do a

276

sound check. I didn't want to go through the set. All I wanted to do was lie in my bunk on the tour bus and sleep — but sleep wouldn't grant me a reprieve. Sleep. I was undeserving of sleep. I kept watch on the clock knowing that it would be the time that Willow would be leaving for the church. Then the time came where the funeral procession would begin. She would walk into the church behind her father's casket and hold her mother's hand. Then I looked at my watch again and saw that it was most likely the time when she was probably at the cemetery. Then I got the call.

Cruz.

The conversation did not start off on a high note. He started it off with, "Where are you, you little fucker?" I didn't know he was going to call. He didn't know about Willow and me. So I thought.

He told me he's known for weeks and weeks about us. Willow told him without her actually coming out to tell him. He guessed it. And I guess we weren't as smooth as we thought we were.

"You need to be here, Max. You need to be here." That's what he kept repeating until I told him to mind his own business. I couldn't face it — the shame. The knife I stuck in her and twisted. He said I was a disappointment. That, by far, is the worst thing he could have said to me. He could have called me every cuss word in the book and they would just be an addition to his vast vocabulary. But to say the word disappointment stings. I'll admit it.

He hung up on me when I had nothing to say

to him except to fuck off.

I did the goddamn sound check and I went over the stupid set. I tuned up my guitar and made sure the stupid amps worked. I played the stupid show that night. The weather was just awful. The thunder rang out above the music and the rain poured down in buckets and they finally called the show after the stupid fans started sliding in the mud in the stupid fields where the festival was and someone cracked their head open. I didn't sleep that night. Even after a bottle of whiskey and a shower. I ignore another call from Cruz and one from Porter. I just lie in my bunk all night. I watch the hours go by in a flash. I toss and turn and get up a few times and go outside the bus. The summer air up north is a lot cooler than what I'm used to. I just stared at the night sky and thought about what she was doing and how much she must hate me. God, she must hate me. I hated me.

Two days have gone by. Two days too long. I haven't eaten. I can't sleep. My fuse is short. I'm sure sympathy is not on my side. All I've thought about was how I could do something like that. I'm ashamed. For the first time in my life, I'm ashamed of myself. Why did I do it? Why?

'Cause I'm a fucking coward.

Alex, my bandmate, comes to my bunk and rips open the curtain.

"Yo, someone's here to see you."

"Who is it?" I ask with a groan.

He shrugs. "That girl from the fourth of July

party."

Cora. Who else would he be talking about? She's called at least three times and I haven't returned a single call. And it's certainly not Willow. The only reason she'd be here is to commit murder.

"We're going into town. Be back later." I wave off Alex and rub my weary eyes and hop off my bunk. When I make my way out to the living room of the tour bus I discover it's not Cora.

"Harlow?"

"Hello, Max."

She sits on one of the leather sofas with her legs crossed and her hands sprawled out on the back of the sofa. She taps her fingers simultaneously and it's not that she has daggers in her eyes for me, they're just not warm either.

I stutter. "I don't... what... why are you here?"

She sits up, uncrosses her legs and stands. She leans in and kisses me on the cheek, sympathetically.

I close my eyes, feeling like I don't deserve this kind of affection from her, from anyone for that matter. When she pulls away she gives me the tiniest of smiles.

"I'm here because you're my friend and I know you need a friend right now. Plus, if I'd sent my larger-than-life fiancé, he'd put you in the hospital. So I'm here on my own free will." She winks at me. "Oh, and to save you from a bloody demise."

Even though Cruz has a strong... well, let's just call it a distaste for Willow, I know he also has a soft spot for damsels in distress so to speak and he's known for a while about Willow and me. So through the yelling he did to me over the phone about me missing the funeral, I know he feels bad for her. He should because I made a prick move. Probably the prickiest move in the entire history of prick moves.

I motion for Harlow to sit back down and I sit across from her. I nervously tap my foot on the floor trying to suppress the anxiety I feel coursing through my body.

"Does he know you're here?"

"Nope. He thinks I'm still in Princeton. We took Willow back to Sandy Cove to get her stuff after the funeral then I drove Willow back home."

"Her stuff?"

Harlow looks sad.

"Yes. She doesn't want to leave her mom so she's staying home the rest of the summer. Besides we start teaching in two weeks."

"Oh." I hang my head. I deserve to hang it as low as it can go.

"I flew here and I'm headed back again in a few hours."

There's silence so I address the big, white elephant in the room.

"I'm guessing you now know about Willow and me then. I knew the big guy couldn't keep it shut after he berated me on the phone."

She shakes her head. "It wasn't him, Max."

My brows meet in the center of my forehead. My words almost a whisper but with question. "Willow?"

"Yes. She gave him permission to spill the beans but he wouldn't really say much, so she did. She told the gang."

I bury my face in my hands and groan.

"Ugh, everyone? Even Porter."

I peer up at her and she lets out a small chuckle. "Yep, even Porter."

I'm not that comfy knowing that Porter knows that his cousin and I were doing it. But it was in the past.

"I should have… we should have told you guys."

"Then why didn't you?" she asks with perplexity.

I shrug, not because I'm trying to be smug but because I feel a bit guilty for hiding it.

"We wanted it to be a secret, I guess. It was the thrill of it, I suppose." A ghost of a smile creeps on my face remembering how it was between us. The excitement. The passion. The longing to be with each other in that way. Then I think how I hurt her and the smile disappears.

"It's complicated… Willow and me. The whole thing, Har."

"So explain it to me."

I look at her dazed. "Explain what?"

She matches my question.

"The complication. What was so complicated about you and Willow?"

I rub my two-day-old stubble and lean my head back on the chair I'm sitting in. I respire. I don't want to talk to Harlow about Willow's and my sex life. It's a little weird talking to her about banging her best friend so I put it all into words that are a little more… gentlemanly.

"Willow and I are oil and water. But in one aspect we mixed and we mixed well. The mixture became mixed… quite frequently. The more we mixed, the more I felt like I needed to mix more with her."

Harlow shuts her eyes and rubs her temples. When she opens them, she looks like she's trying to sort things out in her head. And is a bit aggravated.

"Max, I'm not five. You don't have to use analogies in your explanation. You guys had sex. Lots of it from what I hear. Here, there and everywhere too. I'm getting married, so yes, I have sex as you well know." She air quotes. "I can handle the big words."

I snort. "Yeah, okay. We did it all the time. Everywhere and anywhere. She sort of became my addiction. I've never done drugs but I can imagine something being addictive. She became addictive to me. I couldn't get enough. I'm sorry to be so blunt."

She nods her head and asks me to continue. She listens quite intently.

"Our secret was safe. No one knew. It was that euphoria I think that was most addictive. It was just between us and it was nothing less than… electrifying. Then I was going on tour. She ended it, which I guess made sense. We wouldn't be seeing each other anyway. But Har, can I be honest with you? Like the honest where I think I'm about to bare my soul to you kind of honest?"

Confidently she replies, "That's the only kind *of* honest, Max."

I relax a bit and open the proverbial floodgates.

"The day I was leaving for the tour, when you all were outside waiting to say goodbye to me, I left to go find her because she wasn't with all of you. That's when she broke off our little deal. Which was fine, but then she kissed me. I mean really kissed me, but it felt like a goodbye and I was… I was so fucking sad. It made me so sad. I felt like I was never going to see her again. We promised to email and Skype. We did and there's where my other addiction came into the picture." I stop talking because I feel like such a fool. Why am I saying all of this?

"Go on, Max. It's just me. Judgment free zone where I'm concerned. Okay?" I nod.

"I became addicted to talking with her and telling her about my day and how the show went that I had just done. I looked forward to finding out how her day was. I looked forward to a 'good luck tonight' text from her or to see her on the screen when I finished a show. I counted down the minutes, the seconds even. I *wanted* to see her face. I wanted to hear her voice. At first it was because I think I was a little homesick, but then… I don't know, Harlow, it became something more than that. It was more than the sex thing. I got to know her and, Christ, it's Willow. I mean Willow and me. Can you imagine?" I laugh at that thought. Two people in the universe who couldn't even be in the same room with each other without wanting to rip the others head off.

"Yes, I can imagine. Sometimes, Max, when the oil and the water sit for a while, I think they can mix okay. I don't think right away, but I think in time."

I stand up and pace in front of her. I run my hands rapidly through my hair. The anxiety is tenfold.

"I don't know… with us… we're just so... it's just so complicated.

A beat later — which seems like an eternity — she answers. "So you're telling me that being in love with someone is complicated. Newsflash, Max. I know all about it. First-hand. Love is the most complicated thing in the entire world. So welcome, Max, welcome to the world of love and all of its crazy, mixed up bullshit that's worth so much that you can't live with the thought of *not* having it in your life."

Jump back a minute.

"Who said anything about love?"

She taps the seat beside her. I go and sit next to her reluctantly.

"Max. I am a very good listener. I am also a very good judge of character and at reading people. All the things you just said to me about counting down the seconds before talking to her and how seeing her on your laptop and hearing her voice became addictive but no sex was involved… I'd call that love, buddy."

I shake my head in utter disbelief. She nods her head in total assurance.

"Yes, yes, yes. You are in total slap-me-upside-the-head-I-thought-it-was-Thursday-but-it's-Friday kind of love. Surprising, isn't it?" Harlow looks pretty pleased with herself.

It takes me a millisecond to mull it over. Yes, a millisecond cause for fuck's sake I love her, don't I? I fucking love Willow Taylor. I'm in love with her. I can't live without her. I can't breathe without her and I'm pretty sure I haven't been breathing these last few days. May lightning not strike me dead at this moment because it's the truth. It all makes sense. But then there's the harsh reality.

"I screwed it up."

Her head moves as she contemplates my confession.

"Yes, you screwed up, but I don't think you screwed up the possibility of what could be."

I look at Harlow with such doubt on my face.

"Harlow, when she told me she loved me I was in shock. I think I realized that it was more. I was just afraid to admit it to myself and to her so I took the easy way out which wasn't so easy. She needed me and I bailed. I'm like my mother. She bailed on me. I'm no different." Harlow grabs my hand and holds it.

"Max, you aren't anything like your mom. I don't know everything about what happened between her and your dad but she bailed and that's her cross to bear. Not yours. We make choices in life because we can. We create the destinies we are supposed to be a part of. She created her own and maybe it wasn't the right one, but I believe you can rectify poor choices for the love of others. You just have to put in the effort."

She knows all too well. Cruz thought he was doing Harlow a favor by dumping her when her bitch of a granny told him he was worthless and not good enough for her. But in the end he knew it was the wrong choice and *I* was the one who convinced him to rectify his choice. I did that. I told him truth is love. And my truth is that I love that girl. Willow Taylor is in every song I sing. Every note I play, every word I write in my lyric book. She's everything. She's my music.

Being in love with her — especially her — yeah, I'd call that surprising but I also call it a blessing because, dammit, she loves me too. This is truth. This is love.

"I love her, Harlow."

With her big blue eyes shining at me and her smile a mile wide, she says, "I know you do."

"How do I get her back? How do I convince her to forgive me for doing the shittiest thing on the planet?"

She agrees. "It was pretty shitty. I'll admit that. But you were scared and fear makes us do things without thinking. You weren't thinking, Max. I know Willow and it's not going to be easy — oh no, it's not going to be easy. I mean we are talking about Willow here."

"I'm in for the battle of my life, aren't I?" I look down at my hands. The ones that burn and ache from playing my guitar so fiercely but also the ones that long to touch the skin of a girl who can bring me to my knees in more ways than one.

And now I'm a different kind of scared because what if I'll never be able to touch her again? What if I found the love of my life and forgiving me is the last thing she wants.

Harlow wraps her arms around me in a motherly way. It's unfamiliar to me but I accept it.

"That's why I'm here. To help. Besides, being best friends with Willow Taylor has lots of benefits."

She releases me. Her eyes full of hope for me and I appreciate it.

"Oh, yeah? What kind?"

"The kind where she schemes to get what she wants and doesn't take no for an answer. So I learned a thing or two from her."

My eyes go wide. "You, scheming? Not Harlow Hannum. You're a freaking saint, woman."

She furrows her brows and folds her arms in front of her like a toddler.

"I am not a saint. Take it back." She's totally kidding.

"If you say so."

She uncrosses her arms, looking quite assertive.

"I do."

"So tell me, oh non-saint, how do you plan on helping me convince the woman I love that I'm not a total dick and she needs to be with me because I don't think I can live without her?"

She makes a clicking sound with her mouth and winks at me.

"Oh, don't worry too much. I have a few tricks

up my sleeve."

CHAPTER 17

Oh, Hello Hell
Willow~

Unpacking my stuff from Sandy Cove stings but helping my mom go through all my dad's papers and packing his clothes is just heartwrenching. Everything of his I put into boxes still smells of him even though it's all clean. I can't explain it but my father's scent lingers. I know it's only been a few weeks since his death, but my mother can't bear to go into their dressing room and see all of his things still hanging like he'll walk in the door any minute. I know people will talk about how soon she wanted his things out of there, but it's her business, it's her decision, and if that's what she wants, that's what's going to happen. Fuck everyone else. They don't know what she's going through. Hell, I don't even know what she's going through. My mother can't do it so I man up and I told her I'd do it for her. Aunt Addy and Mrs. Hannum took her away to a winery for a few days. Harlow and Thea offer to help me pack his things up. We start school in two days and they unselfishly decided to forgo time at the beach to be here with me.

"Wills, what suits go in what box?"

I look over my shoulder while I pack up my dad's socks and handkerchiefs.

"The one labeled Suits for Suits."

"What is that exactly?"

"An organization that supplies suits and dress clothing to young men who can't afford to go out and buy those types of clothing for interviews and new jobs. My dad always donated to them."

Harlow looks at me confused. "Wills, these are like two-thousand-dollar suits. Are you sure?"

I nod and a smile creeps on my face knowing that's exactly what my dad would have wanted.

"I'm sure. Just leave the navy blue suit and the black Armani, please. I'm keeping those. They were my favorite." I turn back around to finish what I had started. Thea is putting all of his undergarments in a box for some homeless shelters.

"Hey, when we're done here how about going out for a few drinks?"

I don't want to go anywhere really so I tell Harlow no.

"I need to get this done. I still have lesson plans to do before Tuesday. I don't want to waste any time by going out."

"Willow, you need to get out of here. You can't stay in this house all the time."

"But I don't want to go out, Har. I want to stay here. Don't push me. I'm *fine* with staying here."

She backs off because she knows better.

When everything is packed up — his shoes, his ties, his clothes — I stare at the empty closet and I can't believe it. It's so empty and when my mother comes home I think it's going to be worse for her. I can't cry anymore. No tears can possibly come out of my eyes. I have to keep busy and keep my mind occupied.

For lots of reasons.

As I stand looking at the emptiness that hollows the room, my two best friends come stand beside me and link my hands with theirs.

I allow them to touch me but only for a second. I need to get out of this room and never come back.

It happened exactly how I thought it was going to. My mother sat in her dressing room and cried and cried. I couldn't take it. I hated to see her in such pain. But I knew I couldn't stay in the room. Thank God Aunt Addy was there and she could hold her while she cried. I wasn't trying to be insensitive and Aunt Addy and my mother knew that. I just could not bear to stay in a room that was once filled with him. This whole house is filled with him. Everywhere I look my daddy is here. It hurts so badly. The pictures hanging on the walls. His car keys still hanging on a hook in the kitchen. His wallet still on the butler's pantry counter.

I hate this house. I suddenly can't breathe when I'm in it. Trying to lock myself in my bedroom to prepare for the upcoming school year doesn't help either. But I'm stuck here because I won't leave my mother. I know it seems like I'm a walking contradiction about being here. Harlow has been calling asking me to go shopping with her or out to dinner and I keep telling her I don't want to leave the house, but as I continue to walk around this spacious house — which feels so empty — I want to get out.

But I won't.

I cook all the meals for my mother. I make her bed for her. I do her laundry. I gave Lupe two weeks' vacation fully paid because as depressing as watching my mother in pain, Lupe is right behind her in that department. She breaks down all the time and I'm the one who has to tell her it's okay. I ask my mother every hour on the hour if she needs anything. I've paid all the bills online. I contacted my dad's lawyer. I cancelled all his credit cards. I called the golf course to let them know his membership would no longer be needed. I went to New York for the day to get his personal items from his office.

I haven't left her side except for the day I went to New York and to retrieve my things from the beach house. I was stoic. I wanted no one in the room with me. I needed to pack my shit and go. I couldn't even glance at the other house. I couldn't. Even though I know he wasn't there, I still couldn't look. I tried to push to the back of my mind everything that happened down here this summer. The fun, the beach, the parties. What I didn't want to remember is Max and what happened between us. I looked around my room and thought about the shenanigans that took place here. In the kitchen, the living room, the bathroom and ditto with his house. I can't think about it. I won't allow myself to relish in those memories. It only causes pain.

Mother and I sit at the dining room table and go through all of my dad's legal papers. Insurance, bills that are paid in full, tax items. My dad made sure he took care of us. God bless him. If my mother or I, for that matter, didn't want to work another day in our lives, we wouldn't have to. That's all well and good and I'm pleased my father didn't want us to want for anything. He never did.

I could never do that. I need to continue to do something with my life. I love teaching. I couldn't just sit on some beach somewhere everyday except in the summers. I could never not have a schedule or get up any time I wanted. I couldn't have servants take care of my every need. We always had Lupe to do things around the house but I wasn't waited on hand and foot. Money we always had but my parents never allowed me to take advantage of our good fortune.

Sipping on some tea, my mom announces something that shocks me.

"I want to sell the house, sweetie."

Shock and disbelief blankets my face.

"You do? When did you decide this?" I know I sound a little perturbed but I'm really not. Just very surprised. And a part of me is relieved.

"Honey, I want to make sure you agree with this. This house is huge for just the two of us and you're a grown woman. I work so much and you have your own life. You're not here in the summers and I just don't think we need all of this. This is just… stuff. What I need isn't here." She begins to cry and as my heart breaks a little more every time I see her cry I still don't have any of my own tears. I just hold her and allow her to grieve and wipe hers away.

"Mother, I'll do whatever you want. We can get a smaller place together. I'll do whatever makes you happy. We can go anywhere you want. I'll leave my job so we can go someplace else. Just tell me and we'll go."

She wipes away her tears with a tissue and dabs the remnants of a bit of mascara that has melded underneath.

She grabs my hands and looks at me. Her face breaks my heart.

"No, Willow. I don't mean us, baby. I mean me. I want you to be on your own."

I pull my hands away from her… hurt.

"You don't want me to be with you? I don't understand."

She strokes my face. "No, sweetie. I always want you with me, but Willow, I'm a big girl. I don't need my adult daughter to wait on me hand and foot. I don't need her to give up things in her life for me. Honey, I know that's what you've been doing. Harlow called to see how I was and she told me how she asks you to go out all the time and how you always have an excuse about me needing you here."

I look at her puzzled. "Well, don't you?"

The tiny lines around her eyes expand as she smiles. "Oh, my baby, I'll always need you but you also need to have your own life. I've always had your father but I think I can get along okay on my own. I've always been independent. I'll be fine. I need you to find your way, Willow. My strong-willed girl. You know that's why I named you Willow, don't you?"

I shake my head no. "I thought it was a hippy stage you were going through."

She chuckles. "When I went into labor with you finally, fifteen days after my due date, it took you another forty hours to come out. You flat-out refused to come but when you did, your eyes were wide open looking around and you let out this scream like I've never heard in my life. You refused my breast. You loved your bottle. You refused to allow us to wrap you in anything except for a soft, knitted blanket your grandmother made you. The whole time I was in the hospital and we'd unwrap you from it and try another blanket, you'd scream. We would wrap you back in it and you would stop. I didn't have a name for you for three days. That was until I got to know my strong-willed daughter."

I had never heard of this story before and I'm in awe of it.

"You had these crazy wisps of blonde hair. It was crazy and the fine baby strands had a mind of their own. Daddy thought it looked like the branches of a willow tree blowing in the breeze. And that's how we got your name. That and your strong will."

"I had no idea." I bow my head and a tear slips out. Mother takes her thumbs and rids my cheek of it.

"My beautiful girl, you weren't meant to sit here and watch over me. You were meant for greatness. To live your life to the fullest. To teach. To make a difference in the world. To fall in love and to be happy. I had all of that. I accomplished all of it and even though Daddy isn't here, it doesn't mean I don't have his love anymore. It's all around us, sweet girl. Because we won't live here, doesn't mean he's not with us. He'll always be with us and he would want us to get on with our lives and live them to the fullest. I believe that, Willow. He was the most unselfish man I have ever met."

I swallow back some more tears and I thought I'd feel a lot differently about the whole thing but no matter if I stomp my foot or not, this is what my mom wants. And I don't feel rejected or unwanted. She just wants what's best for me. I want what's best for her. To me it's a win-win.

I grab my mother and hug her because just like my dad, she's the most unselfish person I've ever met. If I ever become a mother I want to be just like my parents. I want to teach them about being unselfish, giving, strong, loving, and able to conquer the world. I want them to find their own place in this world. And no amount of money in this world will ever buy those traits. It's something we are taught.

The first day of school is always the same thing.

All the teachers at Grayson-Elders congregate in the school auditorium. We all say hello to each other and groan because the summer is over and here it is another school year. I have a lot of people express their condolences. I sit next to Harlow, of course. Craw got the job that was once held by Harlow's ex, Daniel. He subbed last year but jumped at the shot at a full-time position here. I tell them about how my parents' house is on the market. We reminisce about the good times we had in that house, but Harlow is genuinely happy for my mother. She thinks there may be a home for sale in her development for me to purchase. Perfect solution. Who wouldn't want to live so close to their best friend?

As we wait for our principal to begin with his welcome back speech, Harlow starts to become restless in her seat.

I lean over and whisper to her.

"What the fuck is wrong with you? You have to poop or something? Sit still."

Her eyes divert from me and she sits up in her seat a little taller but buries her head in a notebook as our principal moves to the podium on the stage in front of us.

"Here we fucking go." I groan. Craw snorts and shakes his head.

"You got that right," he mumbles.

He begins his speech.

"Welcome back to another year, teachers. Hope you all had a wonderful summer. I'll start with giving my condolences to our Spanish teacher, Miss Taylor, on the sudden loss of her father. Miss Taylor, our thoughts are with you and your family at this time." Everyone turns their heads to look at me. As much as I want to roll my eyes because the last thing I want — surprisingly enough — is the attention, I don't. I appreciate it, but I'm here to do my job and leave my broken heart at the front doors of this school before I walk in. I mouth thank you and he continues to speak.

"A few new things this year everyone should be aware of. The cafeteria will no longer be serving meatloaf as part of our menu and I'm sure a lot of the students will be happy to hear this." A few chuckles ring out from some of the teachers. "Second, we will be having an art showcase in December and educational prizes will be given out to the winners in each grade. School trips have been approved for this year and are already dated in the calendars. Also, we have two new members of our staff this year. Please help me in welcoming Mr. Crawford Hannum, who will now be teaching our seventh grade English classes. Mr. Hannum substituted for us last year and made a lasting impression on us and the students so welcome, Mr. Hannum."

I punch Craw in the arm playfully and whisper, "Welcome to the shit show, Mr. Hannum. Good luck." See, I still have somewhat of my witty sense of humor back.

He snickers and says right back, "Oh, no, Wills. *You* enjoy the shit show."

What the hell does that even mean?

Our principal continues to speak. "And, as

some of you might know, there was an unfortunate incident with our band instructor, Mrs. Roberts, and a father of one of the graduating eighth graders last year, and, um… without getting into details at this time, let me just say that personal emails between teachers and a student's parent in a less than professional manner are not condoned by the school district."

Harlow and I look at each other and my mouth is agape but hers isn't, like she already knew. Man, I must really have been in la-la land not to know this kind of juicy gossip. I knew that horny cougar couldn't keep her pants on. She was always flirting with the male parents. I read between the lines.

"So, with that being said, her position was terminated but fortunately with the help of Miss Harlow Hannum we have found a new band instructor. His resume is quite impressive and he happens to be a professional musician who has just returned from an East Coast tour with his band."

Oh, no. No, no, no. Fuck no!

I look over at Harlow even before our principal finishes and I lean into her ear, speaking through clenched teeth.

"I swear, Harlow Hannum, that fat, old man better not say his name. I will strangle you and put you into another coma."

I seethe. My blood pressure raises and my heart beats so loudly I hear it in my ears. I ball my fists up so tight my knuckles turn a whitish hue.

She sits there, her eyes wide with a look of

terror cause she knows I mean it and Craw shields his face with his hands. I elbow him in the ribs. He winces.

"Staff, please join me in welcoming our new band instructor, Mr. Max Vincent."

I feel the bile rise from my stomach as I see him take the stage. I grab Harlow's arm and dig my freshly manicured nails into her skin.

This time I don't bother whispering. "I'm going to kill you, you know that, right?"

She nods and pulls her arm away from me and turns her face to look right into my eyes.

"Yep. I already made out my will."

He begins to address the staff but his eyes are on me. Mine on him… only deathly daggers.

"Thank you so much for that warm welcome. I am very excited to be here and to begin this new venture. I plan on making a lasting impression." His eyes never leave mine and for a second my heart speeds up but then I remember and it ends and I need to get out of here. I stand up and gather my things.

Harlow tugs at my arm.

"Where are you going, Willow?"

"My classroom and to find a new best friend."

He watches me the whole time. I can feel his eyes on me and the need to escape overwhelms me. I practically run up the aisle of the auditorium, not breathing and when I reach the exit doors, I speedily go to my classroom and open the door and lean against the back of it. I fall to the floor and try to compose myself. I try to catch my breath but the sight of seeing Max steals it from me.

And I wish it didn't.

This is what I get for being a cold bitch. This is my punishment. This is my purgatory.

Actually, this isn't purgatory… this is straight up hell.

CHAPTER 18

Groveling
Max~

I pace back and forth in front of the music room hallway. Harlow sits in one of the plastic chairs that lean against the cinder block wall and watches me. My stomach is in knots; my head dizzy from the fear of rejection. After Willow left the auditorium in a huff, which was totally expected, we came here so I could begin setting up my room.

I run my hands haphazardly through my freshly buzzed hair. Yeah, no more faux hawk. I look like I belong in the military with this do.

"I knew this was a bad idea. I knew it, Har. This is going to be bad."

She doesn't seem as nervous as I am.

"Relax. She's in shock. This is when you have to pull out all the stops. Use everything you've got to prove yourself. We talked about this, Max. And, in detail, if you recall."

The details. I have to remember the details.

Harlow came to me in Vermont with a plan. Her mind was set on convincing me I loved Willow and also that I was a shit for leaving her the day of her dad's funeral, but also to recognize that people make mistakes and if you love someone with every fiber of your being, you don't give up when you screw up. You do what you can to win their love back. You fucking grovel. So that's why I'm in the position I'm in.

You'd think with the monstrosity of a brain I have that I would have known I loved the girl. I'd never been in love so how was I supposed to know what I was feeling was indeed love. I didn't get much love out of my mother and even though I knew my dad loved me, he was so focused on me becoming something he never was, I don't know if he knew exactly how *to* show it.

Harlow knew. She's in love. She saw it within me when I couldn't. She said she saw a change in Willow and knew something was up way before she admitted to the gang that she did, in fact, love me. Maybe not now but that's what Harlow was afraid of so she created a plan.

She had heard around the rumor mill from the faculty at the school she and Willow teach at that the school's band instructor, a very married one, had an affair with one of the dads of a kid in the band. They got caught doing it on top of the piano in the band room. Very *Pretty Woman*-esque, if you ask me. Well, she was fired on the spot and they were in desperate need of someone to direct the band for the upcoming school year. Granted, it's only for a few school concerts during the year, but I get to choose the themes of the shows and do some instructing. Not only did I teach myself the guitar but I also learned how to play piano, drums, and bass. Harlow knows I can play the necessary instruments so before coming to see me she called her principal and he requested an interview. With my credentials alone, I was awarded the job. It's only part-time but on the weekends until the beach closes down for the bitterness of winter, I'll be playing at Jax. I plan on putting my own spin on the instruction and prove myself to Willow that I'm serious about my life. I'm not a fuck-up and that I love her. Also, it works out so I'm able to see her or inadvertently see her almost everyday.

Back to the details of 'The Plan.' In order to woo my woman back I need to knock her off her feet, send her hurling into space, then right back down where she belongs. In my arms. I miss her being in my arms. I miss her smell, her wise-ass mouth. Her legs wrapped around me, her smile. I miss the way she made me feel at home when I wasn't there. I miss everything about being with her and she wasn't really even mine, so to speak. I want her to be mine and I want her forgiveness. So insert groveling here.

"She's in room two fifteen. Second floor." Harlow points to the staircase to her left. "Go, Max," she tells me sternly.

"But what if she throws a shoe at me or slams the door in my face?"

Harlow lets out a hearty laugh and snorts. "Oh, please. If it's a shoe or a door you're worried about, that's nothing. Just hope she doesn't have a hatchet or a blender nearby. If she does… well, never mind." She pauses and goes deep into thought. Most likely about Willow chopping off my manhood. "Stick to the plan, Max. Just stick to the plan."

I had a tour of the school a few days ago by the principal so I know where the seventh grade hall is located and when I reach Willow's classroom I peer into the rectangular-shaped window that adorns the door. My breath hitches when I see her sitting at her desk. Her hand is bracing her forehead and she's looking down. Her one leg is crossed over the other and her foot is bouncing up and down a mile a minute. I duck back against the wall and breathe in deeply. Shutting my eyes, I will myself to go in there and speak to her. I'm not expecting a happy reunion, but maybe just a 'fuck off, Max.'

I knock on the door with anxiousness invading every nerve in my body. I hear her say come in so I turn the handle of the door and walk in. Her eyes are still focused on the top of her desk. She's reading something and never takes her eyes away from it. But she knows it's me. It's like she has eyes on the side of her head.

Her voice is low and monotone. "What do you want?"

I keep my feet firmly planted on the floor below me. I don't want to rush right up to her and fall on my hands and knees and beg her for forgiveness and tell her I'm in love with her. Well, I do, but like Harlow said, baby steps.

"I wanted to talk to you." My voice is small and doesn't belong to me when I hear it.

Head still down she addresses me. "Why? So you could tell me you're an asshole. Newsflash, Max, I already knew that. Now get out."

"Wills, listen. I know I made…" She cuts me off and raises her head to look at me. Her eyes are full of rage and her voice is laced with poison.

"Yeah, a mistake. You came here to tell me you made a mistake by not showing up on the one day I needed…" She pauses as her voice becomes slightly raised.

I see her cheeks hollow as she takes in air and lets it out steadily. "You came to say you're sorry. Okay, great, now go." I dare to take a step closer.

She holds out her hand to stop me. "Don't even think about it. You need to leave. Not only this room but my life. I don't want you in it."

I feel a pain in my chest when she says that. I deserve that, I know I do, but I have to convince her otherwise.

"Willow, please don't say that. Please listen to me. I have to tell you something." I sound desperate now. Her eyes look glassy as they brim with tears, but quickly she looks away as soon as she shows any sort of vulnerability. She goes back to reading whatever is on her desk.

Fuck, I don't want her to cry. I never want to hurt her again. She can't even look at me.

"There's nothing else to say. You said whatever it was you wanted to."

I shake my head. "No, Willow. I have so much more to say. Let me say it." She groans and her forehead falls to the desk.

"Why can't you just leave me alone? It's bad enough I'm going to see you around here. By the way, tell Miss Hannum in advance it was me who slit her tires." She raises her head up and looks out onto the sea of empty desks in the classroom. Her neck twitches back and forth. Her eyes are tightly shut as though she's willing me with her mind to leave and when she opens them I would be gone.

"I really thought I had better people in my life. I didn't think my best friend would betray me this way. Helping you get a job here. What did either of you think that was going to accomplish? You know what, don't answer that. I have other things on my mind rather than trying to figure it out." Her voice is weak, and it makes me ache not to hear her normal, tenacious voice.

There are so many things I want and need to say to her, but the words don't come. I'm a pussy. I'm afraid once again and I'm starting to think this was a huge mistake. She needs time, and even though I know I should give her time, I don't want to because I don't want to spend any more time apart from her.

She sniffs and straightens her spine. She pushes back her chair and stands.

My God, she is beautiful. When she's angry she's beautiful. When she's happy she is too, and even when she hates me she's the most beautiful thing I've ever seen. She walks towards her chalkboard and starts to write something on it. A paper is in her hand and she refers to it when she writes. I stand there like a buffoon. The chalk breaks and falls to the floor in a few tiny pieces. I bend down to pick them up at the same time she does and our eyes meet. That magnetic energy that has always been there reappears after a long absence. But it's brief because she tears her eyes away from mine almost immediately. I felt it and she did too. I could read it on her face and see it in the way her body reacted just from me looking at her. She stands up and smooths out her skirt. I place the chalk on her desk.

She turns around and grabs another piece continuing to write on the board.

"Please, just go. We're done here." Her voice is so small I almost don't hear her, but I do. She's struggling and I see that so I won't push my luck right now. I walk to the door and before I step over the threshold I turn to look at her and she attends to her duty.

"Willow…" I trail off and chicken out because I want to scream at her that I love her, but I can't. She's not ready. She stops writing and stands still after I call out her name. At the sound of my voice, she closes her eyes. Her chin points downward.

"I'm sorry." That's all I can say and she doesn't even bat an eyelash. Not that I expect her to anyway. She just stares at the board and with that I leave her.

I take a long pull of my beer before going back to my game controller and focus on the TV.

"I'm not surprised she told you to get lost,

dude. I'm sorry, but did you expect anything less?" Craw's fingers go a mile a minute on his controller as we battle the fake mafia with virtual guns on the screen.

"No, I'm not surprised. I'm just surprised she didn't kick me in the balls or throw me out the window."

Craw snorts. "I'm just as surprised but she is sporting some serious wounds right now. I told you from day one it's going to take a lot to win her over. She's stubborn and difficult. Two things you already know about her."

He curses when I kill his avatar in the game and leans back on the sofa throwing his controller on the table in front of us.

"I know this and that's why I have some heavy duty work ahead of me. I know she's hurting and it's partly because of me."

His eyes give me a sympathetic look, slightly. He knows I screwed up and, like everyone else, was pissed at me but once I explained everything to him he took mercy on me, even insisting I live here in his apartment with him. I pay Craw rent and I have my own fully furnished room. Porter forgave me as well. When I told him I was in love with Willow and that I would do anything to set things straight, he was understanding. Very understanding. He told me he knows all about screwing up with someone you love. I have no idea what he meant by that and I wasn't getting into it with him. But he still wants me to stay at his house on the weekends that I play at Jax.

Craw chuckles. "I still can't believe you got a

job at Grayson-Elders. My sister and her matchmaking ideas. Willow is going ape-shit. I heard them in the parking lot of the school today shouting… well, Willow was doing the shouting."

I sigh knowing that I'm the reason they're fighting. I don't want to come between them, but it was Harlow's idea and she assured me she was fully prepared for the wrath of Willow.

I change the subject because when I think of the girls arguing, my stomach hurts.

"What's up with you and Ally? Haven't heard you talk about her much lately."

Craw finishes the beer and shrugs.

"It's over. She couldn't handle it. I wasn't going to choose her over my sister. After Mr. Taylor died, I realized life's too short to argue with family. I wasn't in love with Ally. I thought I was at one point, but when she got angry with me for leaving her and being with my family — especially Harlow when Mr. Taylor died — I knew she wasn't the one for me. She's young and immature. I started to see it more as time went on. She's going back to England. We didn't leave on the best of terms."

This was Craw's first real serious girlfriend and I'm sure it was hard for him, but he did the right thing as far as my opinion goes.

I smack his knee. "Sorry, man. You did the right thing, though."

"Yeah, I know. Still stings a little, but it's cool." He goes and grabs us a few more beers.

He pops off the caps and hands me one. "Nervous about tomorrow?" Tomorrow being my first day of work.

"A little but it's just meeting the established band members and auditioning some new ones. I'm a little nervous but looking forward to it."

Craw picks up his controller and starts a new game for us.

"I don't think it's the kids you need to worry about." His voice trails off and he eyes me from the side cautiously as he takes a sip of his beer.

I know what he's saying.

"I'm fully prepared for it, Craw, and I don't mean the kids. I know what I'm in for but she's worth it. If I get to call her mine forever, then so be it."

His eyes go wide as he turns towards me. "Forever? God, in a million years I never thought I'd hear those words spoken from you about Willow. And I thought Harlow and Cruz were opposites."

I smile just thinking about Willow.

"Me either and I still can't wrap my head around it, but I know I love her and she was made to be mine. I can't explain it. It's confusing and surprising but true, and I'll do whatever it takes to make her believe it too."

On the first day of school, all teachers must walk the halls in order to preserve order amongst the students. I'm nervous because I know I'm going to run into Willow sooner or later even though my room is on the first floor and she's on the second. I'm also nervous because I sent a present to her room. A bouquet of freesia to wish her a good first day. It's part of the plan. I know they're her favorites. She told me one night during one of our Skype chats. They smell like her too. Fresh and delicious.

I meet the previous members of the school band. They seem like a great group of kids. The school organizes them in sections so I have three classes a day. The rest of the day is for me to arrange music and coordinate with the choral teacher on what needs to be done. I'm busy and time flies. I look at the clock and see it's almost noon by the time I'm finished meeting the kids and auditioning some of the new students. I haven't been out of this room yet and I have to take a piss. When the last of the students leave before lunch, I run out of the room and head to the restroom to relieve myself. When I'm on my way back I hear the clicking of heels in the distance. I look down the slightly darkened hallway near my room, but I see nothing. I head back in my room and there they are. On my desk a bouquet of freesia. Not crumbled or thrown into a million tiny pieces, just laid on my desk. No note stating for me to go fuck myself, nothing. That's when I realize the clicking heels were Willows. I need to try harder.

Flowers. What the hell was I thinking?

The rest of my first day goes as follows: I go into the faculty lounge. I see her at the refrigerator grabbing her lunch bag. She sees me, looks disgusted, and she walks out. I walk into the school office to grab some forms I need to fill out, again upon seeing me, she leaves. I go to the

library to grab a book on Mozart and see her
coming my way down the hall. She spots me
while talking to another teacher but quickly turns
her eyes away when mine meet hers. She looks so
painfully beautiful it hurts. Her long hair flowing
down her shoulders onto her chest, her tight
pencil skirt gracing her hips and the high, black
heels she's sporting drive me crazy. I've had those
same shoes dig into my ass if memory serves. And
I'm not trying to think of her in a sexual way on
purpose. It's just that she stuns me and I can't
help it. I've had her so many times and what lies
beneath the clothing burns in my memory.

The rest of the week I try my best at 'the plan.' I
have one of the band members deliver a huge
basket of gummy bears — her favorite candy —
to her room. I must have bought every bag in the
store and stuck it in the basket. After lunch, I
return back to my room and the empty basket is
sitting on top of my desk. I thought since it was
empty I was getting somewhere. I went to the
closet of my room to get my guitar case out of it
because I promised some of the students I would
play a little for them. When I opened it to retrieve
the guitar, a thousand gummy bears spilled out
onto the floor. Some were lodged in the strings…
ruined. Most of them had their poor heads severed
off. Guess the candy thing didn't go over very
well. Question is, how'd she know my guitar was
in there?

The next gift, a *Goonies* t-shirt I got off of
eBay for her was ripped to shreds like a rejected

314

Bon Jovi t-shirt some teenager from the late 90s would have worn. That was a cool-ass shirt too. It had Sloth on the front with the Superman t-shirt on and it said, 'Hey you guys' on it. I would have worn it. I'm sad.

The mix download I made for her with all the classic rock bands she loves goes without comment. This shocked me. That was until I got an email from Harlow stating that Willow told her to tell me that she wasn't into Journey so I should go fuck myself.

Normally this would be a negative. I think of it as a positive because she told Harlow to tell me to go fuck myself. This is progress.

But I'm not getting my hopes up. I text Harlow.

Me: *I need to up my game, don't I?*

Harlow: *Pretty much. She's sort of the girl you have to take a class on to figure her out.*

Me: *Not giving up, Har.*

Harlow: *I wouldn't expect anything less from you, Max. You'll figure it out.*

Yeah, I'll figure it out before it's too late.

CHAPTER 19

Take your Lovey-Dovey Shit and Stick It Up Your Ass
Willow~

The first few weeks of the new school year are always a big adjustment. This I can handle. What I'm having a hard time with is the fact that my parents' house sold within a few weeks after my mom put it up for sale. It was a quick move. She hired people to pack up and move her to a new, smaller house just a little further away than the one she lived in. She seems very happy with it. I, on the other hand, hate it. I hate living alone and I've only been doing it for a week now. I know that Harlow is only five houses away from me but we are not on speaking terms at the moment. Yes, I'm being stubborn. Yes, I'm being difficult, but she should have thought about that before she sabotaged our friendship by helping what's his name get a job at our school.

Of all the asinine things one person could do.

Well, that's not entirely true. She is marrying a tattooed, butt-muncher with the I.Q. of Barney the purple dinosaur.

Still, I'm not speaking to her. She can kiss my size six ass.

The day I moved in to my new townhouse, Porter, Craw, and the genius otherwise known as Dickcop set up my bed and carried my furniture in. They mounted my flat screen TVs and programmed them. I watched Harlow sitting on her front step watching them move me in. As Cruz carried in a box from the truck, he stopped when he noticed me eyeing her from down the street.

"She misses you, you know?"

I let out a sound of air that resembles annoyance, but I stop and sheepishly reply, "Yeah, I know she does." He winked at me and continued to carry stuff into my house.

Now here I am. Lying in my lonely room, in my lonely king-sized bed, shoving gummy bears in my mouth like I'm Hannibal Lector. Just hand me some lotion and tell me to put it in the fucking basket. I don't care. I don't like this. I keep hearing sounds. I know it's the people attached to my house. The only light that's in my room is the stupid TV that I hardly ever watch and the moonlight coming from my bedroom window. I have an end unit house so I have more windows. I should turn on my bedside light to bring me comfort. So I do. Ten seconds later I get a text.

Harlow: *I see that you're up. Can we talk?*
Me: *That would be a no, Judas.*
Harlow: *Willow, please. I have gummy bears :-*

)

Me: *I already murdered a whole bag of them. I'm in a 'Dexter' kind of mood so it's best you stay away.*

Then nothing.

Good. She got the hint. That's until I hear someone's unrelenting knocking at my door.

Crap. Who the hell is it? It's eleven at night. On a school night. It better not be that freaking munchkin with a delivery.

I stick on my robe and creep down my steps. When I reach my front door I whisper/yell.

"Who is it? I have a gun and a screaming case of herpes so you better get lost." I look out of the side glass panel next to the front door.

Bloody hell, Harlow. She adorns a fuzzy pink bathrobe with a big 'H' embroidered on it. She's chewing on her thumbnail as usual and she looks pathetic. I take in a breath and open the door because, truthfully, this distance is killing me too.

I open the door and to my surprise or not, she's crying.

I'm still stiff when I open it and glare at her.

"Why the hell are you crying?"

She sniffs and tries to speak between sobs like a five-year-old child being scolded.

"I... um, I didn't think you'd open the door if you knew it was me." Her words skip around her. "I just... you live right here, Willow, and I live right there." She points to her house down the street. "And the only time we've ever gone without speaking was when I was in a stinking coma. I... I'm sorry, Wills. I'm so sorry. I can't do

319

this anymore. I can't take another middle finger thrown at me when the students aren't looking, or you stealing my lunch from the faculty refrigerator and smearing my peanut butter and jelly all over my windshield."

I wave my finger at her. "Now listen, I only did that once."

She wipes her snotty nose with the back of her oversized sleeve.

"Once was enough."

We stand in silence at eleven o'clock at night in our pajamas in my open doorway.

"I thought I was doing the right thing. I know how you felt and… I'm just so sorry." She continues to sob like a teenager getting dumped on prom night. And she's my best friend.

I pull her into the house by her arm. "Get in here, you nut."

I hug her and she cries some more and I feel a little tear slip down my cheek.

Dammit.

After a lengthy conversation about how she interfered in my so-called love life or lack thereof, I forgive her for being an idiot and now we stuff our faces with the gummy bears she brought to my house anyway, along with all sorts of sugary concoctions. We sit on my cushy new sofa my mom bought me for my new house.

"This sofa feels like I'm sitting in marshmallows." Harlow shoves more bears in her mouth and mumbles, "This is the best sofa I've ever sat on."

I nod my head as I spray whipped cream directly from the can into my mouth. With it full of creamy goodness I still manage to talk. "I know, right? When my mom took me to the store to look for furniture, I fell in love with it."

Harlow leans back on the cushions, making herself even more comfortable.

"I'm pretty sure I could live on this couch and hide food under the cushions so when I got hungry I could keep myself well nourished."

I reach over her and shove a salted-caramel brownie piece in my mouth. I feel like a stuffed turkey.

Harlow looks at the TV and groans as my compilation of 80s movies I popped in play on.

"*Gremlins,* Wills? Really? Why can't you be normal and watch 80s movies like *Pretty in Pink?* Now that's a classic. I think my mom told me she saw that in the theater."

"You know me better than that, Har. I hate mushy gushy. I don't do mushy gushy. Never have."

She sits up. "Why, though? Why not?"

I shrug. "Just because I love clothes and makeup and girlie stuff doesn't mean I'm into the other kind of girlie stuff."

"That's not an answer."

"It is to me."

She shakes her head. "You're trying to skip around my question."

"Am not."

"Are to."

"Why because I thought I fell in love?"

"No. Because you *did* fall in love."

"Harlow, I said I thought I was in love. I was confused by the sex is all."

She folds her arms in front of her. "Bullshit."

"Excuse me?"

"You heard me. That's not why. You don't say you love someone because of sex. I mean being compatible with that aspect helps, but there's so much more to it than that. Sure, attraction is a factor, but there's more so why not just accept it?"

"Because I'm incapable of it. That's why."

"Of love?"

I nod because that's exactly how I feel.

Harlow switches off the TV and throws the remote down on my table.

"I don't think you give yourself enough credit, Willow. You give off this characteristic of being the tough girl. The one who doesn't feel much. The girl with the 'I don't care' attitude. But it's all wrong. You are so much more than that, Willow." Harlow's face is serious. I'm used to it. She's always serious and sensitive. I look away from her, not believing anything she says.

She grabs both my hands and holds them even when I try to pry them from her gently. She's not having it. She yanks them closer and looks at me deadpan.

"Love is more than falling into it. You don't have to use the word in love to describe love. You're a loving friend. I wouldn't be alive if it wasn't for you. That's love. You're job too. You love teaching and I see you have so much patience with those kids. They adore you. That's love." A tear slips from her eyes. "And you're a loving daughter. Oh God, Willow. Your dad loved you so much and I saw how you loved him dauntlessly." I try to choke back a sob, but it's at an impasse and I fail.

The tears roll down my cheeks faster than I can breathe. Harlow wipes them for me but the sobs come so quick, her fingers can't keep up.

I finally pull my hand away and cover my face. The pain wrenching inside my heart and the river flowing from my eyes is the outlet of my aching heart. My tortured soul.

I cry out, "I miss him so much. I miss him. Why? I just wish I knew why."

She reaches out and holds me and I relinquish my hands from my face and allow her to hug me. She soothes my back with her hands.

"I wish I had the answers. I really wish I did, but I think things happen in our lives to help us be stronger people. Different people. It's not fair that it happens that way, but I believe there's a reason for everything. You are full of so much love, Willow. There's so much love around you and you give it as much as you receive it. The reflection of the love your dad gave to you is shown in everything you do. You need to trust me when I say it. Believe my words. You *are* capable of it."

I pull away and catch my breath. My face is drenched and my mouth feels like a desert.

"You really think that of me? I never thought of myself that way. You know me more than anyone. Why can't I see it?"

She smiles at me so tenderly. "Because sometimes we are blind to the things we are good at. You're good at love. You love fiercely. I've never seen anything like that. With your family, with your friends and with Max. You may not be able to see it, but now that I know the truth about you both, the whole truth, I see it. I think I saw it but like so many other times I was blind to it. I saw a change in you. I didn't know what it was at the time. Maybe I thought you were maturing. I mean you stopped threatening Cruz's balls with a blender. That was a big thing for you."

I shrug. "He's not so bad, I guess."

"A different kind of love changed you in ways. You loved Max. You *love* Max. You stumbled into love with him without even realizing you were. It's a good thing, Willow. When you stumble and fall, there's no warning. It just happens. We can't control it and we can't control how others handle the fall. We can only control how we do as individuals."

I sigh. "I don't know if I can let what he did go, Har. He hurt me. I told him I loved him and he ran. He ran from me on the worst day of my life. How does someone do that and then you forgive them. If I'm capable of love, I'm not so sure that I'm capable of forgiveness. I need baby steps."

She laughs at me. "Yeah, I know and he's trying to get your forgiveness."

"Relentless little fucker, isn't he?" She nods. "Yep. Just hear him out, Willow. Please."

"Why though? 'Cause he sends me gifts? He thinks gummy bears and flowers are going to get me to forgive him? That's just admitting you made a mistake. Fine, he made a mistake, but what else is there? Maybe I wanted him to love me back and he tried to spare me the embarrassment by running because he didn't. I don't need someone who I love to buy me gifts or do sentimental things. My parents did both. They gave me love and all the material stuff. But now I just need someone to tell me they love me. That they're in love with me. I need the words. That's all. Maybe someday."

Memories of my parents and what they had flood my brain and I want that so much. I didn't think I did. I never thought I'd love someone with my whole heart. But I did. And he crushed me. I just want that kind of love in my life. I'm like a chrysalis changing into that butterfly. I allowed love in my heart and it hurt, but I don't want someone to break me of my ability. I just can't. I've come this far... maybe.

"Wills, can you just do me a favor for now? Give the little man a small break? No pun intended. Just hear him out on a few things. Remember, you have it in you."

I want to believe that what Harlow tells me is the truth. I do a little, but like I've said before, rejection is something I've never had to deal with. Anything I've ever wanted, I've had. Cars, money, clothes, my pick of guys to be crazy with and kiss till my mouth hurt. But maybe it was all unfulfilling. Quite possibly I was just going through the motions and allowing myself not to be prepared in case there was a kick to the teeth. A wake-up call. If I'm what Harlow says, maybe I can at least give Max the chance to explain and learn to get over him and forgive. I've never had to get over someone and when I see him my heart still flutters. Working at the same school isn't helping and I refuse to give up my summers at Sandy Cove because I couldn't bear the thought of being denied something I wanted. I am a spoiled girl. Anything I wanted was forever at my fingertips. It was falling in love that I couldn't catch. But, like Harlow said, we can't control how others stumble and it was obvious that Max didn't fall. I think I can hear him out and accept it and go on with my life. I can be a big girl.

I *think* I can.

CHAPTER 20

In The Lyrics
Max~

I've played at Jax the last few weekends. Sandy Cove is still somewhat hopping on the weekends. Even with the crisp October air upon us, people pack into this place.

My nerves for the most part are a mess right now. The girls are coming this weekend because it's Willow's birthday. So I pretty much want to vomit right now. I have a present for her and I hope it affects her the way I want it to. It could backfire or make for a great story to tell our kids.

Fuck, I said *our* kids. Since when did I think about the future in that way? And with Willow. But she's my muse and I have to tell her the only way I can, if she'll listen. I can't lose her.

I've lost a lot since that night. The guys in The Band kicked me out of said band when I ditched the rest of the tour. It wasn't like we had a slew of dates left to play but they were going to go into the recording studio and they weren't happy with my sudden departure. They ran it by Mr. Carpenter first and when he found out I ditched Mr. Taylor's funeral he was pissed. Apparently he tried to talk them into keeping me on but that wasn't the straw that broke the camel's back. When Cora kept trying to pursue some sort of relationship with me once I got back that night after Willow told me she loved me, I told Cora the truth. I told her everything. I told her about it all and that was that. I liked Cora and we did nothing else but kiss a few times, but when I did kiss her I didn't feel like I did when I kissed Willow. I didn't feel that immense power her kiss holds. The electrifying current wasn't there pulsating through my veins. They were just lips that were there to be kissed. I should have known from the first one that there was nothing behind that contact. I wish I wasn't so blind to how I felt, but it wasn't fair for me to string Cora along. She was upset and it's not that she went running back to Daddy to tell him I broke her heart, he just knew something happened. Cora just told him I was in love with someone else. She is actually a classy girl. She didn't spill the rest of the details to her dad but for some reason hurting his daughter didn't mesh well with the way he wanted things to go in what was his perfect world. His beautiful daughter being with his protégé, him making money off of me and my band.

So he canned me. It's okay though. I have other business to attend to.

I sit here and nurse this damn beer because every

sip I take turns my stomach and my persistent foot tapping is pissing Cruz off.

"Would you please knock it the hell off? You're like a kid high on sugar. You see her all the time at work. What makes tonight different?"

I look at him like he's even crazier than usual. "Big difference, dude. I pass her in the halls. Every room I go into she sees me, she walks out. Tonight she's coming here on purpose. I don't know how to act."

Cruz drinks his beer and Porter plays with the label on his bottle and they look so damn calm. What the fuck is wrong with them.

"Hello?" I wave my hand in front of their faces.

"What? I don't see what the big deal is. It's just Willow."

Of course Porter would say such a thing. Being her cousin and all.

"Well, it is a big deal, dumbass. I'm in love with her and she hates me, just in case you forgot."

His head shakes lazily back and forth and he smirks. "Nah, didn't forget."

"How am I supposed to act when she comes through that door?" Porter looks up towards the door. His face goes blank and his jaw slacks. He takes in a deep breath and closes his eyes. When he opens them there's an agitated look on his face. Thea walks up to the table and Porter straightens up his back and bumps his long leg on the table which sends his bottle of beer spilling on the table... and onto Thea, who stands at the edge of it. She raises her arms and makes an 'o' face when the contact of the cold beer goes on her shirt and drifts down her pants. She stands there cold and shocked. We all jump up to find napkins or anything to try to stop the spill from going any further.

Cruz and I wipe the table as Porter uses the sleeves of his shirt to clumsily clean off Thea's shirt, along with her boobs.

"Oh God, I'm so sorry. I'm so sorry." He goes on wiping her boobs as Cruz and I look at each other then back to the awkward scene in front of us. Thea stares at him as he does a diligent job basically feeling her up. Porter still mumbles as he finishes wiping her boobs and goes towards the downtown.

That's when I hear her voice. Beautiful and smooth but still laced with a bit of venom.

"Porter, can you stop molesting my friend? Just go get her a towel." I drop my napkin as soon as I hear her. I stand up straighter but I keep a slight distance as the sight of her takes the oxygen right from me. Do I say hi first? Do I not say anything for fear of retaliation or a middle finger? This is the girl I love. I can't ignore her.

Porter apologizes to Thea again and she says quietly with her eyes downcast, "It's fine, Porter." She turns her head away from him but his eyes stay on her and he looks so regretful and conflicted when he sees her turn away. I see him mouth the word 'fuck'.

Oh boy.

I put my hands in my back pockets and nod

my chin up towards Willow and take a chance.

"How's it going?" It seems like forever but she does look up at me. She rolls her lip over her bottom lip and I can tell she's uncertain as to what to say back but as always she surprises me.

"Fine. You?"

Well, I hit the jackpot then. She gives me a 'fine' and in a very subtle way asks me how I am.

I invade her personal space and I know I'm taking a chance by doing it, but it's worth it. I lean into her ear — taking in the scent of her skin and hair — and whisper, "I'm a mess."

When I pull back, her eyes are closed but when she opens them and those eyes look at me, she steps back away from me.

"Good."

That's all she says and I deserve that. I am a mess. In my head and in my damn heart. But I can accept this. I retreat back as well, grabbing my beer and downing the whole damn thing. Harlow walks in with Craw and she goes right to Cruz for a tiny makeout session because you know it's only been three days since they've seen each other. I haven't felt Willow's lips on mine for weeks upon weeks. It sucks. It fucking blows. What I wouldn't give to though. Even if she continues to hate me, I'd give anything to taste her lips one more time.

Harlow and Cruz finish making out. Thea is dry, Porter looks like he's going to slit his wrists, and Craw grabs a beer at the bar.

We all stand there. Quiet streams through our little circle.

Cruz clears his throat.

"Hey, guys, wait till you hear Max and his solo set. It's fucking amazing. I thought he was good with those other douches, you haven't heard anything yet."

Harlow wraps her arm through mine and squeezes it while resting her head on it.

"I'm proud of you, Max. You guys should see him with the kids at school. He's an amazing band instructor. The winter showcase is going to be amazing."

Everyone but Willow congratulates me. She wanders to the bar after I've been praised, not wanting to hear anything good about me, obviously.

Harlow says in my ear, "Step up the game, Max. Remember." I nod to her and go to the bar and stand next to Willow as she waits for her drink.

"Hi." She looks at me with her peripheral vision and snakes out the tip of her tongue, teetering on whether or not to answer me back.

"Hi."

I turn and lean my back against the bar and continue because I'm doing my best and I can't back down.

"Willow, can we talk? Please. I need to say some things to you."

She takes a rather healthy sip of her drink and sighs, clearly annoyed. "Fine, then talk." She never looks my way just stares straight ahead. "I'm listening."

"Can we go outside to talk? Not in here. I need

you to be able to hear me."

She nods and I motion towards the back of the bar beyond the back exit doors. I touch her lower back to guide her and she shivers but quickly recovers and jerks her body away from my hand. I walk by our friends and Harlow winks at me and I put up my hand to show her my fingers are crossed.

When the cool air hits us as we exit the back of the bar, it's the temperature that makes me shiver, as well as a sense of deja vu because right out here over by the brick wall we had a moment of bliss. Fucking euphoria in its hottest example. We walk towards that wall and she stops in her tracks before we get there. I'm speculating that she has recollection of where we are and the memory has drifted in, but she needs to stop it.

Without turning to me she says, "This is far enough." Then she turns herself around and I'm mush just at the sight of her heels and painted on jeans, accentuating her long limbs.

"So start talking before I change my mind, Max."

Everything is on the tip of my tongue. All the words are there. I just have to get them out. Words I've never spoken. Ones I've never had to and I reach down so far deep in my soul for courage and I do my best to raise it up.

"Willow, I know I've said it over and over again but I am so sorry for hurting you. I'm ashamed of myself for doing what I did. I'm just so sorry."

"You should be." She bites out with poison in

her tone.

I groan, probably when I shouldn't, and roll my eyes. "I know. Can I... can you just let me talk and get this all out first before you comment?"

"I'm giving you the chance to talk but see, you're fucking it up already. You've already told me you're sorry. What else do you possibly have to say?"

"A lot if you'd be quiet and let me speak for Christ's sake."

"Oh, you've got some nerve talking to me like that, you gnome. I don't need another apology. I've heard it come from you. Tell me something I don't know already."

I throw my arms up in the air and growl in frustration and start pacing the damn asphalt under my feet.

"You are the most frustrating woman in the world. Why can't you just shut up and listen to a man who wants to tell you he loves you, Willow. My God. That's all I want to say besides I'm sorry." I gave her a whammy. I stunned her. I shut up Willow Taylor by telling her I love her. I see her swallow several times and no other words come out of her mouth so I take advantage of the situation and keep running my mouth.

"I fucking love that you have a smart mouth. I love that you always have something to say about everything. I love that you care about how you look, that you like to wear heels even to a beach bar. I love that you can look stunning in a rain jacket and boots. I love how you love your friends, and your family, and how behind your pain in the ass attitude, you have a good heart." She stays still but she's listening even if her eyes are downcast.

"I love that you like things that others would think you'd cringe at: 80s movies that aren't love stories, candy, cool music   not hip-hop or dance mixes. I love that after sex you rub the lobe of your left ear." Her head snaps up and her eyebrows gather in the center. Her face displaying confusion but it's not at me because these are the things that I pick up on. The things I've discovered I love about her.

"Yeah, don't look so confused. You do. After we lie there catching our breath, you rub your ear and it's the single-most adorable thing I've ever seen. It makes me melt. You make me melt and I'm telling you that I love everything about you. Everything, Willow."

She goes to speak and I stalk up to her, closing the distance between us and I rest my finger on her soft, pink lips.

"I want it all with you and I'm so sorry I ran, but you're want I want. I want us. Of all the people in this crazy world I want the craziest one... you." She closes her eyes and I cup her face in my hands and I kiss her. At first she resists, then I just intensify it by prying her sinfully gorgeous mouth open with my tongue. She gives in and it's the most achingly sweet thing in the universe. Nothing but tongues and lips and teeth are present along with the taste of her and the explosive vibes our bodies twist with.

She snakes her arms around me and brings me in even closer. So close. We breathe each other in and the subtle flicks of my tongue against hers makes the front of my pants tighter. I slide a hand down to unbutton the front of her jeans and my hand slides down to feel if this kiss is affecting her as much as its affecting me. When I feel her heat and her wetness and all that's Willow, I no longer question it and I revel in the salvation I have found coming from her.

I slip a finger in and she moans against my mouth. I kiss her neck and the shell of her ear. She bends her head back and allows me to taste her skin and make her feel so much just from my touch.

The constant repeat of her name rolls off my tongue. "Willow, baby. Willow… God, you feel so good." Our lips meet again and her hand finds its way to my dick and she softly kneads it through my pants. I lament a sound and allow her to make me feel good. Her touch is a divine act that I've missed so much. I take my hands from inside her and she lets out a whimper when I do. I back her up towards our brick wall and I raise her hands up above her head and I fuck her mouth with my tongue and all I want to do is take her back to my room and make the best love to her. I grind against her front and her hips are in sync with mine. Her body is screaming for me and I know it just by her movements because I'm in the same boat. We battle with our mouths — fighting for territory and some feeling of relief but it's not going to happen like this. I need her under me.

Skin against skin. I need to be inside her and never come out for the rest of my fucking life. I leave her mouth and kiss her ear.

"I need you so bad. I need you, Willow." Then she stops and her body tenses up. I pull away and look at her face. A tear slips down her cheek and I ease up on her hands against the wall. Just enough for her to make her way out of the now gentle grip I have.

I search her eyes and wait for her to tell me why she looks like this. Why is she crying?

She chokes back a sob. "I needed you too but you left me when I needed you the most."

She pushes against my chest and buttons her pants and fixes her shirt and wipes at her mouth like she's disgusted that my lips were just there against hers.

"Willow, I said I was sorry. Please, don't do this. I love you, do you hear me?"

She wipes her tears away and sniffs, shifting her hair over her shoulder.

"I heard you, but you ran when I said it. Harlow told me to forgive you… I just don't know if I can. What you did to me on that day after what we shared the night before? My God, Max. I gave you more than my body. I gave you my soul. I looked in your eyes when you were inside me and I thought, 'God, Willow you found it. What you didn't want wound up finding you anyway.' And I never wanted that night to end. I didn't want anything to end. I wanted you and you knew it and you ran like a coward and I'm not sure I can get over it." I step up to her and try to grab her face so she'll look at me, really look at me.

"Don't you dare. I can't do this. I can't be hurt again. I can't lose anything else and I can't trust you wouldn't run again." I go to speak but it's interrupted by one of the bouncers telling me it's time for me to go on stage. I tell him in a minute and I know that's a minute too long.

"Willow, trust me. I'm not going anywhere. I'd never hurt you again. I swear."

She shakes her head.

"I don't know that. I just don't, Max." She walks away and goes back inside leaving me to struggle with what she said. I let out a huge "fuck" into the night air with no one to hear me but me. I want to chase her but I don't think chasing her would solve anything right now. I wait another minute wanting to rip out my hair and my heart. I go back inside to search for her, but she's gone. The gang sits at our regular table. I go to Harlow.

"I stepped it up." She gives me a quaint smile and pats my arm.

"Yeah, I could tell by her smeared lipstick and the fact that she ran out of here as fast as she could."

"I tried, Har. I really did. I told her I loved her. I don't think it helped."

She rubs my arm. "I'm so sorry, Max."

The manager of Jax announces my name and I have to go sing. This is the last thing I want to be doing, but I have to.

I make my way on the stage. It's just me, a

microphone, an amp, and my guitar. My friends cheer for me and others clap and welcome me. I swallow down the lump in my throat and wish to God I was looking out to the crowd seeing her face amongst them. I clear my throat and start with the song that means the most to me. The one all about her. The one she helped me with but the one I finished after I found the love in her and then lost it so quickly.

"Hey, everyone. I'm Max Vincent. Thanks for coming."

Cruz yells out above the crowd, "Yeah, we love you, you little stud." People illicit laughter and I chuckle.

"Yeah, love you too, big guy. This song is an original and it's about a girl. Of course it's about a girl, but it's more than that. It's about finding her and stumbling into love with her when I didn't even know it. When we fall, we fall hard, people. This one's for her."

I play the song with my heart and soul. My fingers burn with energetic intensity and so does my voice. The song for Willow eats me alive but it's also my confession. She'll never hear it, but I know I wrote it for her and she helped me not even knowing it would be about her.

I go straight home after my set and Harlow and Thea go directly to Willow's room. I retreat back to my house after standing at their sliding door like a lost puppy, but not for too long. It's too depressing. I go to my room but I find myself restless. Now I stand at her bedroom door at the beach house once I know everyone is asleep. I stole the key the girls hide to their house and I run my hand over the front of it and I can hear her cry. I want to bang on it and tell her to open up and let me in. Let me into her heart again, but I need to give her space and time to process all the things I told her. The sounds of her pain are like a million pins in my heart. I know she's hurting from her dad's death, but I also have something to do with it. I have to prove to her in some way that I'm not going to run. I'm not going to go anywhere. She's it for me. I just have to figure out how to do it.

CHAPTER 21

Wearing Me Down

Willow~

Sitting back at my desk this morning, I don't acknowledge the fact that I have to give a Spanish quiz to sixty kids today on my brain, I have *the* song. The one my sneaky little friend Harlow recorded for me to hear on her phone. The one she forced me to listen to. The one Max performed at Jax when I left a few nights ago. She told me it would change everything. But everything *was* already changed. It was painfully beautiful and so recognizable. I gave him some of the words but he finished them, placing words inside of the lyrics so eloquently it made me want to fall to my knees and weep. I almost did.

The lyrics were about me and when we were working on the beginning of it together, I don't really think either of us realized that.

You came in like the wind

making my head a mess.

Your eyes and lips; making me second guess.

I thought I didn't need you, I didn't think I'd care that you came into my life from being kryptonite to flare; igniting something in me that I thought didn't exist, but that was until I saw the flames in your eyes.

I knew I couldn't resist.

Electric heat we couldn't extinguish no matter how hard we tried, but it was more than just feeling your body next to mine; my feelings I just couldn't hide.

I stumbled in to loving you, clarity being my friend, I know how much I hurt you, please don't say that this is the end.

I need you like my last breath; you stole mine that first day.

Please don't let my fear make us end this way.

I fell in love with so many parts of you, the good, the bad, the gray.

I just never thought that my heart would make me feel this way.

I love you like my soul depends on it to live;

all I need for you to do is say that you'll forgive.

I welcome the twists and turns, the doubt and fear, the unknown and knowing only draws me near.

You are my muse, my bird in flight, the one I dream of every night.

You're the tune, the words, the melodies, the song in which I sing.

But my life is nothing if I don't have you, my everything.

Harlow said to me, "Willow, he loves you and he said the words you wanted to hear and he meant them." I know he did and he very well meant each one, but I can't get past why I feel like he'll leave me. Then the hurt would just come back again tenfold.

I had broken down all the components of the mess that are Max and me for Harlow. I had to give her the pros and the cons. But she had an answer for everything.

Cons first because that's who I am.

1. We don't get along most of the time.

Her answer for that - no one ever gets along all the time.

2. We take every opportunity to insult each other.

Her answer - foreplay. Built up sexual tension.

3. He has no sense of style. The complete opposite of me.

Her answer - Opposites attract. And she shrugged and proceeded to tell me to look at her and Cruz. That really didn't help my cause.

Then she made me go through the pros.

1. Talent turns me on. Always has.

My answer - she's correct. Seeing footage of Jimi Hendrix play the guitar upside down - yeah, wet panties. Even though I'm not the least bit attracted to Jimi Hendrix.

2. We have chemistry.

Yes, I know. It's undeniable. He's the electricity and I'm the conductor of it. If we didn't have the spark we would never had made our little deal.

3. We get along better than I think.

I got to know Max more after he left for the tour. When we talked, we'd talk for hours. Even after he was exhausted from doing an intense show. He didn't want the conversations to end during those talks. I think next to Harlow, Max knows more about me than anyone. It's strange really. I don't even think Harlow knows why I'm an only child. I told Max about my mother's many miscarriages after I was born. I told him how at one point when I was ten they thought I had leukemia. After all the tests came back and were negative, my parents stopped trying to have another child. They knew I was safe and I was the only thing they needed.

Max is the only one I ever told that to.

4. Harlow pointed out to me that I fell in love with him.

My answer, yes… yes, I did. Unexpectedly, truly, deeply, madly.

As I sit here still thinking about the lyrics, I still can't believe out of all the people in this goddamn world I fall in love with Max. I remember the first day I met him and how I crushed on him. Not telling anyone, not leading on that the guy turned me on like a fucking oven. I never told a soul that when we were in Sandy Cove and I would see him with a girl, I'd freak out inside. I'd find a guy to fool around with but when I closed my eyes, I'd see Max's face sometimes. I couldn't control it and it made me angry. It made me wish he didn't exist but then where would my heart be if he didn't? I think that's why I was always so mean to him. I was mad at him for making me feel things. He was just this stupid boy who played a guitar and looked hot doing it. But then between the time we first met and now I fell in love.

When I talked to my mother last night she asked how I was. I tried to pretend I was okay. She knew better. I told her it was because I missed my dad so much, but she knew from the sound of my voice it was more. So stepping outside my 'Willow Bubble', I did. I told her about Max. I told her I fell in love with the stupid ass and told her how he hurt me. I told her I wasn't sure I could forgive him and also that I wasn't sure I was satisfied with the way I felt about that decision. She told me she knew it all already.

That little fucker called her.

He told her he was sorry what he did to me and that he was in love with me and since my dad wasn't here he asked her permission to date me. I don't even want to talk to him or look at him but I'll give him credit for his persistency. My mother gave her blessing and told me that Max reminded her of my daddy in many ways. He pursued her until she gave in and they had a love story that people write books about. Maybe it wasn't always a fairytale, but it was one to be admired. Nothing's perfect. I'm far from it but as I sit here and twiddle the compass necklace my parents gave me, I think about not losing my way and who I am… who I truly am. I need to find forgiveness and just let the bad things go that don't matter in the end. In the end they may be the things that make our own happiness slip through the cracks. I don't know if I can stop it. I don't know if I can try.

But what if I don't?

.

CHAPTER 22

I'm Pretty Sure I've Lost the Fight
Max~

As I sit here strumming on my guitar out of sheer boredom, my cell rings. I see it's my dad calling. I haven't heard from in since the Philadelphia show. I have no idea why he's calling.

"Hello?" I hold my breath after I answer.

"Max?"

"Yeah?"

"Son, I think we need to talk."

"What's there to talk about?" I know I sound distant and I have my reasons.

"A lot, Max. I have a lot to say. The first is that I'm sorry and I was wrong. I was so wrong."

My jaw hangs open because these are words I have never heard come from my father. I didn't even know he knew how to say those words.

"When did you come to this realization?"

"As soon as I walked away from you that night, Max. I knew I was wrong as soon as I said what I said. I was just too afraid to admit it. I'm a stubborn man, son. I think me being that way had something to do with losing your mom, but you're my son and I can't lose you too because of the way I am. I have to change and this…" I hear him take in a deep breath and let it out.

"This is me changing. I'm so proud of you, Max. So proud that you chased a dream. It's a dream I should have supported instead of pushing you towards a dream *I* had for you. When I heard you on that stage and saw what you were capable of, I should have told you I was proud of you. I didn't and I'm so sorry for that. You're all I have and I can't lose you. Can you forgive me, son?"

Forgiveness. That word has been running rampant in my brain lately. There's truth and strength behind that word and what sort of meaning would it have behind it if we didn't actually believe in the power of it.

"Dad, of course. I'm sorry that I wasn't what you expected, but it's who I am and that's not going to change."

"Max, you are all I expected and then some. The parts of you that were the unexpected are the ones I'm most proud of, and I am so proud of your talents and where your life is taking you. Not only that, but I'm proud of the man you've become. I tried my best, Max. I've done a lot of it on my own and I thought I screwed it up, but I see I didn't. Guess I didn't give myself enough credit."

"You did a good job, Dad. I love you."

The phone is silent for a second and I can hear

him sniff.

"I love you too, Max. I'm proud to be your dad."

"And I'm proud to be your son."

We talk a little more and I tell him how I quit the band and that I'm instructing music now for kids and he's blown away, but in a good way.

Nothing I do seems to be working with Willow. I wanted her to hear the song I wrote to her. Telling her I was in love with her just made her more upset and run. She can't forgive me. I even called her mom. Mrs. Taylor simply said not to give up on her.

I'm afraid that it's too late for that.

Harlow wanders in the band room as I sit here trying to arrange some music for the students to practice.

"Hey. How are you?" I look up from the slew of music sheets in front of me.

She pulls a chair up to the front of my desk.

"Hi. I'm okay."

She smiles. "No, you're not."

I chuckle. "You're right, I'm not but I'm at a loss, Har. I think I've lost her."

She cocks her head to the side. "I'm not so sure about that. I think you just have to try a little harder. You don't give up that easily, Max. You're a fighter. Fighters do whatever they can to hold on to the things they want. You're that person."

"I'm not so sure of that anymore."

She leans back in the chair and sighs. "Max, love is worth fighting for. It's the only thing that we can't allow ourselves to give up on. If she's worth the fight, then don't give up. Is she worth the fight, Max?"

I run my hands over my face and rub my eyes that burn from loss of sleep.

"Of course she's worth it. It's the fact that I'm not sure she wants me to fight."

Harlow stands up when we hear the sound of the bell signaling the start of the next class. The students begin to shuffle in and take their seats.

"Max, if you don't know by now, that's what you two do best. You wouldn't be Max and Willow if you didn't." She winks at me and leaves.

I look out at the sea of students sitting in front of me. All of them behind their respective instruments and I know I need to finish instructing them on the arrangement they need to play for the winter showcase, but I'm not going to do that. I'm going to go against the guidelines and all the rules because that bright bulb in my big brain flickers on and I can't shut it off.

"Hey, everyone. We're going to do something a little different today and I need to know who is willing to give me a little bit more practice after school for the next few days?"

Everyone's hands go up and I go to my desk and type up a permission form for their parents so they can stay after school for the next few days. After I finish composing it, I send it via e-mail to the school's secretary and ask for copies to be back to me by the end of the day. I stand in front of the kids with my laptop and scan through my play list. When I find the song I want them to listen to, I ask the class, "Have you guys ever heard of AC/DC?"

CHAPTER 23

Guess I Really Did Shake Him
Willow~

Harlow and Thea insisted on a small housewarming party for me even though I've been in my house for a few months. They said better late than ever. Besides the girls, Porter, Cruz, and Craw are here. The guys bought over some beer and liquor and the girls made a few things to snack on. Oh, and gifts. I love gifts. Hey, I'm Willow, remember?

We sit around in my new living room and talk about the annual Halloween party Jax is having this coming weekend and after a lengthy conversation they convince me to go.

It's nice to have them all here with me. I feel like I haven't smiled in a long time and to sit here and laugh with my friends is the best medicine.

After I open my presents, Cruz stands up, opens a bottle of champagne and Thea passes out glasses to everyone. When she goes to Porter and holds out a glass for him to take, I can't help but notice how he looks at her and how he wraps his fingers around her hand when she tries to give him a flute. He lingers there and his eyes are fixed on hers. I watch it play out before me and I can't help but smile a little when I see Thea give him a small smile when he tells her 'thank you.'

Hmm…

Once everyone's drinks are poured, Cruz stands up and begins a toast.

"So me of all people would like to toast Willow on her beautiful new home, on her new venture in life, and may this home bring you happiness and fulfillment and enough room to store all of your heels and makeup 'cause God forbid you don't have enough closet space." I toss a throw pillow at him, which he dodges, and then laughs at me.

"And I'm glad you liked the picture and frame my Turnip and I got you. There was no way in fucking hell I was getting you any type of cutlery or a blender because to me they are just weapons of mass destruction, especially to my balls." Cruz winks at me and I mouth a 'thank you.'

He raises his glass and we all follow.

"To Willow."

The gang repeats Cruz's words in unison and as I down my drink I hear a loud bang in the distance. Then it stops. Then I hear it again. The sound gets louder and closer. I set my glass down and stand up from my place on the floor.

"What the hell is that? Are we being attacked?" No one says a word and I wonder why they aren't jumping up like the maniac I am.

I look at them as they continue to sit around my coffee table and drink.

"What the fuck, people? It sounds like an army marching down the street." I stalk over to my door and all I hear are drum beats coming from the other side of it. I turn the knob and open it with force and that's when I see it.

A band on my front lawn. A band of kids beating drums on my front lawn. Kids from Grayson-Elders. The fucking school band.

The beats of each one in sync with the other but all giving off different sounds.

A horn section joins them, then two girls begin playing violins but they are quick and I can't keep up with how fast they play the strings.

I look over my shoulder into my house and my friends have suddenly gathered behind me and they are all smiling like idiots.

And I still haven't quite figured it all out but then the melodies come together and I know what they're playing. My favorite song. But then, out of the shadows from the side of my house, comes a guitar playing man with crazy hair and a terrible wardrobe and he's playing the tune along with the rest of the band. He doesn't look up. His concentration is solely on his strings and the rhythm of the music.

The beat is a little slower but rings through the chilly October skies like drifting clouds.

And then he sings.

I stand there as his eyes find mine and he steps a little closer as he plays and sings. I feel a shove from behind me; before I know it I pass the threshold of my door and I'm on the small front porch of my house. I look behind me and Cruz shrugs and gives me his best innocent look. I shake my head, give him the finger, and turn back to look at the guitar playing man. My neighbors come out of their houses to look at the concert being performed on my front lawn.

The guitar player sings the words that aren't his lyrics but by the look on my face and his soulful expression, they might as well be.

AC/DC can sure write some good shit.

Every step he makes is closer to me and I see the electricity in his eyes. I hear the way he sings the lyrics and how his eyes are fixated on me now. I can feel his voice go through me and invade my heart and it swells. It swells with love and pride and forgiveness and my God, I love this boy, this man. This one person who was created just for me. Who never gave up on me. This boy who wouldn't take no for answer and the one who was just afraid and has remorse for his wrongdoing. He loves me. I'm his muse, but he's mine. He showed me what it's like to love beyond all comprehension. That anything is possible. That life goes on and so does love. It knows no bounds or depths. It only has a soul and he's the other half of my soul. He always has been.

I step down to meet him as the song begins to wind down and now he's standing right in front of me, singing the final words of the song and looking into my eyes like I'm the only thing on this Earth that exists. When he's finished, he swings the guitar around to his back and gently holds my face in his magical hands.

And it's like they were born to do this.

It grows quiet after the band is done playing.

The guitar player licks his bottom lip and rolls it between his teeth, then he speaks.

"You are a huge pain in my ass. You're cocky and demanding. You're stubborn and impossible most of the time. You make me want to rip out my hair and run for the hills most days. You have the mouth of a truck driver and the demeanor of a petulant child."

And this is making me cry, why? Because he's telling the truth. He's not sugarcoating it. This is who I am. He wipes at my tears as they flow down my face.

"But I can't live without you. I can't stand another day without you in my life. Be mine, Willow. Be mine forever."

I place my hands on his as he continues to hold my face.

"Stop talking for one minute." He nods.

"I hate your hair, I hate your clothes. Your Converse are hideous and you eat like an inmate on death row who's being served their last meal. You're a smart ass and your mouth is almost as bad as mine so don't think you're all innocent here." I choke back a sob and try to catch my breath when he steps even closer to me and his beautiful lips linger over mine. I can feel the warmth of his breath across my face as he scans my face.

"But I love you and I think it's the craziest thing that's ever happened to me. I don't think it's crazy that I love you, but that it's *you* who I love. You have me, Max. You always have."

He brings my hands down and kisses my fingers. Bringing them to his cheeks, he closes his eyes and whispers, "Forgive me, Willow. I will never hurt you again. You're my life. You're my greatest gift, the best song that has ever been sung. I love you."

He lets go of my hands and I wrap them around his neck and gaze into his eyes.

"I forgive you, Max, and I love you with all my heart. But hurt me again and I will make a smoothie out of your manhood."

He throws his head back and laughs then seals the deal with a kiss that's one for the books. I feel a surge of voltage go from my lips to all of my limbs and the deeper the kiss goes, the more I feel like I'm being lifted off this earth. Jilted into space and beyond the stars. But he's my star, my world. My muse.

When we break away from the axis-tilting kiss he brings his forehead to mine and takes in a breath.

"We're crazy, aren't we?"

Our lips touch tenderly once more and I say against his sinful, God-like lips, "I think crazy is what we do best."

And as the cheers from our friends ring out behind us we turn to look at them and laugh.

I turn back to Max and shake my head. "Yes, we are but I think it'll only get crazier from here."

He pecks at my lips then wraps his arms around me and says in my ear, "That's a guarantee."

EPILOGUE

One Week Later
Max, Willow, and The Gang

"Are we really doing this?"

"Yeah, Wills, we are."

"This is nuts."

"Yep. But we do nuts good."

"I do your nuts good."

"Oh, yeah you do, baby. Last night was insane. Who would have thought marshmallow fluff could be so hot."

"I know, right? You have no idea how many times I had to wash down your happy place before all the fluff was gone?"

"See, I knew you should've let me help you."

"Max, you were down there enough, don't you think?"

"No, way. I could live there. It's nice and cozy."

"You're hot."

"No, you are."

"No, you."

"For the love of Christ, can you two knock it off for a minute and pay attention here? Let's get this done with so we can go celebrate."

"Shut it, Dickcop. Don't rush me."

"Cruz, leave them alone. This is their moment."

"Sorry, Turnip. You're right. I still can't believe this is happening though. Not even six months ago Willow was going ballistic that we were even engaged. Now this?"

"You're telling me? That's my cousin and my best friend."

"Would you two please be quiet? Harlow's right, leave them alone."

"Sorry, Thea."

"It's okay, Porter. Let's just enjoy this."

"Ready, Wills?"

"Ready, Max. Now pay attention to the man."

"Dearly beloved, we are gathered here today to witness the marriage of Willow Taylor and Max Vincent. If anyone here has just cause that these two people should not be wed, please speak now or forever hold your peace."

"Cruz, I swear to the heavens if you even…"

"Hey, I like my balls. I'm keeping my mouth shut, Willow."

"Please continue, sir."

"Thank you, Miss Taylor. As I was saying marriage is a sacred bond between two people who are about to be united in love and sacrifice. Max and Willow have decided to write their own vows. Mr. Vincent, you can begin."

"Willow, when we first met I wanted to run

the other way when you walked into a room, now when you do I just want to run to you and never let you go. You are the crazy that keeps me sane. You are my muse, the love of my life, and the truest bad-ass I've ever met."

"Aw, Max. You're going to make me cry and I spent a lot of money on this makeup so let's try not to do it."

"You got it, baby. Anyway, thanks for marrying me. I love you."

"Miss Taylor, your vows please."

"Oh, okay. Max, your hair irritates me, but the rest of you I adore. I fell in love with you when I didn't even know that I could. Love existed in my life, but this kind of love was the most unexpected. I think in life the most unexpected things are the greatest gifts, and you are my greatest gift. Thank you for loving me and accepting all my faults. Thank you for sharing your love with me. Thank you for marrying me."

"Oh God, how beautiful. Someone hand me a tissue."

"Don't cry, Turnip. We'll be doing this same thing soon enough."

"Max, please place the ring on Willow's finger and repeat after me. With this ring, I thee wed."

"With this ring, I thee wed. I love you, Willow."

"Wow, that's pretty. Good job, babe."

"Thanks, Wills."

"Willow, place the ring on Max's finger and repeat after me. With this ring I thee wed."

"With this ring I thee wed. I love you, Max."

"Whoa, this is so cool. I'm so honored. Um, sir? Are we married yet?"

"Right after I say this, Max. I now pronounce you husband and wife. Max, you may kiss your bride."

"You don't have to tell me twice"

"Ugh, Turnip, do I really have to watch?"

"Yes, you do. Now turn around and get your hands away from your eyes."

"Wow, that was some kiss, husband."

"Thanks, wife. Ha, ha. I called you wife."

"Yeah, well, I called you husband."

"Guess it's official now."

"Sure is. I'm glad I said yes when you asked me last week at my house."

"I'm glad all those kids agreed to my plan. They were amazing."

"They sure were."

"Oh, my little girl. I can't believe you're married. It's a little quick, but you're a big girl. I just wish your dad was here."

"He is Mother. He's always here. Every time I look at Max's finger I'll know he's here. Thank you for offering Daddy's ring for Max to wear. It's so special to both of us."

"Mrs. Taylor, I promise to take good care of it."

"Oh, Max, I know you will and no more Mrs. Taylor. You can call me Tessa or Mom, or whatever you would like."

"I'd like to call you Mom."

"Then Mom, it is."

"And Willow? You can call me whatever you

want as well. I know it may be hard to call me Dad, so if you just want to call me Bob for the time being, I'm good with that."

"How about I call you F.I.L."

"What does that mean?"

"It's short for father-in-law."

"Hey, I like it. It sticks. Let's go with that."

"Craw, can we get some of that champagne over here?"

"Coming right up, Mrs. Vincent."

"Oh, that sounds cool. I like it. Willow Vincent. I'm going to keep it."

"You better."

"Would you rather have taken my name?"

"Hell, no."

"Good then shut your trap."

"Here we go already."

"No, you big goof. I'm just kidding. Hey, can we have a toast before Jax opens and a slew of people come in and crash our wedding. Besides, I want to go down on the beach and get some pictures before the sun goes down. It's gorgeous out."

"I'm going to do the toast this time since Cruz did the housewarming toast and Porter did the quickie engagement toast the same night."

"You know you two are crazy, right?"

"Yeah, P. We know. You've only said it about a thousand times since we decided to do this."

"I still can't believe we pulled this off in less than a week."

"Well, thanks to your expert paralegal skills in finding us a judge in Sandy Cove who was willing to do this on such short notice, Thea. It came together quicker than we thought."

"Oh, it was nothing."

"No, Thea. It was something. You're something."

"Um… well, thanks, Porter."

"You're welcome, Thea."

"Now can I get on with my toast?"

"Go ahead, Harlow."

"Thanks, Wills. Okay, to Max and Willow. The craziest, most mismatched-meant-to-be couple on the planet. Thanks for bringing us all into your line of insanity and allowing us to witness your love. You guys are certifiable, but we love you regardless and wish you a lifetime of happiness. Here's to Max and Willow."

"To Max and Willow."

"Thanks, everyone. We appreciate you being here with us. Excuse us for a minute."

"Max, are you okay?"

"I'm fine. I just want to see if you're okay."

"I'm fine. I'm really happy and I can't believe we just got married. We're married, Max. Like, we're married. Do you think we're insane?"

"Yes, we are completely and utterly wacky, but that's us, Willow. You and I never did play by the rules and we will continue not to. This is how we roll, baby."

"I like not playing by the rules. It feels good to be bad."

"Are you flirting with me, Mrs. Vincent? You're a naughty girl, aren't you?"

"Nah, I'm a bad-ass."

"I'd say your ass isn't bad. I personally love your ass, even though you're a pain in it. I mean I am your husband after all."

"Yes, you are and I'm your wife."

"You sure are. And forever you will be an even bigger pain in my ass."

"And you'll always be shorter than me."

"Touché, wife."

"Right back at ya, husband."

The End

Stay Tuned
for Book 4 in The Shore Series, Falling In- Porter and Thea's Story
Coming Soon

Stay connected to M.R. Joseph

Follow her on Instagram @missyreds

On Facebook -

https://www.facebook.com/reunionbookseries

On Twitter @redkar_m

On Goodreads -

https://www.goodreads.com/author/show/6936575

.M_R_Joseph

To sign up for M.R. Joseph's newsletter email her

@ mrjosephwriter@gmail.com

ABOUT THE AUTHOR

I'm a book nerd turned writer who loves the 'Happily Ever After' mixed with a bit of suspense, drama and the occasional cliffhanger! My love of books started me on my writing journey. I began writing my first book in July 2012 and since that time I have created 2 series. The first series 'The Reunion Series debuted in November 2012 and two books followed. My new series 'The Shore Series" debuted in March 2014 and claimed Best Selling status shortly after the release of the first book. There will be 6 Shore Series books in all. I'm also the author of the Romantic Comedy, 39 & Holding. I live in Philadelphia with my adoringly handsome husband, and two pretty cute kids. You can always find me with my Kindle glued to my hands or in my car with the music turned up while embarrassing my children with my mad, car dancing skills.